D0379820

Caroline's hand slipped to the back of Toni's neck. "Kiss me again."

She was irresistible, even though Toni knew it was a mistake to kiss her then, to kiss her as they slowly made their way back to her rental car, to kiss her once they were locked inside.

"Toni." Caroline's small moan ignited something inside Toni's mouth and the kiss turned hotly passionate. "I've wanted you for so long."

Toni couldn't say, "Me, too," because it wasn't true. Instead she found a real truth, which was, "I know."

WRITING AS KARIN KALLMAKER:
*Just Like That*
*Sugar*
*One Degree of Separation*
*Maybe Next Time*
*Substitute for Love*
*Frosting on the Cake*
*Unforgettable*
*Watermark*
*Making Up for Lost Time*
*Embrace in Motion*
*Wild Things*
*Painted Moon*
*Car Pool*
*Paperback Romance*
*Touchwood*
*In Every Port*

WRITING FOR BELLA AFTER DARK:
*All the Wrong Places*
*Once Upon a Dyke: New Exploits of Fairy Tale Lesbians*
*Bell, Book and Dyke: New Exploits of Magical Lesbians*

WRITING AS LAURA ADAMS:
*Christabel*

**The Tunnel of Light Trilogy:**
*Sleight of Hand*
*Seeds of Fire*

**Daughters of Pallas:**
*Night Vision*
*The Dawning*

Feel free to visit www.kallmaker.com.

# Just Like That

## Karin Kallmaker

Bella
BOOKS

2005

Copyright© 2005 by Karin Kallmaker

**Bella Books, Inc.**
P.O. Box 10543
Tallahassee, FL 32302

All rights reserved. No part of this book may be reproduced or transmitted in any form or by any means, electronic or mechanical, including photocopying, without permission in writing from the publisher.

Printed in the United States of America on acid-free paper
First Edition

Editor: Christi Cassidy
Cover designer: Sandy Knowles

**ISBN 1-59493-025-2**

*For Maria, and all the many friends I've been pleased to escort through our wine country—I couldn't have done it without you.*

*This novel is dedicated to the inspiration of Jane Austen, who breathed life into the modern romance novel.*

*Seventeen is prime time*

# Chapter 1

"Everybody knows that a single woman with good money is in want of a wife." Jane waded out of the pond and stood dripping on the old blanket they'd tossed over the soft, early spring grass.

The outrageous statement succeeded in banishing Syrah's drowsiness. "You? Wife material?"

Jane shook water out of her hair. "I figure if a woman's making steady green and she's in her forties, never been engaged, maybe even still a virgin, then she needs a wife."

"You mean she needs you." Syrah plucked a grape from the fist-sized cluster on the blanket next to her.

"Same thing. Are those good?" Jane peered dubiously at the bright green fruit, then picked one for herself.

Syrah bit the bottom from the grape she'd chosen and managed to keep a smile on her face. "I think so."

Ever trusting, Jane popped the grape into her mouth. Syrah allowed the laugh she'd been holding back to escape her lips, then clapped her hands to her throat, trying to soothe her own outraged glands.

"You lying sack of potting soil—it's *sour*!" Jane made a threatening gesture with her arm that Syrah laughingly avoided.

"Yes, I know. And it's good, don't you think?"

"You're trying to poison me. Gods-on-the-vine, that's painful."

Syrah passed over her water bottle to make amends for the lack of warning. "It's too early for ripe. You of all people should know that. Take a little sip and then let it roll around in your mouth. Just think about it. That grape and thousands like it, this fall, next year, ten years from now, will taste like today, this sky, the breeze, those soft clouds, the hint of fog maybe tonight." Tipping her head back, Syrah closed her eyes to the rolling vista of checkerboard greens as she savored the layers of flavors still assaulting her taste buds. "These grapes will be our memories in a bottle."

"Like a painting, but drinkable." Jane passed back the water bottle, then shimmied into her boxers. "I'm afraid I've got more than wine on my mind."

Jane tended to put her clothes on before she was dry, and today was no exception. As she watched her friend try to wrangle her tank top down her still wet torso, Syrah had no trouble recalling a hundred similar afternoons. A swim in the pond, a bask in the sun, snacks purloined from Bennett's kitchen—a beautiful May lunch hour was worthy of nothing less. Syrah arched her shoulders into the sun. A few minutes more and she'd get dressed, too. "Is there more than wine to life?"

"Yes. A love life. A hot woman with a warm body and an inventive spirit. That's what's on my mind. I'm tired of being alone. I'm tired of being your date at the Spring Fling."

Syrah's eyes flew open. "You mean you don't want to go with me this year?"

Jane flopped down on the blanket, her shirt stuck to her back. "Well, yeah, I do, now that you're back for good. It sucked going alone. I hope you had fun in Europe, because I was bored out of my mind without you around."

"But enough to go thinking of yourself as somebody's wife? What's gotten into you?"

"The old Netherfield place finally sold, and I've heard rumors about the woman who bought it."

"Rumors fly fast around here." A breeze tickled over her nearly dry breasts and Syrah rolled over to reach for her tank top. "She could be straight."

"No. Definitely a dyke. And femme, so, hey, I'm thinking she needs a wife like me. I've got all the qualifications. I can fix stuff, dance, like to talk and think sex is really fun. My only strike is the money thing."

"You're an artist. You get to have no money. I'm not an artist and I've got no money either."

"You have a vineyard. A very large, old vineyard."

"Belongs to my father."

"And will be yours one day."

"A long way in the future, I hope." Syrah couldn't help the flicker of concern she felt thinking about her father. He wasn't as physically vigorous as he had been before her sojourn in Europe. "Meanwhile, gas money can break the bank."

"Good paint costs more than gas." Jane idly shooed away a buzzing bee.

"Besides, you won't be the only one checking out the new woman in town, you know. Move into this neighborhood and everybody thinks they automatically own you." Syrah didn't mean to sound bitter. She'd not been so popular when she'd left. But the four years in Europe had somehow reactivated her as dating material, and the fickleness irked her. She was the same woman now as she had been then.

"It wasn't that way in France?"

"Not really." Syrah yanked her tank top over her head and shoved her dark, not-quite-dry curls over her shoulder.

"From your e-mails I gather that you had a line out your door."

"For fun, yeah. I don't know what's with California since I left. There is a positive *mania* to get married. I don't just mean the

3

piece of paper. I thought the drive to pair up was bad before I left. Hell, it was one of the reasons I left. I don't need a wife and I don't want to be anybody's wife, either."

"And all those fun French girls didn't want to settle down?"

"They were fun and that was the whole point. But I'm home now."

Jane was quiet for a moment and Syrah appreciated the restraint. There was no point in rehashing the scorching European summer that had decimated last year's wine harvest and left this year's in doubt, or the undeniable reality that Ardani Vineyards needed another Ardani on the premises. Her father could still tell which hillside had birthed any given grape, but his energy for supervising crews and maintenance had definitely waned.

She drew on her panties and shorts, squinting into the hot sun that danced along her skin. The pleasure in it was so sharp that for a moment she could not breathe. She had thought she'd love Europe, the independence especially. She certainly enjoyed herself, and enjoyed a small amount of respect from the vintners she worked for from season to season. But she had pined for the Napa Valley sun and the blazing blue sky. Since her return to the States in December she had waited through the long, wet winter for the glorious spring to arrive. No matter the reason she had come home, this *was* home. She wasn't going anywhere else again.

"I think," Jane finally said, "that I am tired of pleasing myself."

Syrah glanced up in surprise. "But you've always prided yourself on pleasing the ladies."

"That's not what I mean." Jane stretched her long neck and closed her eyes. "So I have a good time one night with some lovely Chiquita up for the weekend from San Francisco. She goes home happy and I've certainly had a blast. Dinner and breakfast have been had and it makes me think about lunch."

"Lunch?" Syrah sat up to slip on her sandals, letting her hair hide her smile.

"Don't laugh." Jane was frowning into the sun. "Maybe it's hormones, maybe it's that, like you, I'm finally looking back on thirty.

But I don't know. I feel like I want to make somebody's entire day wonderful. Not just dinner, bed and breakfast. I want twenty-four-seven. To mean something to somebody all the time."

"Just because some woman has moved into the area doesn't mean she's your type. What if she's got no brain? No style? What if she doesn't get Jane the Artista?"

"Some artist." Jane shrugged and Syrah was surprised at the downward turn Jane's mouth had taken.

"An artist," she repeated. "You create. You have flair and substance. French women would spread you on a cracker and gobble you up."

"I don't want to be someone's trophy. I want . . . oh, hell, I don't know what I want. I know what I *don't* want. I don't want another summer of lunches by myself."

Syrah couldn't think of a response that made sense of Jane's abrupt abandonment of the very life she'd been striving to perfect since high school. What had happened to the cocky butch who had once declared, "Happiness is putting her to sleep so you can wake her up"?

She found the keys to the truck in her pocket and gathered the grapes and bottled water. "It's got to be nearly one."

Jane grunted and scrambled to her feet. "Drop me at the job site?"

"Sure. Want to have a burger or something tonight?"

"Okay."

Syrah nearly said that she'd gotten more enthusiasm from Hound the last time she'd said "burger" to him, but she resisted. She and Jane had been friends too long for a temporary fixation with romance to interfere. "I'll pick you up after the tasting room closes. I'm pouring until six."

She coasted the truck down the incline from the pond, braking carefully to keep dust from billowing in their wake. Jane opened the gates as they made their way to the shady back road. The tires finally crossed onto packed dirt and she punched on the CD player as they increased speed to the public road that would get them to

5

Jane's current job site. With the windows rolled down and Stevie Nicks bawling a witchy song they might have still been in high school.

The green-smudged hills and canopies of trees had not changed since then. Neat rows of vines lined both sides of the winding road. Rieslings in the sun, Syrahs in the lee of a curving hill, Pinots tucked into the shade—none of it had changed. The annual cycle of budbreak, leaves and harvest were only temporary. What was underneath—the vines—were as permanent in her mind as the soil itself.

She watched Jane heft a roll of irrigation hose after greeting her boss, then tromp into the atrium of a new office building. Syrah didn't care for the impersonal glass-and-mirrors architecture, but at least they were putting in a lot of greenery, keeping Jane employed for that much more of the spring. The job would end and her friend would haul out her paints and go back to her first love. That was what Jane had done for the baker's dozen of summers since high school. She hadn't changed, Syrah told herself. Not Jane. Not anything.


"I'm back," Syrah called out as she dropped her keys into the bowl next to the back door. Hound promptly greeted her with snuffles all around her knees, fanned her briefly with his tail, then he gracefully reclaimed his bed, curiosity assuaged.

There was no human response, however, and a quick check of the tasting room confirmed that it was empty. She headed around to the patio overlooking the sunny hillside that curved down to the road. With a grin, she beheld her father in mid-snore. The glider had always been his favorite place for a quick doze.

Setting the grapes down on the seat next to him, she tiptoed back to the tasting room to turn the door sign to *Open*. In a few weeks, early in June, they'd be open all day. A noon dip in the pond would be only a memory until September.

She tidied the bar, frowned over the tasting listing—why were they still offering the best reserve? Its reputation was growing and she thought it was time to put it away. A bang from the kitchen announced Bennett's arrival so she went in search of a snack. Sour grapes and a few crackers hadn't dented her hunger.

"You'll never guess the news I heard." Bennett set out a container of her homemade tapenade just as Syrah opened a box of sesame crackers. "News that you should be overjoyed with, I might add."

Syrah dug up some of the chopped olives and sighed happily as she savored the delicious blend of garlic and pesto. "Netherfield has been bought."

"How did you know?"

"Jane told me."

"Jane." Bennett's eyebrows joined into a single line. She slapped Syrah's hand away from the tapenade. "Get a plate. Honestly, all the years I've tried to teach you some kind of manners. Jane doesn't know anything about it. I've been asking around and the new owner is apparently some businesswoman with money—retiring in her forties, a lady of leisure. Get a napkin."

"Mm-hmm."

"She's very pretty, everyone says, and agreeable and has already offered to host a Wine for March of Dimes get-together once the house is habitable again. There are already people there working on it."

"Jane should offer her services for landscape design. She's good enough to do it on her own. It's that artistic flair she has."

Bennett finished with the last of the groceries and rinsed her hands. Another thing that had not changed, Syrah mused. Bennett's hands were as strong and gnarled as they had always been. Those hands had mesmerized Syrah as a girl, watching their hard strength turn out lighter-than-air pie crusts and biscuits. "You are the most eligible woman in the area and this very afternoon you need to go over to Netherfield and see about meeting the new owner."

"Mm-hmm."

"Don't you even want to know her name?" Bennett gave Syrah the look that suggested Syrah must be ill not to have demanded that piece of information at the outset.

"I'm sure you'll tell me."

Tomatoes squished between Bennett's fingers, pulp and seeds falling into a bowl while the beautifully ripe flesh headed for the cookpot. "Perhaps I won't, if you're being snippy. You are very tiresome sometimes. All I want is to see you happy and settled."

"Bennett, you've never been settled and I think you've been happy."

"That's me, not you. I never was the settling kind." She rinsed her hands again with an air of finality.

"Maybe I'm not either."

Bennett snapped the lid on the tapenade shut. "I knew your mother, and you are just like her. Some people are meant to go around in pairs, and Jane Lucas should have nothing to say to a woman like Missy Bingley."

"Why not? A woman named Missy seems exactly like Jane's type."

Drawers were being opened and examined with increasing agitation. "I don't know why you persist in being so obtuse. Jane is a very nice girl but she's eccentric."

"You mean she works with her hands."

"If you insist, yes. I know she calls those paintings art, but it might as well be mud she's slapping onto the canvas. Cheaper than all that wasted paint. She is hardly suitable as a partner for someone like Missy Bingley, who I'm told is extremely cultured and affable."

Syrah knew better than to argue. Bennett had lived all her life in the valley and had spent the majority of it ruling the Ardani household with her iron fist. Not for the first time Syrah marveled at the traditionalist values that kept Bennett going to mass three times a week but somehow blended with her staunch loyalty toward all things Ardani. She'd play matchmaker between two lesbians and go to confession for having brought about such an event, then sleep like a baby.

Syrah was rescued from further comment by her father's tread outside the kitchen door. He held the bunch of grapes Syrah had left for him in one hand and looked both sleepy and pleased at the same time.

"What did you think?" He hoisted the bunch at Syrah.

"They'll be some of the best Gewürz' we've had in a while."

He grinned. "You got that right. Not a lot to mellow them yet, but the early rain brought the peach blossoms on early and the overtones will be there."

Bennett bustled between them. "Netherfield has been bought, finally, and Syrah refuses to go and meet the woman. A very wealthy woman, I must say, and an asset to the community." Bennett relieved Syrah's father of the grapes, plopped them into a bowl and hurried out to the tasting room to leave them on the bar. The swinging door between kitchen and tasting room allowed Bennett's continuing remarks to arrive in bursts. "You would think . . . can't be single forever . . . Jane Lucas indeed . . . suitable and eligible . . . never see thirty again . . ."

Syrah watched her father pat his pockets. As usual, his glasses were in his breast pocket, which he checked last. "There was a letter in the post last week that I didn't understand. Found it this morning and thought I should ask you." He put the glasses on his nose and repeated the patting process until a folded envelope was discovered in his back pants pocket. He unfolded the enclosed letter and reviewed it with raised eyebrows before handing it to her.

"'Mr. Anthony Ardani, Chairman of the Board.' Huh?" Syrah gave her father a puzzled look. Chairman of the Board? "'We regret that your lack of response to pressing concerns of Ardani Vineyards, Incorporated, creditors has required the retention of a consultant appointed by the court to examine and recommend a course of action for the resolution of shareholder concerns.'" She scanned the rest of the letter, growing increasingly confused and dismayed. "Dad? When did we become a corporation?"

He shrugged. "A few years ago. While you were away. It seemed like a good idea. They all invested money and then we could borrow to renovate the bottling and replace the large barrels. I bought the Tarpay fields they auctioned, too. Didn't cost me a dime."

"But, Dad . . ."

"Everything will be okay, pumpkin."

"But, Dad, these people who signed the letter, they own more of Ardani than you do. They've hired someone to tell us how to run our business and if we don't do what this consultant person says—" She glanced down at the final line in horror. " 'Creditors may choose to call their loans due, resulting in the forced sale of assets sufficient to repay the debts.'"

"That's the part I don't understand." He regarded her with faint worry clouding his brow.

"Our land, the winery, that's what they mean by assets, Dad."

"But I didn't sell those to anyone else."

"You gave away shares."

"Yes, but I didn't sell anything."

Syrah closed her eyes. "They became the same thing when you incorporated." With a rising feeling of dread, she added, "You're the smallest shareholder, it says here."

"But I'm Chairman of the Board."

"Oh, Dad . . ." She sank into a chair at the kitchen table.

"There's two cars pulling in," Bennett announced as she reentered the kitchen. "One's a Mercedes."

"I'll pour," her father offered.

Syrah nodded numbly. She read the letter again and tried to take in the situation. She didn't know much about corporations, but it seemed like very bad news when a judge was involved in making decisions about a business's future. The voices from the tasting room washed over her, the familiar rise and fall not providing any comfort. Finally she quit the kitchen for her father's office and sat down at his desk with a sick feeling in her stomach.

He'd refused all help she'd offered with business details when she'd arrived home last December. Instead, they spent the winter examining the winery equipment while he imparted long lectures about the mix and barreling, as well as the health of the slowly evolving vines. Business was booming, he'd explained, and it certainly seemed like that was so, based on the shipping she supervised, and it had recently become legal to ship wine to individuals across state lines. Crews for planting, culling and weeding were running smoothly and on schedule. The excess from Tarpay Chablis grapes were already assigned to the big mass-market winery. It was destined to be the best season Ardani Vineyards had ever had.

She lifted the most recent water bill and was confronted by a legal-looking document titled, "Receivership Update."

It was too much to take in. She glanced out the window at the rolling greens and soft golds of the fields she'd known all her life. This vineyard had been owned by Ardanis for more than one hundred years. The vines didn't belong to a bunch of banks and businessmen in New York.

She shuffled papers, trying to locate anything helpful. The fax machine whirred on and off again and she retrieved an order from an upscale market in Napa. In the tray under the new arrival were papers that had been faxed in this morning.

They announced that somebody named Toni Blanchard would be calling to make arrangements for a site visit. The phone chose that moment to ring and Syrah could only stare at it in horror. She let it switch to voice mail as she went in search of her father.

The customers, bearing bags sagging enough to contain at least three bottles each, were heading out the door.

She proffered the papers and waited while her father again located his glasses.

"Who is this woman? The name is familiar." He glanced at Syrah. "A woman, at least, pumpkin."

"I wouldn't bet on that helping us out."

"Oh, I remember." He gave her a relieved smile. "A feature in *Inc.* a couple of years ago, the issue we were featured in. This is very good news—this is Bill Blanchard's daughter. I probably still have the article."

"Bill Blanchard?"

"An old, old friend. We went to Oregon together. He decided to become a lawyer and now he's a judge."

Knowing her father's pack rat propensity, Syrah wasn't surprised when he produced the magazine. He couldn't find the tax returns from last year if he had two weeks to look, but a magazine that had mentioned their wine three years ago he could locate in two minutes.

Page forty-nine featured a breathtaking photograph of the vineyards from the tasting room and a short article about Ardani wines. Just opposite was one of the magazine's profiles. The short article detailed the rising star of Toni Blanchard, corporate turn-around specialist.

Her father peeled away the yellow sticky note that had served as a bookmark, revealing the photograph underneath. "She looks like a nice woman."

Dark hair twisted at the neck and East Coast stylish, Toni Blanchard gazed out from the page with an expression Syrah could only describe as haughty. If the toes on her shoes had been any longer, they'd have curled like some court jester's. Everything about her dripped wealth and superiority. "She's never set foot on anything but concrete," Syrah said.

"She's smart and she'll be on our side. Bill will do us right—decent fellow, very decent. I'll give him a call, how about that?"

The phone rang and Syrah again let it go to voice mail. She could imagine the affected voice that went with the cold expression on Toni Blanchard's face, and she had no desire to hear it right now. She wasn't reassured in the least by her own father's forty-year-old college friendship with this woman's father, not at all.

Feeling as if she'd eaten lead, she dragged herself back to the office and began sorting papers in earnest. The situation couldn't be as bleak as it seemed.

# Chapter 2

A shred of lettuce dangled precariously from the end of her fork, and so Toni Blanchard didn't hear what her lover of several years had said. Annoyed that the waiter had forgotten she wanted her dressing on the side, she shook the fork to let the lettuce fall safely back to her plate.

"I'm sorry. I missed that." She looked expectantly at Mira.

"I don't love you anymore."

For a moment, all Toni could do was blink. She shook her head and replayed Mira's words.

Their gazes locked across the table. When Mira's fell back to her food, Toni's pride wouldn't let her ask Mira to repeat it one more time.

Then it hit her that *la belle dame sans merci* Mira Wickham had brought her to this hushed, expensive, off-Park Avenue restaurant to dump her, on the belief that of course Toni wouldn't make a scene. They'd end things and depart as composed as when they arrived. Toni stared at pools of dressing on her salad and pictured them running down Mira's face. The coffee was still steaming. It would look great in Mira's lap. An earlier Toni might have given in to the brief urge to mark the occasion of their breakup with such an emotional gesture, but not now. She and Mira had been heading toward this little scene for too long for it to end any way but civilized.

She put down her fork, salad untasted. Mira could have at least waited for her to enjoy the twenty-five-dollar Aquavit signature strip steak she'd just ordered. She supposed that was a petty thought under the circumstances. Mira had always chided her for being "thrifty," as if having a bank balance meant you'd lost your common sense.

"It's been fun, sweetie, but it's time to move on. I emptied my drawers today and I'll be home in London for a while. Um, Nancy will be going with me."

"Of course," Toni said. Nancy. Fine. She ought to have seen this coming. Mira didn't deal in forever. At one time in her life, Toni might have thought two years of dating was more than a dalliance. She had few romantic notions left, thank goodness. Otherwise, Mira would be eyelashes deep in salad dressing.

Because she knew when to cut her losses and move on, had in fact made a considerable living knowing when to invest and when to sell, Toni smiled pleasantly, picked up her handbag and walked out. Their business was concluded. The salad remained on the plate, the coffee in the cup.


Any other day Toni would have paused to appreciate the cool air of a lovely New York spring evening, but the echo of Mira's voice made it hard to think.

*"I don't love you anymore."*

That statement implied, didn't it, that Mira had once loved her? Why hadn't she said in answer, "Did you ever?" As usual, Toni reflected, she had thought of the perfect reply far too late. Put her in a boardroom or in front of a room full of shareholders and words never failed her. It was the one-on-one where she faltered.

Certainly at first Mira and she had sparkled together. They'd enjoyed how the love affair between a self-made daughter of a country judge and an heiress with blue blood in her veins earned them the occasional shocked glance.

*"I don't love you anymore."*

She felt numb. Surprised she didn't know about Nancy. Shocked by the suddenness. Even so, the avenue was crowded with cabs, yet she didn't want to throw herself in front of any of them. The thought of waking in the morning without Mira there didn't make her want to wrap her neck with a noose. Numb, yes. Heartbroken, apparently not.

After a half-block's walk up Madison Avenue, and giving it considered thought with every step, Toni formulated her "Breakup To Do List." Maybe it was because she was still in her work clothes—power suit, heels, cell phone clipped to her waist—that made the necessary process seem like a daily inbox exercise.

By the end of the second block she'd used the cell phone to change the PINs on various accounts. She had no idea if Mira even knew them, but it was prudent.

While eyeing the busy avenue for a cab with its medallion lit, she cancelled the credit card Mira had upon occasion borrowed when her spending outstripped her trust fund stipend.

Crossing against the light at Fifty-Eighth Street, she demonstrated the art of flagging a cab for a slow-moving tourist. While seated in the back for the short ride home to the Upper West Side, she tapped out a brief e-mail to her business manager announcing that she would no longer be extending use of various vendors and services to Mira. Good-bye, car service; good-bye, spa; good-bye, tee times. Over meant over.

She walked in the front door of her condominium a mere twenty minutes after leaving the restaurant. The signs of Mira's departure were subtle, but there. Photographs on the piano were gone. She smiled ruefully over the obvious absence of a very, very old bottle of Scotch. Absent clothing and toiletries left holes in the closet and bathroom.

Only when she was putting away her watch and earrings did she notice that several pieces of jewelry were gone. She expected anything she'd given Mira to be taken, of course, but among the missing were a few pieces she'd been very clear were just a loan. Ouch.

She glanced at her pale face in the hall mirror and said aloud, "What else did you expect?" and realized she was glad it was over. Just like that, in the blink of an eye, it was over, like it had never been. Other than the occasional very good sex, and the rare evening out with Mira's friends that Toni had actually enjoyed, their dating had seemed to have no purpose, no goal. It had been a way to spend time, but Toni had precious little of that.

It was for the best.

Bottom line: she was dreading calling Missy because Missy had been certain that Mira was a leech and would eventually dump her, but only after lulling her into a false sense of forever. She didn't want to call Missy. Sometimes an old friend was the last person you wanted to talk to.

"So where is Lady Mira *reech beech* now?" Missy, thankfully, had skipped right over "I told you so" and gone directly to outraged support.

Sometimes, Toni allowed, an old friend was exactly what you needed. "I have no idea. I decided there was no point in lingering over the discussion."

"There's somebody else."

"Nancy, her skiing buddy she met last year. But it's not like we agreed to be exclusive."

"If I recall, she said those were tedious details that would get in the way of . . . what was it? Letting your love mature to its fullest?" Toni would have bet money Missy was rolling her eyes. "There are way better fish in the sea, my sweet."

"I'm done with trying. It's exhausting."

"Come to California for a while."

"I've got plenty of work here, but I might be somewhere in the state briefly. A business review for the court—another idiot who has no business running a corporation. Someplace south I think, near Santa Something-or-other. If so, we'll hook up."

"There are hundreds of Santa Somethings in this state, so maybe you'll be close. I'm still in San Fran weekdays, but I can't wait to get out to my house. You'll love it. I love it. The people are very nice and you wouldn't believe the social life for lesbians. I'm going to a dance for the local ladies, even."

"Sound fun," Toni said automatically.

"Sounds deadly dull to you, I can tell. It won't be Saturday night in the Village, true, but honestly I have never seen so many attractive, vibrant-looking women in my life. And that was just at the local grocery store."

Toni could hardly believe that Podunk, California, or wherever it was Missy was moving, could offer much of interest. She changed the subject. "How come we're not in love with each other? It would make life so much simpler."

"I don't know," Missy answered. "Maybe because Caroline would scalp me if I made a move on you."

"You know as well as I do your sister and I never even made it to the bedroom. It was never serious."

"I know. But I also know that Mira was a shallow bitch who liked your bank balance."

"Gee, thanks."

"You know what I mean. Mira might be Lady Whatever-it-was, but she has no real capital for, what, another four years? In the meantime, she needed you." Missy clucked her tongue for a moment. "I'm sorry, I'm being brutal. I swear, she's the first time you've been semi-serious about anyone since that woman across the hall in the dorm. You deserve better than being treated like that, way better."

"Oh, I don't know. She's a butterfly socialite. I never expected Mira to treat me seriously. Maybe that's why she didn't." Her

Blackberry chirped and Toni glanced at the caption. "I've got a call I need to make."

"Call me later," Missy insisted and Toni promised she would.

"About this e-mail from you," Kyle, her business manager, began with no other preamble. "Is this about Bookworthy Enterprises?"

"No. Mira and I aren't seeing each other anymore, that's all."

"Since when?"

Unused to him prying into her personal affairs, Toni didn't keep her surprise out of her voice. "Since about an hour ago. Why?"

"She called this morning, asking if I thought investing in Bookworthy was going to be worth it. I didn't know it was a rush—"

"It wasn't. What did you tell her?"

"I said I didn't think it would pencil and you'd pass on it. She said okay and that was that."

She thanked Kyle absentmindedly for the information, reluctant to make any link between Mira's conversation with Kyle and her pronouncement at dinner.

For a short while she gazed across Central Park, watching the lights change and the traffic flow below her. She could only think of a long list of things she ought to do and feel. She ought to make plans that celebrated being single again. Take a short trip, reassure herself she liked solitude. She ought to be angry, or hurt, or crushed.

She was saved from making a decision about her emotional state by the ringing of her home phone. Since most of her business contacts went through her cell, it was probably a telemarketer.

"How are you, little girl?"

"Daddy! To what do I owe this honor, your honor?"

"We'll get to that. First, how are you? How did that business in Georgia end up?"

"Not well. Everyone was too stubborn. Nobody wanted to believe it was share some sacrifice or all sink together, not until the water was over their heads."

"That's a pity. I know you had high hopes."

Fifteen hundred jobs gone overnight, Toni reflected. She'd hoped to save a third of them with the workout proposal, but sometimes things just didn't happen. "I did, yeah. So did the rest of my team. How's Carlyle?"

"Getting old, like me. It's easier on a dog, though. At least he gets to sleep most of the day. I've found people notice if I nod off in court."

"You need to perfect sleeping with your eyes open."

He sighed. "I've tried, little girl, I've tried."

"So . . . what's up?" Toni relaxed into the sofa.

"I had a call earlier from an old, old friend. A very nice fellow, a country gentleman, you might say. Met him at Oregon. His family owned a winery—guess it's all his now."

"Mmm-hmm?" She kicked off her heels and rubbed her aching toes.

"Seems you're on your way to visit his place. Ardani Vineyard?"

"I am?" Holding back a sigh, she stretched for her Blackberry.

"Northern California. Receivership review."

"Oh. I didn't know it was a winery. After a while, all the cases seem alike." A business was a business, Toni thought, though you couldn't convince any owner of that fact. The basic principles applied across every corporation. "Why did he call?"

"He recognized your name from Christmas letters from me, I guess."

Toni frowned. "Did he think you'd have some influence over my work?"

"I think he thought I somehow got you appointed on his behalf."

"Right. The receivership court is in Delaware."

"I don't think the subtlety of that is something Anthony Ardani would appreciate."

"Then he's got no business running a corporation." Toni shrugged. "I always try to do what I can for the principals, but I'm working for the court."

19

"I know that. All I told him was that I'd give you a call, and I am. Thing is, he's a nice guy. He introduced me to your mother."

"Oh." Hell. Sentiment had no place in the kind of decisions she made.

"His daughter is in the business with him now. She was in Europe for several years."

How lucky for her. Living the good life while the family business failed—how typical. Home now that the money had run out? "I'll do what I can."

"We have one thing in common, that's for sure. We both think we have the most beautiful daughter on the planet, and both of you are gay. So maybe you and his daughter will be able to work together."

As if Toni had any intention of getting involved with anyone anytime soon. Let alone some debutante fresh from her European tour. "There's no secret gay language that guarantees that, Daddy."

"I know that. I did meet her once when she was two or three. You must have been twelve—the year you went to your mother's retreat for the summer."

"I remember."

"They tried for years and ended up with a sweet little girl. I wouldn't be surprised if she's grown up to be Sophia Loren. She had the eyes for it."

Great. Some debutante with fine eyes. "Maybe she remembers you."

"I doubt it. Too young, and that was the year her mother died. I was there for the funeral. Anthony and I corresponded fairly regularly at that time. Then we drifted apart. He buried himself in the winery."

And you buried yourself in the law, Toni wanted to say, when Mom died the following year. "I'm sure he's a very nice man." Business was overflowing with nice people who had not a clue how to keep their enterprise running.

"Well, I hope that whatever it is you have to do, Bill and Syrah come out of it okay."

"Sir-rah?"

"His daughter."

"Is that Italian? Sir-*ah*?"

"No, I think it derives from French—at least the grapes by that name come from France."

The debutante with the fine eyes was named after a grape. How *quaint*. "I see."

They chatted a little while longer about more general topics, but Toni found herself afterward feeling annoyed and agitated. How dare someone call her father for intercession in a business deal? She'd get to California and discover, like she always did, that business had been bad, money was spent on the wrong things, and nobody wanted to take the blame. Just like in Georgia, everyone would be stubborn and, in the end, everyone would lose. Nobody cared about anyone else, just their own skin. These Ardani people were just like everyone else.


Her mood had not improved much by the morning, but she arrived at the small Midtown office they called the bullpen by nine.

Toni pushed open the door, reflecting as always that it didn't look much like the consulting offices of a multi-million-dollar firm, to be sure. Only the administrative staff had permanent workstations, while the rest of them worked from home offices or were on the road too much to need a base. Toni skirted a pile of luggage near the door and took note of Sanje and Mike, both gesticulating as they talked on their cell phones. Crystal and Bobby were sipping from tall coffeehouse mugs as they pecked away at their keyboards.

"Hi, all. Who's leaving? Or just getting back?"

"Those are mine," Crystal volunteered. "My flight to Fairbanks was delayed so I thought I'd stop in."

"Fairbanks, that's right." Toni gave Crystal a steady look. "You'll be just fine if you've got a parka."

Crystal, oddly, wouldn't meet her gaze. "Parka and boots—got them both."

Valerie, Barth and Tracy, the Queens of Admin, appeared from their respective cubicles waving hot sheets.

"Be with you in a second. General announcement, everybody, just an FYI. Mira and I have decided not to see each other any longer. I know a lot of you chatted with her, so feel free to continue contact with her. I just thought you ought to know." Toni finished her speech and was about to turn to the waiting cluster of admin staff when Crystal leapt up with a gasp.

"It's okay, I just spilled my coffee. Damn." She blotted at her desk with a wad of napkins, trying to capture the runoff. Hundreds of deli napkins appeared from desk drawers. "I'm sorry about the carpet."

"No worry—if you let it keep dripping it'll cover up the ink stain." Toni waved Valerie into her office and settled into her desk chair as she rapidly reviewed the call sheet that Valerie proffered. "Tell Henry that for something at this level of urgency, he can call me direct. I'd have talked to him last night."

"He's new. He's still afraid of you. Thinks you're going to fire him or something."

"I keep reminding him he works for himself. I'm just the fixer."

"He'll get the hang of it." Valerie pushed her glasses back up her long nose. "Sorry about Mira."

"Don't be. It was overdue, really." She ran her gaze down the list a second time, just to be sure nothing required her immediate callback. Their loose-knit group operated on a system of trust: you needed help, you asked and you got it. Consulting and finders' fees for ailing businesses were their bread and butter. "Oh, a call from Doc Burbidge."

"Yeah, said he needs a word of advice." Valerie gave a contained but obvious wiggle.

It was the best news she'd had in the last twenty-four hours. Doc's requests for advice almost always led to large contracts. "I'll call him at nine-thirty. Would you let his assistant know?"

She was about to ask Barth to bring in his list when Crystal appeared in the doorway.

"What can I do for you?"

Crystal closed the office door, which brought Toni's eyebrows up. "I need a private word."

Puzzled, Toni waved at the chair and watched Crystal carefully perch on the edge. "What's up?"

"It's about Mira. She called me last night."

"Did she?" Toni knew that Mira and Crystal occasionally went out for drinks but had presumed it was innocent since Crystal was married. "What was the call about?"

"She, uh—I feel like a fool, except she's been . . . I mean . . . Robert and I were having problems, and slowly breaking up, and she listened."

"I didn't realize you and Robert were separating. I'm sorry." Toni kicked herself for not noticing the new fine lines around Crystal's eyes.

Crystal swallowed hard, then rushed on. "It's okay. Almost old news, now. I should have told you. Anyway, she said she couldn't get a hold of you and had to go home to settle a business deal right away, and she needed cash. She knew I'd just gotten the payout from Bronson."

"She didn't say we'd broken up?" Toni wanted to ask how much money Mira had asked for, but Crystal obviously had more to tell.

"No. And, well, she said . . ."

"Yes?"

"She said you'd covered her before and knew about this but had forgotten to leave a check and she couldn't locate you and her flight was going out at midnight."

Toni felt as if her heart had stilled. "She said I'd pay you back, is that it?"

Crystal nodded. "It was a lie, wasn't it?"

"Yeah."

"And I was supposed to be gone this morning but my flight was delayed. She counted on my not being able to talk to you." Crystal blinked rapidly, her eyes glistening with tears. "I can't believe she lied to me. I feel like . . . such an idiot."

23

"I'll cover it and believe me, I'll get it back from her." So much for wondering about her emotional state—Toni could feel anger starting to pulse in her fingertips.

Crystal wiped away a tear. "I thought it was too good to be true. Someone like her. I mean, she's rich and titled, and British, and when I said I thought maybe I liked women, too, she *listened*. And didn't act like I was sick."

You could have talked to me, Toni thought. Then she had to ask herself if that was really true. She'd mentored Crystal through the years, giving her all the benefit of her experience. But what if Crystal had hinted of personal problems? She didn't have time to play therapist. "Mira is a good listener."

"So last night I met her at this place in the Village and gave her a check. And . . ."

Uh-oh, Toni thought. *Oh, please no.*

"And we . . . she had to leave for the airport and said she wouldn't be back for several weeks and she'd miss me. And she didn't expect to feel so sad. And . . ."

Toni closed her eyes. Mira must have gone to Crystal after the restaurant. *If I'd stayed, she might have asked me for the money.* But instead, she used Crystal. Then, in a hurt rush, Toni remembered the first time she'd been with Mira. How irresistible, how heady, how sexy and forbidden it had been. "Were you by any chance in the ladies' room when she said that?"

"Yes, we were alone. Otherwise, I wouldn't have, and I couldn't think."

Quick and fast, hard kisses and a steady, sure hand. Toni felt slightly ill.

More tears trickled down Crystal's cheeks. "I'd had a drink and my head was pounding, and I'm not excusing myself. I said yes. I felt terrible after, because of you. I didn't sleep at all, and thought I'd be on a plane, then I realized I'd have to face you."

"That's what Mira thought, too. That by the time we were face-to-face, you wouldn't feel . . . conflicted."

24

"I'm so sorry, Toni. You don't have to cover the money. I've been a fool." Crystal rose shakily and hurried toward the door.

Toni quickly cut her off, back against the heavy oak. "Crystal, please. Mira—I don't know what her game was with you. But not all women are like that. And I'll cover the money." She took Crystal's hands. "You know how we say take emotion out of the deal and then what to do with the money becomes clear? I think in this case if we take money out of the deal for you, what to do with the emotions will be more obvious to you."

Crystal gave a little sob and Toni had to put her arms around her. She was like a little hurt bird. Toni thought again that if she hadn't walked out on Mira, none of this would have happened.

Crystal mumbled, "It's thirty thousand dollars, Toni. How could I have just handed it over like that?"

"Because she had all the right moves." It was chump change to Mira. Mira didn't care that Crystal had worked herself to a frazzle on the Bronson merger and was still paying off her Harvard loans. "It's okay. I'll have Kyle transfer the money and you can do some serious thinking about who you are and what you want in your future while you're in Alaska."

Crystal nodded and gratefully accepted the tissue Toni snagged from her desk drawer. "Part of me, after she left, part of me felt like I finally made sense. But right now, I'm so confused."

"Take your time. You're gone a week, right? Just take your time." Toni didn't know what to do with her own emotions at the moment. She knew she was angry, but it felt far away. Too hot to touch. She tried for a comforting smile. "But stay out of ladies' rooms."

Crystal made an attempt at a laugh. "Who knew?"

I did, Toni wanted to say. She could have told her Mira liked to pounce in semi-public places. But she never talked with Crystal about that kind of thing. "I certainly didn't know Mira was capable of this."

Crystal gave her nose one last wipe and Toni let her leave. She would find Mira and somehow . . . it wasn't the money. Crystal had been lied to and her trust abused.

The intercom chirped and Barth announced it was time for her nine-thirty call to Doc Burbidge. She picked up the line and heard it click through. Moments later she was focused on what Doc wanted, but a part of her was trying to figure out what to do about Mira.

The call ended well, with a request for a proposal to analyze the validity of a merger in which Doc had a majority shareholder's interest. She wrote the particulars down automatically, sent them off to Valerie to record and post. She had come to no conclusion about Mira, however, which rankled. Mira had told both of them she was going home, but that, too, could have been a lie.

The intercom chirped again and Barth said, "Sorry, boss, it's Rafi. Something about a car and not knowing what to do about Mira. I didn't know what to tell him."

Toni's stomach did a strange twisting swirl. "Sorry you're in the middle of that. I'll take it." She snatched up the handset. "Rafi, what's the problem?"

"Well, Kyle he call this morning and said, uh, Miss Wickham no more car. But she call and insist and say it a mistake. I don't want you mad."

"Sorry, Rafi. Did she say where to pick her up?"

"Omni, Central Park. She want to go JFK."

"Tell her you'll be there promptly. But pick me up first."

# Chapter 3

"It's a pleasure to meet you," Syrah said, infusing every word with as much sincerity as she could.

If Missy Bingley was having to try as hard to be courteous, it didn't show. Her broad smile was all too engaging and Syrah felt her intention to dislike the woman slip a little. "And you, too. I've not been in the area for very long, but everyone told me I had to get to Ardani. I think this is where I confess I know nothing about wine and throw myself on your mercy."

Syrah gestured at the tasting counter. "Step right up."

"Now, what is it that makes this a tasting room and not a wine bar?"

"Do you want the boring legalities while you sip our two-year-old Chardonnay? It's a good place to start. Light, fruity. There was late rain that year so you might get a hint of sweet molds after the mild acidity."

"I will never get the hang of all the wine lingo. And yes, bore me with legalities." Missy set her handbag, as petite and trim as the rest of her, on the old oak bar.

"The lingo of wine is easier once you've tasted a lot of variety. We're not selling you a full glass of wine, just a taste, that's one legality. And you've already noticed there's no place to sit. The assumption is you're here to taste and will move on fairly quickly. We're also not licensed to sell food. Just to let you taste our wine and shop in our little store."

The couple at the end of the bar, a picnic hamper between them, gestured. "We'll take the 'oh-three Cabernet and the 'oh-two reserve. It's wonderful."

Syrah nodded. "Be right with." She watched Missy taste the Chardonnay and recognized a few signs that Missy knew a little more about wine than she let on. "There is a small fee for the tasting, but we'll only charge that if you don't buy a bottle of wine."

"This is delicious," Missy said. "A little bite on the end, but it eases off on the way down."

"That's the late rain talking." Syrah went around the bar to the store that shared the rest of the tasting room's space, picking out the two bottles the couple had requested. "Do you need me to wrap these for you?"

"Not the Cabernet," the man said. "That's for the picnic."

"You got it." She carefully wrapped the bottle of reserve and totaled the two at the register. Credit card and wine were exchanged as she finished the transaction. "And as you can see," she said to Missy, "what you do with that bottle of wine when you walk out our door is your business. You just can't drink it in here."

"Hence your beautiful patio, and that gazebo just down the hill."

Syrah nodded. "Ready for the Riesling?"

Missy tipped the rest of the Chardonnay into the crock nearest her and Syrah rinsed the glass with a swish of water, tipping it again into the crock. "Oh, it's got a lovely color on it."

"It does, and good legs for a Riesling. We've done better, I'll be honest, but this is a fine white wine for a party. Good quality and taste but won't break the bank."

"That's actually why I came. I'm hosting a—"

"Miss Bingley!" Bennett emerged from the kitchen, busily wiping both hands on a tea towel. "You've made a beeline for us, how flattering. You've met our Syrah, I see."

"That I have, Mrs. Bennett."

"Bennett—everyone calls me Bennett. You would like a plate of my strawberries and cheese, I can tell. Syrah here picked those strawberries this morning. She's very useful and everyone agrees she's easy on the—"

"I can't pour for her and serve her food at the same time, Bennett. You know that."

"Silly rules and nonsense." Bennett swooped down on Missy Bingley, taking her by the arm. "You'll put one foot in my kitchen and I will serve you food, and Syrah will pour for you from her side."

Missy laughed, and Syrah had to admit it was charming and seemed genuine enough. "I actually had a sandwich before I came, because I didn't want to get tipsy. But thank you very much, Bennett, for the offer."

Bennett stepped back as Missy picked up her glass of wine. "Are you considering an Ardani vintage for your Wine for Dimes get-together? Such a neighborly thing to do." She fixed Syrah with a hard look.

"Yes, it is," Syrah belatedly chimed in. "And when the order is for a charity event we extend wholesale prices and could be easily talked into donating a bottle or two of something special for auction. Our 'ninety-four reserve Cabernet Sauvignon is coming into its prime."

"I do like this one," Missy said. "It's very cheerful."

Syrah grinned. "And you say you don't know the lingo of wine. A well-balanced pH to me is cheerful to you. Would you like to try the Gewürztraminer?"

"No, I rarely care for it. But the Pinot Noir is a must." She extended her glass.

"You'll be at the Spring Fling, won't you, Miss Bingley?"

"Everybody calls me Missy, Bennett. And yes, I will be. It sounds like a lot of fun."

"It'll seem a bit of a country dance after San Francisco," Syrah observed.

"Nonsense." Bennett wrapped the towel around her hands as if she wanted to snap Syrah with it. "It's an enjoyable evening."

"You've never been to it." Syrah watched Missy taste the Pinot and could tell Missy liked it from the way she took a deep breath after she swallowed.

Missy's gaze flicked to the pricing sheet and Syrah could almost see her asking herself, "Yes, but do I like it twice as much?"

The door chime tinkled and Syrah glanced up. "Goodness, is it noon already?"

Jane had a sour expression as she crossed the room. "Yeah, and I'm filthy. I need to wash up." She disappeared into the kitchen with Bennett in hot pursuit.

"I don't have many strawberries, Jane, so no poaching." The door swung shut behind them.

Missy finished the Pinot with a slight shiver of delight. "This is extremely tasty. I thought the Chardonnay was good, but in comparison, it's not in this league."

"That's why I served the Chardonnay to you first. You'll find a lot of our Chardonnay in the markets, but only a specialty shop will have the Pinot."

"I can really taste the difference."

The kitchen door swung open again. "You'd think the strawberries are made of gold," Jane complained.

Missy transferred her gaze from Syrah to Jane and Syrah was abruptly aware that Missy's eyes were a light, twinkling shade of blue and the color that flushed her pale skin quite attractive. One slender hand needlessly tidied her short blond curls, and the carefully crimsoned lips were parted as if she was going to say something but had forgotten how to speak.

After several seconds, Syrah glanced at Jane and nearly did a double-take. Jane's color was rising, too, but only someone who knew her well would be able to tell under the tan. She seemed frozen in place and was uncharacteristically quite, quite still.

Bennett bustled out of the kitchen again, then paused to take in the tableau. She looked first at the blushing Missy, then the deer-in-the-headlights Jane, and finally gave Syrah a look that said, "And look what you've missed out on now!"

The silence was broken by the arrival of her father, who beamed at Jane. "Haven't seen you in a dog's year."

Jane, flushed to her ears, managed to say, "Hi. Yeah," before she went back to staring at Missy.

Syrah hoisted the first bottle of red on the tasting list. "Cabernet?"

Missy's batting eyelashes could have fanned a forest fire. "Yes, please, unless you've . . . got a date." Her gaze darted to Jane, who, Syrah decided, looked exceedingly stupid with her mouth hanging open.

"Not a date," she started to say.

"I'll finish pouring, Syrah. You could use a break after dealing with the testing meters all morning." Her father took the bottle of Cabernet out of her hand and turned his genial host's smile on Missy. "I'm Anthony Ardani. What have you liked so far?"

"This is Missy Bingley, who's just bought Netherfield," Bennett explained.

Syrah marched across the room to clamp onto Jane's arm. "Let's go for a swim," she said pleasantly, all the while dragging Jane toward the door. "What the heck was that all about?" she demanded once they were in Jane's old truck.

"Who was that?"

"Missy Bingley. You said she needed a wife."

"Wow."

31

"I thought I should get you two a room or something."

"Wow." Jane's turn onto the back road was distracted. "She's the most beautiful woman I've ever seen."

Syrah rolled her eyes. "Beauty is in the eye of the beholder."

"Oh, come on, Syrah. Wasn't she gorgeous? And that smile!"

Syrah had to grin. "I'll admit she's very pretty. And quite charming."

"Did she notice me?"

"Gee, I don't know. She just blushed and stared for two full minutes."

"Not on account of me."

"Well, it wasn't over me, and it wasn't over Bennett."

"I have to figure out how to see her again. Maybe I can get onto one of the landscaping crews she's going to need."

Jane was incapable of speaking on any other subject for the duration of their dip in the pond. She took forever to get dressed, which made them late, and was still in a rosy, puppy-love state when she shoved Syrah out of the truck at the foot of the road.

Hiking up the winding road to the house, she saw that Missy Bingley's car was still there. If only Jane had known, Syrah mused, I wouldn't be getting all sweaty walking up the hill.

Her father was chatting with Missy in an easy fashion and wrapping several bottles. Missy turned when she heard the door chime and smiled sweetly at Syrah, but her gaze searched behind her, then fell.

"Jane was late getting back to work and couldn't stop in," Syrah explained.

"Of course."

Syrah sighed to herself. She didn't want to lose Jane to some doomed romance for the duration of the summer, but they'd been friends too long for her not to help Jane when she could. "She's an artist, most of the time. But right now she's making the rent money landscaping."

"Jane's quite talented," her father observed. "I can't say I under-

32

stand her art, but she has a way with plants. Our hillside was orig-
inally her creation."

Missy glanced out the window. "Is it? It's lovely, all the different
shades of purple and red, with oranges along the crest. I love those
feathery sages mixed with the spikey ones—is that aloe? All that
variety but it's beautiful as a whole, too."

"You should see her paintings," Syrah offered.

"Yes." Missy's tone made Syrah want an insulin injection. "Yes,
I should."

# Chapter 4

"Gotta love being able to work at thirty-two thousand feet!" The man in the seat adjacent to Toni's plugged his laptop into the outlet and reached for the snack the steward had provided just after they reached cruising altitude. "This is what makes first class worth it."

Toni shrugged. "I actually enjoy being unreachable for the duration of a flight. Sometimes it's the only rest I get." She finished the water she'd requested and reclined in her seat. Turning her face to the window she hoped the fellow would become quickly engrossed in his work. Airplane small talk could be tiresome.

Her nerves quieted and she went through her To Do list for arrival in California. Missy was going to pick her up in San Francisco and they were frantically driving to someplace north in order to get to a dance on time. She hadn't intended to make the trip so quickly, but after the scene with Mira she had found nearly everything about her apartment, New York and the office intensely irritating. She wanted to be away from it all, for a little while. California was as good a place as any, even if she'd have to go out into the country.

When she'd gotten to Mira's hotel, Rafi had called up to announce he was ready for her party. Toni hadn't been surprised when Nancy had appeared along with Mira. It was very Mira, to have Toni pay for the cab ride to get Mira and her new lover out of town. Mira cared very little who paid for things in her life, as long as she didn't have to—that much was becoming exceedingly clear.

Both women had been surprised to find Toni in the back of the waiting car. Nancy drew back hastily, as if trying not to be seen, while Mira merely gaped.

"Nancy, Mira and I are going for a short drive through the park. We'll be back in just a few."

"I don't think that's necessary." Mira dripped haughty disdain into every word.

"It is. Trust me, it is. I had an interesting talk with Crystal this morning."

Mira had enough decency to look momentarily chagrined, then she nodded at Nancy. "We'll be right back. Don't worry, we can always get another flight to Houston."

Nancy, having not said a word, faded into the background of Toni's thoughts as they pulled away from the curb. So even the bit about going home to London was a lie. The divider was up between them and the driver, so she didn't bother to mince words.

"I've covered the money you stole from Crystal."

"I stole nothing! I knew you'd cover it."

"In that case, it's the money you stole from me."

"I'll pay you back when I get my estate."

Toni opened her portfolio and extracted a single sheet of paper. "This is the total of the cost of the jewelry you borrowed from me, and Crystal's money."

"What did you do, take an inventory after you walked out last night? Did you count the teaspoons, too?"

The sneer on Mira's face was unattractive and Toni had to stop herself from pointing that out. She didn't want to get into a shouting match. "I noticed the amethyst bracelet was gone, and then of course, I looked for the earrings."

"I'll send them back."

"Of course you will. I'm glad we don't misunderstand that they're mine."

"You are being a bitch about this." Mira stared out the window as she sulked.

It was a sunny day in Central Park, but inside the car it felt like winter. Toni tried not to remember how Mira had made her laugh sometimes. There was no laughter left, making the past irrelevant.

"The jewelry doesn't mean anything to me. It's Crystal—I can't believe you lied to her and took her money. You could have called me. I might have even said yes."

"Given the way you took the news of my leaving, I had no reason to think so. You weren't open to talking about anything."

"What was I supposed to do, Mira? It was over. You said it yourself. You'd already cleared out, already helped yourself to what you wanted."

"I didn't think you'd walk out like that. It was humiliating. I had to make up a lie to a waiter."

"You didn't seem to mind lying to Crystal." Before Mira could protest, she went on, "Were we supposed to dine and kiss goodbye at the door? I don't get it."

"No, you don't. I didn't realize that until you walked out."

"Wait—you are not going to make this situation into a guessing game where I have to figure out what I did wrong. I walked out of a restaurant. You were walking out of our relationship. You ended it, not me."

Mira glared at her across the space separating them. There was no charm in her now, and no remnant of the graceful, easy, seductive woman who had first attracted Toni. "Yes, I did, and now you're being petty."

"Thirty thousand dollars cheated out of one of my employees—

seduced out of her—that's not petty." Toni couldn't help her rising tone.

"Is that it? Is it because I gave Crystal what she'd been craving for months?"

"You and Crystal are adults and can do anything you want. But you tricked her out of money, fucked her and left her feeling shitty because she thought she'd betrayed me. And then she discovered you'd lied to her about the money. But none of that matters to you, does it?"

Mira leaned toward Toni, her eyes dark with anger. "First of all, I knew you'd pay her back—you are incredibly predictable. And I was done with you and could have fucked anyone I wanted without your middle-class values getting all up in arms. And she was not thinking about you when she dragged me into that bathroom. If she's guilty, that's not my problem, and now she knows she wasn't getting it on with her boss's girlfriend, so where's the injury? Exactly what have I done?"

Toni was nonplussed. "You caused Crystal a massive amount of anxiety and pain. She feels like a dupe."

"But it's all better now. She'll forgive me, even. I bet we hook up when I get back. She was very . . . eager."

Toni couldn't look at Mira, and in her mind's eye all she could see was Crystal's tear-streaked face. What a horrible first time with a woman—Crystal might never trust a lover again. Hell, Toni thought, I might not either. She'd had no idea Mira could be like this. "I was supposed to beg you to stay, wasn't I? And when I didn't, you decided to hurt someone else."

"You give yourself too much importance, Toni, dear." The modulated, sexy British accent that Toni had found so attractive became a stabbing pain behind her ears.

"You resigned, and I was supposed to make a counteroffer to keep you. Oh!" Another thought occurred to her and she slowly smiled at Mira. "Thirty thousand—that was the finder's fee you expected from the Bookworthy deal. But Kyle told you yesterday morning it wasn't going through. You figured you were owed it anyway and Crystal was handy. How efficient—you used the fewest number of people for the maximum return," she ended sarcastically.

"I learned it from you."

"I don't use people."

"Oh, really? What do you call your business tactics?"

"Honest. I don't deny they're brutal sometimes. But I am honest with people."

"Tell that to all those people in Georgia out of work because you wouldn't budge on your investment rate."

"I'd compromised all I could on behalf of the potential investor consortium. The owners, the union, the city government—they refused to compromise at all. So I walked. I told them that I would, I gave them a deadline, and then I walked."

"And all those people lost their jobs."

Wounded by the memory, Toni said fiercely, "That's not my fault. I'm not representing a charity that will give millions of dollars to keep a poorly run company in business, a company that will keep wanting more and more while everyone selfishly thinks they are *owed* what they have. The union needed to come down ten percent, and I wanted the owners to give up fifteen. The city needed to extend tax incentives already in place for three more years, and then and only then were my investors willing to take on risk at a low rate of return because I really wanted to save those jobs. But everybody wanted the money for free." Toni gave Mira a scathing look. "Money is only free to people like you."

Mira was smiling and Toni hated that Mira had successfully goaded her into a tirade. "And here we are at last. I knew sooner or later you'd resent that I inherited my money and you had to get lucky in a few business deals to have yours."

"That's not what I meant, Mira, *darling*. I meant you taking money that's not yours, and thinking you're owed it. You have no intention of paying me back."

38

"I don't now." Mira shrugged, coolly assured. "I wanted to end things as friends."

"I am not some aging executive who needs to pay for a young pretty thing on his arm to look successful. Did you really think I was going to beg you to stay, and pay you to do so?"

There was an abrupt suspicion of tears in Mira's eyes, but Toni didn't believe them. "I thought you loved me. I thought you'd show it. And once I knew for sure that you did, I was going to ask you for a loan. But you've no idea how hurt I was last night. You cut me to the bone when you didn't even answer me."

*I don't love you anymore.* Toni made herself replay that phrase, and she ground the shattered glass of it into her brain again and again. Remember the facts, she told herself. Gritting her teeth she said, "Your Plan A didn't work out, and you executed Plan B. You would have been long gone if Crystal's plane hadn't been late. So here's the deal."

"I'm not signing that paper." Mira waved a hand. "You can forget that."

"Fine, don't sign it. I'll sue your estate for it, with interest."

"You'll look stupid if you try that."

"No. You see, I don't need the money and everybody knows that. It must be about principle if I'm willing to sue over it. Some people might get the idea you're Not Nice."

"You'd have to drag Crystal into it."

"You're right. I don't want to, but I will. And she's angry enough that she'd agree. It'll get ugly, mostly for you. You're nice to that bombshell heiress with her own reality TV show, and you'll even party with her, but behind her back I know what you and the other Blue Bloods really think of her. You don't want to be her, with a sex-and-money scandal hanging around your neck, Lady Wickham."

Mira said nothing, but Toni could tell from the tiny flinch that she had scored a point.

"You shouldn't have fucked her."

"I was mad at you." Mira picked at a fraying edge of the seat leather.

Poor Crystal, Toni thought. She hadn't even been real to Mira. "So here's my offer. We'll agree the money is a gift. Keep the jewelry. Stay away from my employees and my business deals, for, oh, forever. We'll part *friends*."

"This conversation wasn't even necessary. That was how I felt."

"I'm sure you did. But I think a business deal is better spelled out, don't you?"

Mira went half-limp, all the fight apparently gone. After a sigh, she said, "You don't really know what it's like to be me."

Poor little rich girl. Toni stopped herself from rolling her eyes.

"I'm supposed to be rich. I'm not supposed to work for a living. But until I'm thirty-five I'm supposed to live on an amount that won't even pay your rent. What am I supposed to do with my time if I can't have a job? What except hang out with other people like me? And they expect me to have the money they do. And I *will*." Mira's eyes again glittered with tears, but this time Toni knew they were real. "But not for another four bloody years."

Toni thought, you could have gone to a top university and walked out the other side knowing your quarter million in student loans would be paid off like magic. You could have volunteered with the Peace Corps and seen what poverty really looks like. You could have studied art in Tuscany, or written that novel you talk about, and almost certainly have gotten it published. You could have done anything. But you only wanted to dance, ski and travel in your private flock of pretty birds. "There are billions of people who would love to have your hard life."

Mira's eyes flashed. "I am what I'm expected to be. I was what you wanted, wasn't I? You may not need someone like me on your arm to prove you're successful, but you liked it all the same. You wanted a foot into my world and thought the admission could be bought. Only you didn't fit in, no matter how hard you tried."

Stung, Toni said, "I loved you. I didn't love your world. I didn't like your friends. I didn't think you were really as shallow as that whole scene, but I was wrong. Just like that, I realized I was wrong."

"That's right, Toni, dear. You have all that money you made and you tried to get into the rich and famous category. But since it's so obvious that you don't fit in, now you're saying you never wanted it. Right. Fine. You keep talking that talk. Take me back to the hotel."

Once upon a time Mira had made her laugh and feel like a lucky, happy woman. They'd enjoyed hot dogs from pushcarts and warm Friday nights strolling in the park. They'd made love slow, fast, soft, hard, everything in between. Mira had been adventurous and intense.

"I loved you," Toni had said then.

"At least Nancy knows who she is and what she expects from me." Mira had crossed her legs and retreated into wounded silence, not saying another word.

A shaft of light made Toni flinch as the plane slowly banked, and she hurriedly pulled the shade down partway.

I was not in love with her title, future money or social set, she told herself angrily. *I was in love with her, with who I thought she was. I'm proud of who I am, and what I do with my life. I wasn't trying to be something I'm not.*

It was getting harder to make herself believe it. When Doc Burbidge had accepted the preliminary contract Toni had faxed him later that day, she'd realized she needed to get the California trip out of the way before he demanded her full attention. It would be good to see Missy again, even though she had serious doubts about the beautiful women, the wonderful wine and assurances of lively song at some local dance, no doubt held in a barn. She expected nothing but a rapid conclusion of her business.

"Is she here yet?" Jane bounced on the balls of her feet, looking so much like a puppy that Syrah wanted to whop her on the nose with a rolled-up newspaper.

"Not yet, for the tenth time in ten minutes. Dance with me. I'll watch the door with you."

Jane dutifully, if unenthusiastically, pulled Syrah onto the still uncrowded dance floor. The Fling would not be in full swing for another hour, but the prospect of being a wallflower even this early in the evening was daunting. Syrah loved dances and dancing but she didn't like feeling as if she were once again in high school. She normally didn't have to ask Jane to dance with her, but Jane was irrevocably fixated on Missy Bingley. Syrah wanted to believe it was temporary, but the way Jane was behaving was so very Not Jane that it was starting to scare her.

They gyrated in time with "Don't Leave Me This Way." Jane was a good dancer, full of exuberance and willing to let go to the music. Her arms raised, she snapped her fingers as she twisted to the beat. Her nipples strained against her purple muscle tee, which had ridden up enough to display a washboard stomach.

Not for the first time, Syrah thought if she didn't love Jane like a sister, she'd want to jump her very graceful, elegant bones. Her own dancing, and attire, was slightly more reserved, but tonight it liberated her from her worries.

The Fling was getting off to a slow start, and at the moment less than half of the thirty to forty women were dancing. Toes were tapping and many bright eyes cast around for someone willing to make the first move. There was a small flash of light as the bar door opened and closed, foretelling of new arrivals. Syrah turned in place to see Missy enter, followed by a stranger. Missy was smiling broadly, already nodding at women she knew. Her gaze was sweeping the room when it suddenly froze about two feet behind Syrah. The easiness of the smile waned, then redoubled.

Syrah glanced behind her at Jane, who had frozen in midstep, then hastily recovered her poise.

In that flash of an instant, Syrah had a terrifying but undeniable thought. *Someday I will be the best friend toasting them at their wedding.*

She was so absorbed in the palpable exchange of electricity between Missy and Jane that she didn't immediately study the stranger at Missy's heel. When she did focus on the taller, black-haired woman, what she noticed first was the complete lack of any kind of smile. The Dark Shadow, Syrah thought, then she connected the unsmiling reaction as the woman watched Missy greet Jane.

She felt a surge of protectiveness for her friend and did what a best friend ought to do. "Lovely to see you again," she said heartily, and she gave Missy a decent dyke hug while clearly ceding her position as Jane's dance partner.

Missy introduced Dark Shadow to Jane, and then Syrah, but a blast of music drowned out what she said. Syrah had no desire to ask again. Wherever this woman was from she had gone out of her way to overdress. Missy was fittingly clad in jeans and a tank top that was woven with something that sparkled when she moved—a casual, stylish femme to the max. Dark Shadow's black slacks looked like raw silk, and the long-sleeved blouse was crimson silk, and shot with golden threads to boot. Given the rising temperature inside the bar, she'd be soaked with sweat in ten minutes, and with the way she was continuing to glower at Jane, Syrah was going to revel in the woman's discomfort.

Jane and Missy continued to smile at each other without saying anything deeper than "This is fun" and "Yes, it is" back and forth. Jane abruptly offered to buy drinks—an extravagance Syrah wouldn't have allowed, but Dark Shadow quickly said, "I'll take care of it."

Syrah frowned. Dark Shadow seemed to think that Jane was penniless or something. She shook her head with a distant no when asked what she would like. "Thank you, but it's a little early for me. Besides, I want to dance."

"Fine," Dark Shadow replied, with that steady, frozen regard. The dark hair thick around her shoulders was so glossy Syrah wanted to believe it was fake. "Your usual, Missy?"

"I feel like a Long Island iced tea tonight," Missy said, her soft gaze still fixed on Jane.

Dark Shadow quirked an eyebrow and for just a moment Syrah thought she looked familiar. A visitor to the tasting room, perhaps, but not recently. It might have been several years ago, before that discontented furrow had marked the olive-tinted brow. The hint of silver hair at each temple further stumped her memory, and Syrah gave it up.

"A beer, no glass necessary," Jane said when queried. "Thank you very much."

Becky Argost swooped down on Syrah at that moment, her gamin grin a welcome sight. "Two-step, come on!"

Jane didn't exactly seize Missy's hand but they were right behind Becky and Syrah as they swung into the rhythm of the Johnny Cash song. The music brought more women onto the floor and they circulated with a flurry of laughter and flashing arms and shoulders. From over Becky's shoulder, Syrah delighted in watching Dark Shadow waiting virtually alone in one corner, a tall glass in one hand and two beers by the neck in the other. She was sure the beer was an attempt to slum it with the local yokels.

Briefly, just before Becky steered them through a thick patch of other dancers, she thought Dark Shadow was studying her, but later, she wasn't sure.

"Toni, I'm in love. I am absolutely in love. Isn't she gorgeous? A wonderful dancer and her fingers—I mean, what they felt like on my back was giving me incredibly explicit ideas!"

Toni, having endured an hour of watching Missy dancing with Jane, handed her friend another cocktail napkin to mop her brow. "Do you want another drink?"

"This water is fine, or I'll fall down. The only place I'd want to fall tonight is on top of Jane. She's an artist."

"Will she show you her etchings?" Toni gazed across the empty field that the bar's back patio overlooked.

"God, I hope so." Missy drank deeply from the bottled water, letting out a refreshed gasp. "I don't think I've ever met anyone quite like her."

It wasn't the first time Toni had heard Missy voice similar sentiments about other attractive butches. "How successful is she in her career?"

"I asked her if there was someplace I could see her work, and it's displayed in a local gallery. But she's so unpretentious. She said she sold enough paintings to keep her in landscaping work."

Toni knew when to keep her thoughts to herself with Missy, but her tone was overly dry when she observed, "A riveting success, I take it then."

"Oh, don't be disagreeable and dour, T.B. You are not going to take the fun out of this for me."

"Have fun. Have lots and lots of fun."

"Oh, and by that you mean, fun and nothing else? I'm in love, I tell you."

Missy's eyes were sparkling but Toni suspected the Long Island iced tea was responsible. She merely nodded.

"And have you ever seen such a great group of good-looking women? Must be the country air. I hope it does me as much good. You should dance."

"I don't see anyone I'd like to dance with."

"What about Jane's friend? She has wonderful eyes."

Toni grudgingly agreed about the eyes—large, luminous, dark and expressive. Of course, the expression in them hadn't been very welcoming to either her or Missy. "Really, you've lost your perspective. The women here seem no more exceptional than anywhere else I've been, in spite of all the hype about California girls. Several are definitely below the par. You think everyone is beautiful tonight."

"Well, someone else then. There are plenty of women obviously waiting to be asked."

"They can dance with one another, can't they?"

Missy heaved a sigh. "I don't know what to do with you when you're in this mood. The *reech beech*, she was very, very bad for you."

45

"Oh, I don't doubt it." Toni might have added more, but like a faithful slave, Jane arrived in the patio doorway. She followed the star-struck pair back into the bar, although it was much cooler outside, and all she saw of Missy for the next hour was her backside, increasingly covered by Jane's hands.

"Yes, yes," Syrah said for the fiftieth time. She frowned into the dark outside Jane's truck window as she rested her forehead on the cool glass. "She's beautiful and nice. But she has poor taste in friends. You should have heard that woman going on about women here being 'below the par.'"

Jane slowed for a yellow light. "Perhaps you misheard."

"I could hear perfectly fine from the other side of the tree. 'Below the par' is exactly what she said. And you didn't have to give me a ride home—you could have gone with Missy. It wouldn't have been the first time we arrived together and left separately."

Jane gave an indignant snort. "Aspen was angling to take you home and you're drunk."

Syrah hiccupped delicately. "That's true. Thank you. Go home with Aspen and next thing you know you're joined at the hip."

"Plus, well, Missy and I were really hot together and, um, I got scared."

"Scared? You?" Syrah slowly turned her head to look at Jane. Well, there were two Janes, so she focused on Jane-on-the-left. "Since when has sex scared you?"

"Not sex, it's the morning after. I take her to my place and in the morning she realizes it's an aircraft hanger."

"A very comfortable, spacious artist's workspace, a studio, not an aircraft hangar. You think she's going to freak on you?"

"Maybe."

"Then she's not worth your time." Syrah experimented with opening and closing her eyes and eventually found just the right amount of open so there was only one Jane. "Not worth the time of the most gorgeous woman in the room, my friend Jane."

"You are going to be so unhappy in the morning."

"I'm not that drunk." Syrah rubbed the side of her nose and Jane-on-the-left came back.

"Sure. I'll pour you into bed."

"I'm worried about business. Worried about that business consultant. Sooner or later she's going to show up, or call or something."

"If you want, I could make sure whoever it is ends up in the peat moss, no questions asked."

"Doesn't solve anything. There are a million more like her. The banks won't stop charging inner-est. Okay, stop. Stop now."

Jane rolled to the side of the road and leaned across Syrah to push open the passenger door. The fresh air was nearly enough to stave off the sudden spasm in Syrah's stomach, then she stumbled onto the dirt and unceremoniously threw up in the weeds.

The small part of her that was sober was spewing invectives at the rest of her that had just *had* to have one more drink, then one more. She'd not been this drunk since high school, and she had thought she was over being so foolish.

Jane, like a good friend, provided napkins and even had a slightly stale bottle of water to sip from. Syrah was starting to feel like maybe she wouldn't die when, just then, headlights illuminated them.

Within a few moments a low-slung sports car slowed to stop. "Are you okay?"

Jane hurried to the car. "We're fine, Missy, really. Syrah . . ."

She couldn't hear what Jane said but she kept her back to the car because the headlights were going to stab her eyes out if she didn't. It was a mercifully short while before the car resumed its journey and Syrah was left in peaceful darkness.

Great, just great. Jane's fixation-of-the-week had seen what class of company she kept. Her best buddy Syrah, barfing on the side of the road, great. And Dark Shadow was probably there, too, just great.

They were underway again before she muttered, "Below the par, my ass. She never did dance with anybody."

"Maybe she's married."

"Married women can dance. Nothing wrong with that." Syrah thought about the chiseled, humorless face as she kneaded her hands into her stomach, willing it to settle. "If you ask me, that woman needs to get laid. But who'd bother to seduce her, let alone marry her?"

"She's very attractive. And has that money thing, I'm sure."

"Like money builds character." Syrah stared out the window, fighting the urge to cry. Great, she was an unhappy drunk now. She didn't really know how much money they needed to get out of their problems with the loans and shareholders. Even thinking *shareholder* made her stomach turn over.

The truck lights illuminated the driveway entrance to the winery grounds and Syrah was grateful for Jane's strong arms as they navigated the stairs to the second floor. The tasting room had been renovated several times over the years, but the rest of the house rambled in a grew-like-Topsy way, and Syrah didn't have the balance to navigate the twists and turns. Alone, she'd have probably passed out on the kitchen floor.

Horizontal felt heavenly. She was aware of Jane being a good valet by pulling off her shoes and socks, and she didn't protest when her jeans hit the floor. She felt so much better.

"You," Jane said in the dark, "are going to be very, very sorry tomorrow."

"I know," Syrah thought she said, then a hammer hit her between the eyes.

# Chapter 5

"I'm usually better prepared, but I haven't even looked up the directions." Toni twisted her hair back and clamped it firmly with a comb. It had felt good around her shoulders last night, but today was not about Warm and Friendlies. The late night hadn't helped the jet-lag bags under her eyes, either.

Missy lounged across the guestroom bed, still in her robe. "I don't know my way around very well, but if it's a winery I might know it. I went tasting for the charity thing." She smiled nostalgically. "Very nice things can happen in wineries."

"You look besotted," Toni said, trying not to be irritated. Missy was almost unreasonable with her gooey reminiscences about Jane.

"I am besotted. She's such a gentleman. She knew I'd have gone home with her, but didn't ask."

It had surprised Toni, but all it meant was that Jane was far more clever than most of the attractive, brooding butch women in Missy's life before now. She glanced at Missy in the mirror. "Well, she had her friend to get home. She probably has to do that all the time."

"Do you think? Syrah doesn't strike me as a drinker, and after my mother, well, I can spot an alcoholic a mile off." Missy put her head down on her arms, leaving Toni alone with her own reflection.

"Is that the friend's name?" She slowly buttoned her blouse. "Syrah Ardani? That was Syrah Ardani, Ardani Vineyards?"

"Yeah, didn't you hear me introduce her?"

"It was too loud."

"How do you know the—" Missy lifted her head to regard Toni in the mirror with horror. "Oh, no. That's why you're here. Oh, that's awful. She's very nice. And her father is *adorable*."

Hell. Now she wondered if the borderline hostility in Syrah's greeting had been because she knew why Toni was there. Frankly, however, she'd have thought Syrah Ardani would be *much* more hostile than that—she might not have heard the introductions either. "I've no doubt they are swell people, but I can't say more than that."

"Business can suck." Missy looked almost tearful. "I don't know how you do what you do, T.B. It would kill me."

Toni steeled herself against a flurry of images—her father meeting her mother for the first time, at the introduction of the man she would be evaluating in less than an hour. A little girl with eyes that had left an indelible impression on her father. She thought of the way Syrah Ardani's very grown-up eyes had sought her out for just a moment when she was dancing and she made herself remember the cold, hard facts. Syrah Ardani was the debutante who'd just gotten back from Europe. Given her roadside performance after the dance, she was still a party girl.

The party was over.

"It's not easy, sometimes," she admitted to Missy. "Especially when people who've not done anything wrong get hurt. There's nothing wrong with thinking if you go to work every day and do an honest day's work you ought to be able to go on doing that, live your life, raise a family."

"But the world changes too fast for that these days. I know why you gave all that money to the Inner City Education Fund. You don't want to be laying them off because they don't have a flexible mindset or the skills to change jobs if they have to."

Toni fastened her cuffs. "It's just guilt money, nothing more."

"Shut up," Missy snapped. "I hate it when you say things like that. Mira—"

"Mira occasionally spoke the truth. I've gotten very rich."

"Playing by the rules!"

"Rules that favor me in every game. There." She patted her hair.

Missy appeared behind Toni and slipped her arms around Toni's waist. "You're a good person, Toni. I'll never believe otherwise."

Light and dark, Toni always thought, when the two of them were side-by-side. "Why don't we love each other?"

"I thought we did."

"You know what I mean."

"Maybe . . ." Missy patted Toni's stomach. "Maybe we are meant to be the best friends ever in the history of the world."

Toni laughed, marveling as always how Missy could make life seem very simple. Her laughter faded as she made herself ask, "So, how do I get to Ardani Vineyards?"

Syrah awoke with the certain knowledge that her head was stuck in a bottling machine. *Thump-click-slam-whuff-zzzzzzzz-thump-click-slam-whuff.* For quite some time she could only pray for the machine to stop.

She feared the creak of the bedroom door was Bennett bearing anything that could be food. Instead she had only a mere warning of claws on hardwood before the bed exploded in motion.

"Hound!" Syrah clutched her head. "Get off the bed, please!"

Hound licked her face, and the smell of dog breath was Syrah's undoing. It was nearly an hour before she reached the stage of being able to put her sheets and shirt, clothes from the floor and the bathroom rug into the washing machine.

Bennett said nothing when Syrah made it to the kitchen. She gave a pointed look at a mug of coffee on the counter and went back to rapidly chopping nuts. Machine-gun fire pinged between Syrah's ears.

When she opened her eyes again, head still on the kitchen table where she'd slumped, it was just after twelve. Her nose was being tickled with the scent of fresh coffee and this time it didn't make her want to die.

"So you had quite the fun night," Bennett observed. Her hands were smoothing what looked like—in the very brief glance Syrah gave the food—pesto chicken wraps.

"It was fun until I was stupid." Syrah cautiously sipped the coffee. It stayed down. She heaved a sigh of relief. "Don't make me anything to eat for lunch."

"This isn't for you. Some woman showed up to see your father and they're in the office."

"Oh." Syrah frowned. "Who's pouring?"

"Nobody here yet, but it's a beautiful day and I bet we get busy soon."

Syrah nodded and regretted it. The thought of smelling wine was threatening her equilibrium.

Bennett set a small bowl of steaming something in front of her. "Just a couple of bites and you'll start to feel better."

Halfway through the bowl of chicken noodle soup, salty but otherwise mild, she did feel better. A small of glass of water and some Advil went down next and then a few crackers. By the time the first tasters arrived she felt nearly human. She still had to breathe through her mouth when she uncorked the first bottle but the food in her stomach stayed put.

When the customers left she was aware of the low sound of voices from the office and recalled that someone had stopped in. It had been a long meeting, and on a Sunday. She crossed the tasting room to blatantly eavesdrop and heard the woman saying, "I really didn't plan to go into all these details today."

"Sooner the better," her father answered. "I'm sure it's all a misunderstanding, as I've said."

"I wish I could say that it was, but when payments haven't been made for so long, and there appears to be no means to begin making them, the lenders are understandably anxious."

Syrah closed her eyes, feeling dizzy. She tried to make sense of the words but nothing was tracking.

"Couldn't the investors make those payments? Can't we give them more shares?"

"They have to want them, Mr. Ardani, and I have no assurance from any of them that they do."

"But Ms. Blanchard, not two years ago everyone was saying how great it all *penciled*, I think that was the word. Why doesn't it now?"

"That's why I'm here—"

Syrah pushed opened the door and stared dumbly at Toni Blanchard. She first connected the haughty curve of neck with the *Inc.* magazine photograph, but in another moment, Syrah recognized Dark Shadow.

They regarded each other in silence but Syrah could have sworn she saw Toni Blanchard's dark gray eyes replaying that charming scene by the road with Syrah throwing up in the weeds. There was a brief roar in her ears as she heard again "below the par" and recalled the disdain the woman had shown toward Jane, and all of them.

"You're finally up, pumpkin. That was some dance." Her father pulled over a chair but Syrah declined to sit.

"It was. I'm listening for the bell. I wasn't aware you had business appointments today, Dad."

"Not today, tomorrow. Ms. Blanchard just dropped by."

Sure she did, Syrah wanted to snap. Why hadn't he told her the woman had been in touch for an appointment? She nearly demanded an answer from him but didn't want to admit in front of the viper that he had kept her in the dark.

Searching for something appropriate to say, head pounding, Syrah was relieved to hear the tasting room door open.

She turned to see Jane, who glanced around the empty room, then espied Syrah. Heartily, she said, "Well, you look like the cat dragged you in, then dragged you out again."

She gave Jane a wide-eyed glare of warning, then headed her off before she got any closer to the office. "In here," she hissed, dragging Jane into the kitchen.

"What? There weren't any customers—"

"The receivership woman is here!"

"Today? It's Sunday."

"Like that matters to business types. It's Monday somewhere in the world. It's Missy's friend, too. Toni Blanchard."

"No way." Jane regarded Syrah as if she'd just said aliens invented nacho cheese.

"Yes, it is."

"Oh, so Missy's not here. I saw her car and thought . . ."

"I don't have time for you and Missy news right now."

"Syrah, you don't have to be that way." Jane crossed her arms over her chest. "I know you're under a lot of pressure."

"And I'm hung over. The woman who decides if we keep our land or not saw me puking in the bushes last night. She thinks I'm dirt."

"I'll talk to Missy—"

"Don't you dare! Don't you even dare." The tasting room door opened again, and Syrah closed her eyes. "I'm in hell."

"I'll pour," Jane said immediately. "I've heard you enough I can do it."

"I just need a minute to find my wits," Syrah said. She gave Jane's arm a grateful squeeze. "I like Missy. I'm being a bitch. I'm not me right now."

Jane smiled. "It's okay. I know."

There was a clatter behind her and Syrah saw Bennett hastily arranging the wraps she'd been making on a tray. "I didn't know," she said. "I had no idea that was Toni Blanchard or I'd have been done already. The nerve of someone coming to talk heavy business like that on a Sunday. It's so ill-bred, I can hardly believe Missy has anything to do with her."

"Bennett, please, keep your voice down."

"Why should I? Is this her house already?"

The mere thought that someone else would take over this place stabbed so hard into Syrah's brain that she momentarily could not breathe. "I won't let that happen. She can't be that arrogant . . ."

From the frozen look on Bennett's face Syrah knew that the Blanchard woman had to be behind her.

She turned with all the dignity she could summon, which wasn't much. "Can I help you with something?"

"I came to apologize for my intrusion on your hospitality. My hope was to make everyone's acquaintance so that tomorrow we could settle down to business. Was there anything in the list of records I'd like to review that you didn't understand?"

"What li—" Syrah cleared her throat. "No, it was all clear."

The woman's eyes narrowed slightly and Syrah felt like a bug on a stick. "Then I'll see you at nine, if that's not too early."

"I'm usually up at sunrise," Syrah said truthfully.

Toni Blanchard looked skeptical. "Then nine o'clock it is." Her gaze flicked to Bennett, standing at the ready with her tray of food. "That looks lovely, but you didn't need to bother."

"The Ardanis have a long history of hospitality." Bennett sniffed. "Under all kinds of circumstances."

"I have no doubt of that." Toni turned to Syrah with a slight smile. "Your father got a phone call and I thought I ought to give him some privacy."

Bloody hell, Syrah thought. She'd have to entertain Dark Shadow now. "I'll show you the tasting room, then. Perhaps you'd like to begin Bennett's wonderful lunch with a glass of wine."

"That would be lovely."

Oh, aren't we cool and courteous, Syrah thought. They left the kitchen for the tasting room and Syrah pointed out various appointments in the store—local pottery and textiles that complemented various Ardani labels. "The tasting room is not the only way we sell wine, but it allows us the space to provide special events for buyers, not to mention the regional awareness of our vineyard. There are a lot of big names in this neck of the woods. We're a specialty vintner, relying on my father's skill to blend and create unique wines."

"What would you say is the average price of a bottle of wine that you sell?"

"Open or reserve?"

The woman's dark gaze swept over Syrah's face for a moment, then lit on the bar where Jane was chatting with several women. "What's the difference?"

We don't know everything, do we, Syrah thought. "Reserve wine has reached a limited quantity and is only for sale at our discretion. Its value is increasing as collectors anticipate its peak. Every wine has a range when it is at its best. Sometimes a wine is reserve from the moment we open the first bottle." She shrugged. "We taste it and we know. We put it on reserve because it will go up in value. An open wine is expected to sell out and no one will exactly tear their hair out. It's consumable, certainly tasty, but it's not one you'd keep for a couple of years. Our open wines are considered very good in their price range."

"Which is?"

It's all about the money, Syrah scoffed to herself. "Twelve to eighteen dollars a bottle. Reserves can start in the low thirties and range up to the hundreds. The highest, our 'seventy-four Syrah, is over five hundred and will go up for three more years, when it peaks."

Blanchard nodded. "Your namesake wine."

"My birth year wine. Dad was so pleased that my mother said he spoke of little else. When I was born in December my name was a done deal."

"Well, I went to school with three other Tonis, two of them boys, so there's something to be said for unique."

Jane, from the bar, said, "Could have been worse. She could have been named Riesling or Gewürz."

Everyone laughed and Syrah kept a smile on her face. Her temples were throbbing with purple lightning from the effort of making nice with someone who couldn't wait to pounce on every weakness.

She rescued Jane from pouring duty and offered up the first of the reds to the waiting trio of women. They were all cute in that twenty-something way, and she got definite couple vibes from two of them. "This is our 'oh-two Cabernet."

Toni Blanchard was wandering around the store, but occasionally her gaze flickered to Syrah and every time it did, Syrah felt breathless and annoyed. Jane went over to chat and that, too, annoyed Syrah. She didn't like the way Toni Blanchard's eyes seemed to be tallying up the cost of Jane's clothing or haircut.

She briskly moved the three now giggling women to the Merlot and poured two modest glasses to accompany Bennett's lunch. She carried them into her father's office to find him staring pensively out the window.

"Call over?"

He nodded and took the glass she handed him. "Thanks, pumpkin."

Her voice low, Syrah asked, "Why didn't you tell me she was coming?"

"I didn't want you to worry. You've been on pins and needles since I showed you the letter." He breathed in the scent of the wine, though Syrah knew he had to have done so a hundred times already. "Let me take care of it."

"I need to be part of it, Dad." He'd been handling things for too long, maybe, she thought, then called herself disloyal. He'd run the vineyards for most of his life and done so successfully. She didn't understand why they were having problems now, all of a sudden. "This is my home and my land, too."

"I'm sure Toni will do right by us. She just needs lots of information."

"Show me the list later and I'll help—" She stiffened at the sound of footsteps approaching. "I'll ask Bennett to bring in lunch."

"Join us, pumpkin."

"No, I'm pouring, Dad. You enjoy yourselves." She stepped back to let Blanchard go past her and hoped she looked gracious. She suspected, however, that she did not.

Bennett muttered her way to the office while Syrah poured the reserve Cabernet Sauvignon. A new couple had arrived and Jane was chatting with everyone as she headed out the door. Syrah put out glasses and knew she'd be grateful for the arrival of full summer, when their vine manager's wife would run the tasting room.

She was distantly aware that the Blanchard woman had finally left but was too busy to do more than silently celebrate. If only she would be gone forever.


Missy's convertible was fun to drive but Toni found herself too deep in thought to really enjoy it. The road meandered through the rising and falling countryside and she thought distractedly that it reminded her of Bolton Landing. She knew her father still owned the bare bones cottage on Lake George but he hadn't been there in years. Decades.

Too late she realized she'd missed her turn and she found herself on a side road to another winery. She'd already seen more of one than she'd wanted to in a day, but when she pulled into the small parking lot the view was so pleasant she sat for a minute.

Riotous greens gave way to hints of golds on the hillside below her. She was fanciful enough to think—for just a moment—that the countryside held its breath in preparation for the explosion of summer. Most of what she was looking at had to be grapes, but there were trees aplenty, and the sunlight occasionally sparkled on moving water. A creek trickled nearby, pushing the beep of cabs and bustle of business a long way away, but she knew she couldn't forget where home was. She had a dozen phone calls to make and wasting time looking at grapes grow wasn't on her schedule.

She didn't want to leave the view, the sunshine. It helped her not think about Mira, and Mira seducing Crystal, or the prospect of a very unpleasant task ahead of her with the Ardani business.

She banished the flicker of Syrah Ardani's eyes from her memory. The real tragedy, she already suspected, was that Anthony Ardani was a sweet, thoughtful man who couldn't find his checkbook if it was nailed to his forehead. She was certain her examinations of the books and bank records would find that the vineyard had survived under his management only because they'd not borrowed heavily. The recent influx of cash had likely led to unwise spending and unwise borrowing. She'd seen it a hundred times. And she knew how the story ended, damn it.

She was revising her opinion of Syrah Ardani, however. She was no debutante, but certainly she was unused to facing life's hard realities. Her workday began at noon and she'd barely made it on time. Her friend, Jane, for all her show of affection for Missy, had promptly begun flirting with the women at the bar and she was certain the pair of them spent a great deal of time doing just that— flirting in bars. It reminded her too much of Mira. Different bars, different women, but the same lack of direction and ambition.

Annoyed at her temporary lack of focus, she found her way back to the road and followed Missy's directions to the highway. It was clogged with weekend traffic, but she didn't have more than a few miles to go. She knew that off of some of these exits were private roads leading to even more private estates. Somewhere in the area an uncle of Mira's had "a little place" of several thousand acres, and among the other things kept there was a collection of cars most museums would envy.

She liked the money she'd made, but Toni sincerely hoped, having seen the inside of Mira's world, that she never had so much that she traveled from place to place to visit her things.

She didn't know why she was thinking about Mira. She left the slow-moving highway behind, taking instead another country road that passed the tasting rooms for wineries with names she recognized, like Glen Ellen and Mondavi. She turned west and left what little town there was. The temperature dropped under the canopy of trees and a quick right led her past the tiny marker reading "Netherfield."

The driveway, cracked in places, wound through more trees, and even the car sounded hushed. The house, Missy had explained, was over two hundred years old but was structurally sound, if in need of some serious repair. It seemed like the kind of place where spirited heroines swooned into the embrace of heroes with dubious morals.

The shade of an ancient oak tree, circled at its base by cement benches, dropped the temperature around the back of the house several more degrees. Three men were huddled over the empty pool, discussing, no doubt, the equipment spread out on the ground. How Missy had found someone willing to work on a Sunday Toni didn't know, but the prospect of a swim some quiet afternoon was highly appealing.

She parked the car, disturbing a yellow-eyed cat enjoying a nap in the corner of the garage. Jingling Missy's keys in one hand she crossed the badly patched driveway to the house. She could appreciate what had caught Missy's eye about the house and grounds, but there was a lot of work ahead of her.

A door opened with a loud creak and she turned, expecting Missy, but the hair was slightly darker, the frame slightly smaller.

"Toni! Darling!"

She returned Caroline's hug with some warmth, then regretted it when Caroline's hands went too far down Toni's backside. "I had no idea Missy was expecting you."

"She wasn't. But as soon as I got her note about the house and that you were out to explore it, too, I realized how dull Santa Monica was and headed upstate." Caroline tucked her hand under

Toni's arm as they went into the house. "What a great old place this is."

"You were just calling it a rattrap," Missy said from the kitchen table. "You were gone a while, T.B."

"I didn't think I'd be made so welcome. They have a cook and everything."

Missy smoothed the newspaper in front of her. "I need a cook, a butler, an amanuensis of some kind."

"Or cooking lessons," Toni observed.

"I made Pop-Tarts just this morning."

Caroline reclaimed her own seat at the table and picked up a glass of wine. "So you've had lunch, Toni?"

Caroline swirled the liquid in the glass idly, and Toni found herself thinking of the wine Syrah Ardani had served her. It had been undoubtedly good, and listening to Syrah explain to her customers about legs, color, light and fruits of their wine had been educational. "I have. It was very good."

Caroline pouted. "You'll still take me to dinner, won't you? We can even leave Missy here. She's hoping some creature named Jane will call."

"I saw Jane at the Ardani place."

Missy's head shot up. "You did? What did she say?"

Toni didn't want to admit Jane had been flirting and pouring wine for three very cute women. "Not much. I was busy."

"She looked okay? She was well?"

Caroline groaned. "All I've heard about since I got here was Jane this and Jane that. Who *is* this woman?"

"She's an artist," Missy said.

Toni volunteered, "She also does landscaping."

"A landscape architect? Well, Missy, you could certainly use one of those around here."

"No," Toni said carefully. "She does landscaping."

"As in . . . plants grass?"

"She's an artist," Missy said again. "Toni, now that you've seen the Ardani grounds—Jane did a lot of that. I consider her an artist through and through and I don't care how she makes money with her hands." She sighed. "I want to monopolize her hands the rest of the time."

"How long has she been like this?" Caroline frowned across her wine at Toni.

"I only got here yesterday."

"Will you two stop acting as if I'm nuts." Missy tossed her newspaper onto the table. "Neither of you has a clue about feeling the way I do. Neither of you even has a heart!"

She stormed out, leaving Caroline to look at Toni archly. "Hormones?"

"I'm willing to bet Jane arouses something hormonal, yes," Toni said.

"This woman sounds extremely unsuitable."

Toni agreed, but abruptly she did not want to say so. There were aspects of Caroline she did not like, and finding herself in agreement about Missy's love life was unsettling. It wasn't Jane's job that bothered her, it was a sincere doubt that Missy was more than a fling for Jane. "We may have to leave it to Missy to decide."

Caroline shrugged. "She has been going on and on about the women around here. Are they really all that?"

Last night Toni had not thought so, but honesty and the memory of Syrah Ardani's eyes compelled her to say, "Some are."

"Well, take me someplace I can see the choices. Since, I am assuming, you continue to be . . . unavailable?" Caroline arched one eyebrow.

"Mira and I broke up."

"Missy told me. I'm so *sorry*."

Toni laughed. "No, you're not. I'm not either."

Caroline was grinning. "There's a restaurant called French Laundry. Let's go there for dinner."

"I've heard of it," Toni said. "And I don't think we'll be getting in on the spur of the moment."

"You could buy the place on the spot and I'm sure we'd get a good table."

"What would I do with a restaurant?"

"Feed me. I had the most wretched flight into that tiny airport in town and I was lucky to get a rental car at all."

"They told me I couldn't get one until tonight, so you were lucky." Toni found herself smiling indulgently at Caroline. There was a lot she liked about Caroline, too, particularly that she admitted to animal appetites with ease and made no secret of her pleasure in having them fulfilled. "Okay, I'll feed you. But let me go talk to Missy."

She found Missy in the large common room, at war with the wallpaper. A crew was arriving first thing tomorrow morning—Toni had agreed to let them in and get them going while Missy headed for work in San Francisco—to remove it properly, but Missy had started the job on her own, with her fingernails.

She was just digging into another large piece when Toni caught her hand and trapped it under one arm. "You'll spoil your manicure."

"I don't care."

"You're not behaving like you."

"Like I don't know that. Don't you think I'm scared to death? I don't know what hit me when I saw her. At first I thought it was just lust but I feel . . ." She squeezed her red-rimmed eyes shut for a moment. "I feel like sunshine when I'm with her. All that sappy, emotional crap from some second-rate movie. That's how I feel." A smile broke through the anger and tears. "I feel just like that and I'm loving it."

"You're very different people."

"Oh, don't start on her job again—"

"That's not what I meant. At the winery she seemed very comfortable chatting up the women there. I wouldn't want you to get in over your head and find out she's not capable of being serious."

"Oh." Missy crumbled rotting wallpaper between her fingers.

"Well, thanks, I guess. I mean, I'm sure it was innocent and I think she can be very serious. But I appreciate you caring enough to tell me. Listen, take Caroline away, would you?"

"My pleasure," Toni said. "I need some fresh air. You were right about Ardani Senior."

"Adorable, huh?" Missy dusted her hands. "And Ardani Junior? How was she on closer examination?"

"Who are we talking about?" Caroline leaned in the doorway, and Toni took a moment to appreciate her undeniable elegance.

"Syrah Ardani. She has gorgeous eyes." Missy gave Toni a teasing look. "Wouldn't you say?"

Toni nearly made a joke but something compelled her to be honest. "They'd have been quite fine if she hadn't been hung over." She thought of their expressive depth, the shifting shades of gold, brown and black, and her own awareness that she was the last person on earth Syrah Ardani wanted to behold. "They'd have been fine indeed."

"Well," Caroline said, her own eyes sparkling with curiosity, "I can't wait to meet Syrah Ardani and her *fine* eyes."

# Chapter 6

"Maybe it's the meter." Syrah resisted the urge to give the device a good shake. "We should test it again."

Carlo filled another small clear plastic cup from the barrel in question while Syrah reset the testing meter. "We're low on L.A.B."

"We're low on everything, not just the reactive acids. I hope to know by the end of the day what kind of order I can place that will get us to harvest."

As always, Syrah dipped the testing strip into the red-pink liquid, then tasted the wine herself without swallowing it, spitting the mouthful back into the cup. She did not have her father's palate, but she was learning. Still, her mouth didn't say last year's zinfandel was destabilizing, but the meter did.

"Trouble, pumpkin?"

Carlo drew another small cup and Syrah watched her father evaluate it. "Let's get some L.A.B. into it today."

"We're low on it."

"We'll lose the barrel," he said. "This one is closest to the morning sun and always has some trouble with stability, but it can produce complexity. It's not going to take very much. The natural yeast has done its work."

Syrah frowned at the meter, which confirmed her father's assessment. Lactic acid bacteria would shut down the rising pH, but she was going to have to rely on his help for the formula. She didn't yet have that kind of skill.

"I'll see how much we've got of what and let you know," Carlo said.

Syrah nodded her thanks. They were lucky to have Carlo's expertise, and knowing that one of the big outfits had been chatting him up didn't make her happy. They couldn't compete on anything except their charm. "I appreciate it."

"No problem. Means I have to stop in and say hi to Bennett."

"Cheese toast this morning," her father said.

"I am already there." Carlo left them to the quiet of the largest fermentation barn.

"That woman will be here at nine," Syrah said. "I wish you'd let me help get things together."

"I think I have it handled. She's Bill's daughter all over—has his dry humor."

True, there was very little residual sugar in the woman, Syrah wanted to say. "Well, I'm here and I did go to college, too."

"I'd rather you spent time learning the barrels."

"Me, too. I wish that was all there was to running this place, but we owe money to people."

Her father gave her one of his frustratingly sunny smiles and said, "So what did you taste in this one?"

"Too much acid by the time it settles. Delawares can do that."

His smile broadened. "How did you know there were Delawares in there?"

"Aren't there?" She recalled the complex acidities of the wine against the sides of her tongue.

He nodded. "Only Carlo and I knew that. And a few temporaries who helped load the crusher that day. They came on with just the right late acids. This is the only barrel I did a blend for and it's going to be reserve from release day one."

Pleased with herself, Syrah said, "It had Alsatian tone and was more pink than a pure zinfandel, I thought."

"Excellent. Anything else?"

"Once we treat the acid, it will have an intense flavor without being buttery. Peppery without the acid."

"Very good, pumpkin."

Syrah felt a glow of pleasure. "Oh, I told Carlo I didn't think the top row caps had been pushed down in the last round. Row four, the Pinots."

He frowned and headed for the ladder. "I'll check and do it if need be."

"Dad, let Carlo send someone up there." She watched him climb the ladder and wanted to say, "I'm not a little girl and you're not a young man," but arguing with her father never worked. He just didn't hear what he didn't want to. "Dad, please."

"I've done this a million times and I'll be fine." His head appeared over the edge of the third-level scaffold. "I've got the safety gear on."

"Well, that's something," Syrah muttered under her breath, then with a start she realized they weren't alone. Even with the morning sun streaming in the open door, it wasn't hard to tell who the tall silhouette had to be. "Ms. Blanchard."

She stepped out of the sunlight at her back and Syrah could see her poised, angular face. "Please call me Toni. I'm early, I apologize. I thought the traffic would be like it was yesterday."

"Monday mornings are much better. You don't have to take the highway, either. I can draw you a map from here to Netherfield by back roads."

"I'd appreciate that."

The silence was awkward enough that Syrah broke it with an anxious, "Have you had breakfast? Can Bennett fix you anything?"

"When we settle down to work I'll admit coffee would be welcome." Toni took two more steps toward Syrah, gazing up at the barrels.

She wore jeans today, Syrah noted, creased and new, with a short-sleeved top of deep blue that was cotton, not silk. Both were undoubtedly acquired from one of the boutiques in Napa's prime district. Casual but obviously new mocs didn't give her the same height as the *Vogue* pumps had, but she was still at least five inches taller than Syrah. Five-nine, Syrah thought, or five-ten. "Would you like to get started?"

"I don't want to take you from your work. I thought, actually, you could show me a little bit about the process so I know what I'm asking questions about."

"They missed the lot of them," her father called down. "Tell Carlo they're capped now. Just one more to do."

"Someone left the caps off?" Toni touched the barrel nearest her, fingertips running over the roughly polished oak.

"No, caps are the stems and skin and other pieces of the grapes that float up during fermentation. They're essential to the flavor, so it's necessary from time to time to gently push them back down into the wine. Plus, if they sit on top too long they could start their own spoilage process, and we don't want to add that to our wine." Syrah cast an anxious look upward as her father started the climb down the ladder.

"Forgive my ignorance, but I see pulleys, and the barrels appear to be moveable. Why wouldn't you bring them down to ground level to check them?"

"Many wineries do," Syrah said. "We prefer not to move some of them, though, because sediments can get stirred up. These barrels have some of the most delicate of our wines."

"Of course."

"I'm sure it's more efficient to move the barrels." She didn't mean to sound defensive.

"Possibly." Toni shrugged. "How many buildings are there like this?"

"We have seven more like this, another of stone for the slowest reds and two large fully automated buildings for the single-season whites. We're not a mass producer of wine. We grow a lot of grapes, though."

"From the papers I reviewed, I was surprised to see that your largest income is from grape sales, not wine."

"It's why we're a vineyard, Ms. Blanchard." Syrah's father dusted his hands on his khakis. "Ardani grapes are legend. We can claim part of ninety percent of the award winners every year."

Syrah wanted to whisper to him not to tell this woman who had so much power over their future that their competitors would jump at the chance to buy their vines.

"How interesting," Toni said. "How does that work? By that I mean, why would another winery need your grapes?"

"Not everyone has zinfandel grapes from hundred-year-old vines. Our soil, on the upper two hundred and extending to Honeysuckle Bench, has a clay loam base. But the middle two hundred sits on more gravel and our Syrah can be intensely flavored . . ."

Syrah watched them walk toward the house, torn between admiration at her father's poise and aggravation that he was and always had been so trusting.

Carlo brought a tally of the chemicals on hand, and she knew it wouldn't be long before she had to order calcium, sulfur dioxide—the list went on and on, and that was just to treat the wines fermenting or aging in barrels. She also thought that it was time to bottle a full row of noble casks, which meant an order of long-necked flasks that set the dessert wine apart. She was afraid to spend a dime, afraid if she told Toni Blanchard anything, they'd end up with nothing.

It was only half-past nine when she couldn't stand it any longer, and her footsteps took her from barrel-testing to the house to see how her father was faring.

"I'm sure I don't know anything," Bennett snapped. "It's not as if he'll say one word to me, and he knows how it vexes me when I have to guess."

"You know at least as much as I do." Syrah paused to finish a wedge of cheese toast. She was about to brave the office when the clearly audible sound of a car gearing down broke the still of the morning. A few moments later a plain sedan crested the driveway's steep hill. Curious, she watched the plain sedan turn into their small parking lot. There was nothing plain about the woman who got out, however, and stood looking about her as if confused.

With a heavy sigh, Syrah went to offer her help.

"I'm looking for Toni Blanchard," the woman promptly said. She held out a beautifully manicured hand. "I'm Caroline, Missy's sister. You must be Syrah."

Aware of how tanned and rough her own hand seemed next to Caroline's delicacy, Syrah could only nod. "She's inside. I can show you where. Would you like some coffee?"

"Oh, I couldn't. Toni won't want me to linger." Caroline was, if it was possible to be so, even more feminine and petite than Missy, and their resemblance grew stronger as she talked. "She says I'm distracting."

Not sure what to say—or think—about that assessment, Syrah led the way. She didn't spend a lot of time worrying about high fashion, but between Missy and Caroline she was feeling like a first-class frump. Jeans, old tee, even older boots completed her daily outfit. For haute couture she might find a shirt without some advertising logo on it. Saturday night had been the first time in ages she'd felt attractive and interesting to other women. The numerous dance partners had been very good for her ego.

"You left your cell phone and it's been ringing for an hour." Caroline handed it to Toni, who flicked it open with an expression of annoyance.

"Thank you." After a short distracted pause, Toni clicked the phone shut as she rose to make quick introductions. After nods and handshakes, she added, "I'm going to be most of the day, Caroline."

"That's fine. I'm going back to that shop we were at last night

70

and then I thought I might drop by that Laundry place and see about a table for tonight."

Syrah choked back a snort. Right. French Laundry took reservations two months in advance and within ten minutes of answering the phone in the morning they were booked. Napa was full of the rich and famous, especially during the summer, and she'd never heard of anyone getting a table on the spur of the moment.

She watched the way Caroline Bingley's shoulders moved as she and Toni conversed, how her head tipped and her long earrings outlined the curve of her throat. She was sensuous and Syrah was quite certain Toni Blanchard had a standing invitation to take a bite from the invisible apple Caroline was dangling.

Toni, on the other hand, was much more subtle, but Syrah equally had no doubt that she found Caroline attractive. The smile was astonishingly indulgent as her gaze traced the line of Caroline's neck. The two of them needed to get a room. But wait, she reminded herself, Netherfield has dozens of rooms, lucky them.

"All right then, I'll get out of your hair," Caroline finally said, and Syrah offered to see her to her car. On the way through the tasting room, Caroline paused to touch the display of Rieslings. "Syrah, I know this is awfully presumptuous of me, but could I get a bottle of wine for later?"

"Certainly," Syrah said automatically. "What did you have in mind?"

"This Riesling is probably perfect. Well-chilled, for a picnic."

"It's wonderful drunk out-of-doors."

Caroline flushed. "Well, I was thinking of an indoor picnic."

Of course you were, Syrah wanted to say. "I'm sure this will be perfect. It's sharp, with a lot of tannin for a white wine, so it fades to a nice afterglow."

"Just like some of the best things in life."

Syrah laughed—really, it was nearly a giggle, and it was just the two of them, giggling girls together hinting about sex and

Caroline giving sly looks in the direction of the closed office door. "I think you're on to something there."

"Well, I hope to be. You can take a credit card, right?"

Syrah kept smiling as she wrapped the wine. "Yes, but this is on the house. Welcome to the neighborhood."

"Oh, how sweet of you." Caroline took the wrapped bottle and smiled ever so warmly at Syrah. "My sister has been over the top about how wonderful the women are here and I can see she had cause. Now if I can just get her looking at the right *kind* of woman, I'll be very happy for her. Missy has always liked them heavy on muscle and light on brains, so I'm sure it won't last long."

Though her lips hurt, Syrah somehow kept smiling. She waved good-bye like she and Caroline had just formed the very *bestest* friendship ever. It took all her strength not to change that wave to a one-fingered salute. Her hand dropped to her side and she said forcefully, "Bitch!"

They were all bitches, these outsiders, thinking they knew anything about any of them. Thinking Jane was stupid and trash because she worked with her hands for a living—and what must they think of her, by extension? Missy was a shallow bubblehead looking for a hot butch to take her to bed and this Caroline creature, what a piece of work. She and Toni Blanchard could have each other.

She didn't go near the office for the rest of the day. Another dismissive look from Toni Blanchard was more than she could take.

"Okay, you have to tell me how you pulled this off." Toni took the heavy menu from the waiter and nodded her thanks.

"It took two days." Caroline leaned forward, her shoulders gleaming in the candlelight. "I'm glad you found the time for me."

"I want to finish and get back to New York." Toni's gaze flicked over the menu. Asparagus soup with black truffle syrup caught her eye.

"You disappear in the morning already on the phone, come back in the evening already full from another woman's cooking—"

"A woman could get spoiled by Bennett's food."

"Sure it's not other attractions?" Caroline idly ran one finger along her neck.

"What do you mean by that?"

"Well, I see what you meant by the eyes, that's all. If she were my type I'd not mind gazing into them for hours at a stretch."

"We've not talked at all. My business is with her father."

"Business, business, business. You spend half the night waking up poor souls in other parts of the world. Who is Crystal and why the long talks?"

"A colleague and someone who needs to talk." She wasn't going to discuss Crystal or Mira with Caroline. "So you didn't tell me how you managed this. I did call but couldn't get through."

Caroline sat back, looking pleased. It was impossible not to observe the welcoming hollow between her breasts as she moved. "I posted a French Laundry wish on eBay. Someone parted with their reservation for the right compensation."

Toni laughed. "How ingenious, and how typical of you. The menu looks wonderful but it may not hold up to that kind of extravagance."

"The look in your eyes, just now, was what I was after, not the meal."

Toni made herself study the menu. "Fresh king salmon sounds good to me today."

"Why do you do that?"

"What?" She had to glance up.

Caroline's expression still had that molten invitation in her eyes, but there was a mild annoyance there as well. "Every time I say something intimate you divert me."

Surprised by Caroline's directness, Toni said honestly, "Maybe I'm avoiding intimacy."

"I know that Mira has many things that I don't."

"That's true."

73

Caroline's sigh was exasperated. "You really know how to hurt a girl."

Toni frowned as she idly played with the dinner knife. "I don't understand that. I agreed with you, honestly."

"Sometimes a girl doesn't want honesty."

"If I'll lie to you about something trivial, how will you trust I'm telling you the truth when it's important? Mira has qualities that you do not." Caroline took a quick breath and Toni instantly regretted her lack of clarity. "Caroline—I'm sorry. Most of the qualities Mira has that you do not aren't good qualities. You are a much nicer woman than she turned out to be."

"Oh." Caroline's lower lip quivered for a moment. "I thought you meant—"

"She is beautiful." Toni shrugged. "I'm not going to lie about that. You are as well. That dress is a walking crime."

"I thought you'd never notice."

"I noticed the moment you came down the stairs. Mira is beautiful like a razor. You're as beautiful as that wine you opened last night. Warm and light."

Caroline laughed, her sultry smile completely restored. "And oh so good going down?"

Toni gasped with laughter and was glad the waiter had reappeared. Choices were discussed and as always Toni liked that Caroline knew exactly what she wanted and would enjoy. "Tiger prawns in spicy remoulade?"

"I'm feeling very like that tonight." Caroline glanced at the waiter. "Is there an Ardani vintage you'd recommend for our main course?"

But as always with Caroline, Toni reflected, there was a moment when she didn't know if she was being nice or just being the Caroline who could combine nice with just a touch of spite. Did Caroline suspect that the Ardani review was turning out to be painful for her? She liked the old man, she really did, and yet there was no money to bail them out.

The wine was ordered with no input from Toni and she decided that Caroline had meant to compliment, not annoy. "That dress really is a walking crime."

"It has some secrets. If I move my left shoulder just so . . ." Caroline gave a little shrug as a hint. "The entire thing will end up around my ankles, and wouldn't that be a shame?"

"I don't think anyone with eyes would mind."

"What about you?"

"I appreciate beauty and art."

Toni could tell that wasn't quite what Caroline wanted but she let it go. The meal was delicious and wonderfully presented. Caroline's pleasure in the food was engaging as always. They shared tastes and stories of mutual friends and Toni even found herself telling Caroline how close Mira had come to wearing her salad on their last so-called date.

They were finishing the fifteen-year-old Ardani Cabernet Sauvignon as the waiter cleared their entrée plates. "You know I'm not much of a wine drinker," Toni said, "but I can really taste the difference with this one."

"Compared to that little wine last night? It was tasty enough but, yes, this one is in a different league." Caroline held her half-full glass up to the candlelight and the deep cherry-burgundy color blossomed into a multi-layered shimmer of pinks and reds. "Not that I want to be grateful to Syrah Ardani for anything."

"Why not?"

"As if you don't know. You went on and on about her fine eyes."

"I did not."

Caroline took a slow sip from the glass, her gaze never leaving Toni's face. "I've known you ten years, at least, and you've never said a word about any woman's eyes. So mentioning them at all is tantamount to a love letter."

"I've never mentioned your eyes?" Careful, Toni, a little voice said, but something about the wine made the cautious voice very faint. "I'm no poet. Right now I can't think of any other word than blue, but they are beautifully blue. Don't tell Missy, but I like your eyes better than hers."

Caroline blinked. "Don't play with me, Toni. I thought you'd agreed to be honest, even if I don't like the truth."

"I am being honest."

"I think if you just gave us a chance, we could find something more than me fishing for compliments and you being just tipsy enough to give them."

Was she tipsy? She gazed into the depths of her wine, wondering if it was higher in alcohol content than she anticipated. Away from the candle the deep reds seemed almost black and she fancied she saw a flash of gold. They *were* fine eyes. She ought to tell her father he'd been right about a little girl who had grown up to become Sophia Loren. "I don't think I'm drunk."

"Maybe not drunk, but you did flush, just now."

"It must be the peppery aftertaste."

"Just a few days and you've picked up all the lingo." Caroline wasn't really smiling.

Dessert, a delicate caramel brulee with apricots poached in white wine, seemed to melt in her mouth. She was indeed tipsy, Toni realized, and dwelling far too much on Caroline's undeniable charms. Caroline was no angel but she didn't deserve to be used merely because Toni was suddenly aware of how long it had been since she'd felt a woman's body against her own. Mira had been adventurous and Toni suspected Caroline wasn't shy. That Caroline had made it plain she wanted Toni didn't make it smart to give in.

"Let's walk a bit," Caroline said. "I don't think either of us should drive right now."

Caroline's hand through Toni's silk blouse felt warm and familiar. Yountville's small town square wasn't far but most of the shops had closed. The streets were slowly going quiet.

"How much longer do you think you'll be here?" Caroline paused to look at artisan glasswork in a window.

"Just one more day at the winery. Then I can do my report for the court."

"So you're going home."

"I do need to get back, but with satellite hookups and wireless connections, nobody is missing me. As you noticed, I'm on the phone a lot." Doc Burbidge was eager for her to dig into his proposed merger, but she could easily do half the analysis next to the now sparkling pool for a day or two. Her team members knew where she was and the staple of her seven a.m. hour was a long talk with the Admin Queens.

"I'd like to think you're staying because of the scenery." Caroline turned from the window, her tight silk dress slipping a little on her left shoulder.

Oh, hell, Toni thought, too late, because Caroline was already on her tiptoes, pulling Toni down to her for a kiss that was as easy and heady as the wine at dinner had been.

When she could talk, which was several minutes later, she tried to find some reason. "I don't want to lead you on, Caroline. It wouldn't be nice."

"Tonight, I don't think I care about tomorrow."

"Tomorrow you will care about tomorrow." The curve of her shoulders was tantalizing.

Caroline's hand slipped to the back of Toni's neck. "Kiss me again."

She was irresistible, even though Toni knew it was a mistake to kiss her then, to kiss her as they slowly made their way back to her rental car, to kiss her once they were locked inside.

"Toni." Caroline's small moan ignited something inside Toni's mouth and the kiss turned hotly passionate. "I've wanted you for so long."

Toni couldn't say, "Me, too," because it wasn't true. Instead she found a real truth, which was, "I know."

"Touch me."

"Cari, we shouldn't do this."

"I don't care." The next kiss bruised Toni's lips. "I want your hands on me, Toni. I don't care who you're thinking about, or what. Just make love to me tonight."

There were alarm bells, deep down, sounding like an urgent

order to sell the stock before she got burned. The prospect of getting burned was too pleasurable and the heat she found as Caroline straddled her was too tempting. Her fingers tingled and Caroline's sharp cry made the bells go away.

"Please, there." Tears were choking Caroline's voice and Toni shushed her.

"It's okay, it's okay."

"Please," Caroline gasped. "Toni, please."

Caroline ground down on Toni's palm with a ferocity that made Toni momentarily pull back. Then Caroline's hand was wrapped around her forearm, pulling Toni hard against her as she shook. Her dress slid off her shoulders, leaving her breasts bare. Toni's fingers ran from collarbone to nipple and they kissed again as Caroline gripped Toni's arm even harder.

"God, yes."

Caroline was beautifully passionate in her abandon and Toni wanted to fall into the depths with her. It had been ages since sex had seemed this simple. But even as she felt yet more wetness against her palm and Caroline froze against her, she realized she had no idea, and had never had any idea, why Caroline was attracted to her. At least it wasn't my money she craved, Toni thought. *Caroline is not Mira wanting my checkbook more than me.*

She cuddled Caroline against her, shushing the soft tears and feeling like a cad. This obviously meant something to Caroline.

She finally found a tissue in the glove box and Caroline blotted her eyes and nose.

"I'm sorry, I didn't mean to get so emotional. I love the way you touch me, Toni."

"I wasn't even thinking about you," Toni could have said. "At some point, anybody could have done that for you," she might have added, wanting that to be true. Wisely, she said nothing of the kind. Other truths, luckily, were easy to find. "You are beautiful, Caroline."

"Thank you." Caroline melted into her arms and they stayed

like that for several minutes. Finally, she stirred. "You have always excited me."

"How?" Please don't let her be in love with me, Toni pleaded silently. She had never wanted to hurt Caroline that way.

Caroline slowly raised her head, her smile slow and sated. "You're kidding, right?"

"No, I'm not. I don't try to excite you, I really don't."

She laughed. "Well, hell, woman, just think if you did try what might happen." Her smile slowly faded. "You're serious."

"Yeah."

"You are sexier than the day I met you, and even then you had what it took for me."

"Whatever that is."

"You're complicated. Intelligent, attractive. Powerful, decisive, *tall*."

"I knew it was genetics."

"Ten years ago, you didn't have that line, right there." Caroline's thumb traced the curve from Toni's nose to the corner of her mouth. "I think it's gorgeous. You have depth and awareness that I just don't find in many people. I keep hoping that you'll put those qualities to work on me. On us."

They kissed sweetly and Caroline shifted on Toni's lap. "I'm not that complicated," she demurred.

"Don't sell yourself short—it's bad for business." They kissed again until Caroline drew back. "I have been wondering for so long if you made love the way you analyzed a business deal. Totally rapt, and every ounce of your intelligence focused on the matter at hand."

She shifted again on Toni's lap. Toni ignored the invitation. Her head was now too clear. "I don't know what to say, Caroline. If only something like this was governed by practical rules."

"We're so suitable for each other. Same friends, similar background, we like many of the same things, like golf, when you give yourself the time."

Toni could only think of how her father had never been the same, how part of him had never grown back after her mother died. She'd never loved anyone that way and she'd known Mira wasn't capable of it either. Caroline, though, might be, and playing with her expectations wasn't nice. Softly, she said, "I think it takes more than that."

"How will we know if we don't give it a chance?"

"I think we have." Ten years of occasional meetings and Toni still didn't feel more than she had felt the first day.

"This? Tonight? Oh, Toni, darling, you have no idea what I can do." Caroline's lips slid seductively over Toni's mouth, her tongue soft and nimble. "You have no idea how exhausted you would be by morning. Missy wouldn't need anyone to peel the paint for her— you and I could manage that all on our own."

"Caroline, I'm sorry—"

Caroline's fingertips pressed Toni's lips to a stop. "No, no. Don't you say that. Let's just see what happens, okay? I'll stay as long as you're here."

The drive to Netherfield was silent, and they parted at the bottom of the stairs after one last kiss. She knew Caroline would presume that the longer Toni stayed the more interested she was, and so she ought to finish up her report tomorrow and go home.

The report could have been done in a day.

The last kiss had said that if she wanted she could be in Caroline's bed, even now, but looking at the smears on her slacks in her own bedroom mirror, she knew that wasn't why she wanted to stay in the area. She ought to go home and the reasons she didn't had nothing to do with Missy's sparkling swimming pool. The real reasons were yet too foreign to be given credence. They were unquantifiable and therefore, in the matter of rational choices, they did not exist.

Syrah Ardani avoided her and Toni was not ready to go home.

# Chapter 7

Fed up with the information blackout, Syrah prowled quietly through the papers in her father's office. He was out discussing fertilizer with Carlo. Toni wasn't due for an hour.

Her search turned up nothing of interest, though. Piles of bank statements were just what she expected to see, and the letters from the lenders she'd already read. She had no idea what was taking Toni Blanchard so long—she'd been here three whole days. What was there to know that wasn't already apparent?

She turned on the computer, finally, and printed out orders that had been sent in from distributors. Her e-mail was next and she was surprised to see that something had arrived in her personal box since the previous day. She had nothing against e-mail but a phone call was always preferable to her and all of her friends knew that.

Not recognizing the sender's address she almost didn't open it, but the subject line of "About Toni Blanchard" was simply too hard to resist.

"Dear Ms. Ardani," she read, hoping it turned out to be something she could quickly delete.

> You don't know me and at this time I cannot give you my name. We have a mutual acquaintance in Toni Blanchard, however. I had the misfortune to have dealings with her in the past of such a painful nature that I cannot tolerate that what happened to me should happen to you as well. I think I might be able to enlighten you about the temperament of this woman, if you are interested in more details. Please write back if so.

It was signed only, "A Friend."

She didn't like anonymous letters, and for a moment she remembered all the trouble that had resulted from an unsigned note in high school that purported undying love between two boys. It had been a hoax, and a cruel one, and the coward who'd done it had never fessed up.

She nearly deleted the message but couldn't. This was her family's heritage, her livelihood, her father's entire life. She would take everything with a grain of salt, but knowledge could be power.

She wrote a carefully worded missive back, expressing her misgivings but indicating a willingness to listen. She heard someone coming through the house from the kitchen and quickly closed the mail window.

Toni had been early the three previous mornings and today was no different. Syrah ought not to have been surprised. She was again cool and poised in new jeans and a simple eggplant-hued pullover.

"I was just leaving," Syrah said quickly.

"Could we talk for just a moment?"

Surprised, she nodded. "I hope you can give me some information. I am capable of understanding what's going on."

"I'm sorry about that. If you were a shareholder or member of the board I could be much more candid. But as it is, you're an employee, technically."

"An employee with grape DNA."

The smile Syrah received in reply was tight. "I am well aware that you are integral to the vineyard and I have been hoping against hope that something would show up unexpectedly, but I've only got one thing I could report to the court as helpful. It's a Band-Aid at best but could buy you time. Your father wasn't very open to the idea, and I didn't understand why. I thought you might be able to shed light on his resistance."

Syrah said firmly, "I'm not going to talk him 'round for you."

"That's not what I want. My proposal was to lease more future grapes. I know next year's leases are committed, but why not the year after that? At least some of them. Enough to bring the loans to within sixty days current. If that's done, the judge will put a stay on the case and the creditors will step back, for a while."

The thought *had* crossed Syrah's mind, but she knew her father's feelings. "The growers and vintners who could afford that are mass-market producers. It will sound like snobbery, but we don't grow grapes for the mass market."

"Would they pay you what your usual leases would bring?"

"Yes, probably."

"So . . . you don't charge a premium rate for your grapes, you're just picky about who gets them." Surprisingly, Toni didn't seem judgmental, merely reciting back their business practice to be sure she understood.

Syrah nodded. "Essentially, yes. My father can also tell you whose grapes that year will need what from our vines." She tried to speak without undue pride, but she was very proud of her father's reputation. "There are those who think my father has elevated the overall quality of wine produced from this region in his lifetime."

"I understand."

Syrah didn't believe Toni possibly could, not after a couple of days. "Every harvest is different. Every time the vines produce it's another chance."

83

"I do understand. Thank you for explaining it to me. Your father was not so forthcoming."

"We've been called snobs and it isn't easy to tell an old friend he can't have your zins that year."

Toni said softly, "I can imagine that would be difficult for him."

"So, if he agrees, it's just a Band-Aid? He'd give up a whole year for no guarantees?"

Something in Toni's eyes flinched, but she continued to meet Syrah's gaze. "If nothing is done, I can guarantee that you'll have to sell more than half your land, based on the most recent appraisals."

Syrah swallowed hard. "I don't know what went wrong. I wasn't here."

"I wish I could explain more."

"Sure you do." Syrah was almost out the door when she made herself stop. "I'm sorry, that was rude."

"It's okay." Toni was already looking at her laptop screen. "I know this isn't easy."

As she picked up her satchel, Syrah noticed a series of bruises on Toni's forearm. Four bruises, more or less in a row. Fresh bruises. Syrah was certain if she turned Toni's arm over, she would find an opposing fifth to complete the picture.

Was that why Toni seemed nicer this morning? Had she gotten laid? Three days of stumbling over the woman and Syrah had only received dour looks. There was only one candidate to have done the honors, but Syrah didn't feel at all thankful to Caroline Bingley.

Fertilizer, she thought. *I don't need this. She's nothing to me, and she can have every woman in town for all I care.* What was it about that hostile, haughty air, anyway?

The walk through the vineyard calmed her nerves as it always did. Grapes were still tight, small and bright green, but soon they'd hang lower and heavier and she and her father would begin assessing water content and anxiously studying advance weather reports.

She would hate to give up any of them to an unknown fate, but there didn't seem to be any other way.

She could have been blind and known she'd reached the latest fertilizer site by her nose alone. The full day's sun wasn't yet on them, but the air was dank with nitrogen and sulfur. Two crowds of workers were ready to begin walking mulch down the rows while others followed to press the mix in.

"Phew! You guys stink," Syrah announced, repeating herself in her marginal Spanish. She was happy to pitch in for a while, losing her worries in caring for the vines. When she found herself with her father for a few moments' privacy, she said, "I think she's right, Dad. It's hard, but it would buy us time. This is going to be an exceptional harvest." Though she didn't believe it, she added, "We could get lucky."

"I know. I'm trying to square it in my mind. Which grapes, though? I don't want to lose control of the zins, Pinots or Syrahs."

"But the zins are our biggest crop."

"Exactly."

"Dad, I know it's drastic."

"It's never a good idea to pay for today with tomorrow."

Syrah could only nod. It seemed like sound advice for life, not just grapes.

"I shouldn't have bought the Tarpay fields, and with the grapes on them pledged to the sellers for two years we're paying interest on the loans with no income against it. I was anxious to get hold of them and overpaid."

"And that was after all the modernizing and upgrading."

"We needed those new barrels."

But maybe they hadn't needed the new bottling equipment. She'd thought the old one had another ten years on it at least. "I'll tell her, if you want me to."

"No, I'll do it. She shouldn't have brought you into it."

More sharply than she meant to, Syrah asked, "Why not, Dad? Someday these will be my decisions to make."

"I know, pumpkin, but you're still young. I was glad to see you go to Europe. You don't need to be married to this place yet."

"Dad, I already am. I was born married to this place. I bleed grape juice, just like you."

He laughed a little. "I'll try to remember. Seems like yesterday you were going to the prom."

"I'm thirty-one, Dad. I'm all out of proms."

"Guess I'd better go talk to Toni, hadn't I?"

"Might be good. Shall I walk back with you?"

"Sure."

From the patio outside the tasting room, Toni watched the two Ardanis making their way toward the house. Yesterday she might have thought they were blissfully unaware of their woes, but both knew some of what they were up against. Still, they paused to talk over the vines, the father occasionally emphasizing a point with a gesture of his right hand. Both handled the plants as if the vines were infants. She was beginning to suspect that neither could walk past a vine without stopping to touch it and think about its future.

Corporations were, however, all alike in the ways that mattered. She couldn't allow herself to get caught up in the vagaries of their business. Syrah was picking a grape now and apparently tasting it. Whatever the result, it made her laugh and the peal of it carried up the hill.

Toni carried her coffee back inside, banishing the image of Syrah's dark hair glinting in the sunlight. She tried to make herself think about Caroline, about Mira, about her schedule, her work, but she could still hear Syrah's laugh. Syrah was young, she reminded herself, young and not jaded and tired from too much money and too many people.

A truck laden with workers on their way to fields below passed the office window and Toni recognized the slices of pesto-brushed toast from Bennett's kitchen they all carried. Yesterday she might have dared to suggest the economy of not paying for a personal chef, though she'd known the woman's role was far more than that. Bennett was as tightly woven into this family as the family was to the grapes.

Remove the emotion, she reminded herself, and what to do about the money becomes clear. If the Ardanis wanted to buy some time, they needed to give up part of their control of the year after next's harvest. She understood it was unpleasant, but then so were foreclosure auctions. They *were* babes in the woods, the vines, whatever. Why had it fallen to her to take their tranquility from them?

Anyone else would have been home by now, report filed and onto the next contract. The recommendation would be simple: sell the major assets and replace management.

She made her way to the kitchen, unsure as always of her welcome. Bennett had made very clear the standards of her hospitality, which was that if one wanted something one asked or she took great offense. She also made plain her belief that Toni was just this side of evil incarnate. Toni figured, with a tiny pull at the waist of her slacks, she was damned either way and the pesto bread looked good.

"Nobody tells me anything around here," Bennett said by way of greeting. "You're like all the rest in that regard."

"I have a duty to the court." She felt a little faint from the pungent aroma of roasted garlic.

Bennett withered her with a glance as she plated a slice of still-bubbling pesto toast with an egg over hard alongside. "It's still an excellent idea to buy time with a future lease. A baby could tell the sense of it, but that doesn't mean Ardani himself can see that."

"You have a knack for acquiring information," Toni said, halfway through the egg after two bites. "Thank you for this and for remembering it over hard. I don't eat breakfast normally, but I've been ravenous since I got here."

"Clean air. I can't imagine how you can breathe in New York City."

"Ever been there?"

"Heavens no. This is home, and I must say more people ought to stay home."

Ouch, Toni thought. She finished the egg, helped herself to coffee and took the toast to savor as she settled down to work in the office.

By the time the two Ardanis noisily entered the back door of the house, Toni had finalized her five-year expense and debt projections. Neither chart had an advantageous trend.

She surreptitiously licked her fingers and tried not to be swayed by the fact that the best deli near the office in New York would never compare to Bennett's cooking. She had to go home. She was not getting addicted to country air, or anything else they grew here.

"Good morning, Toni. Hard at work already?"

"You've already done a half-day. I feel lazy by comparison."

"I'm sure you were awake when the markets opened." Anthony settled into his desk chair, coffee in one hand.

Toni nodded an admission. "But I only had one eye open."

"Same here." He sipped from the mug, then said, "Let's lease some future grapes."

Astonished by how pleased she was to hear him say that, Toni found herself grinning. "I know you don't want to, but time is hard to buy and that's what we'll get."

Bennett bustled in with a plate and bustled out again saying, "Finally you're talking some sense, I must say."

"Glad to know you're happy," Anthony called after her. "The woman's a menace, weaned on a pickle."

"I heard that, you curmudgeon. Get your own coffee from now on."

Toni fought down her own laughter, not able to recall when she'd felt so relaxed. It was a dangerous feeling, she knew that, and yet she couldn't conquer it. Not right then, with the cool, clean air blowing in from the open patio door, not with Syrah framed in the light, leaning comfortably against the jamb as she gazed out at the rolling fields.

I've caught something from Missy, she thought. "How can we get that process started?"

"I'll call a couple of people and invite them for a glass of vino and a casual auction. They'll call a few and end of day we'll see what happens."

Toni blinked at the rapidity of it. "Aren't there papers to be drawn up?"

"Got the boilerplates in this machine. I just need to write up the zones I'm willing to part with. It has to be the zins. Everybody can benefit from our zins."

Nodding, Toni left him to work as she adjusted her projections. Using the last two years' results of leases, she made a conservative estimate based on a few questions.

She was aware of Anthony Ardani's pride as he made those few phone calls. She guessed it was the first time he'd said the words "cash flow" to people he had to consider colleagues.

Wanting to give him privacy for his painful task, she took her cell phone outside to field calls from the office and paced the patio as she talked. Syrah Ardani appeared from one of the fermenting barns, then later from around the corner of the house carrying a large basket of vegetables from the garden Bennett tended. The morning wore on, with glimpses of Syrah, who did not seem the least bit like a lazy debutante. Watching Syrah deep in conversation with their manager, she revised her earlier thoughts—Syrah was full of youthful vitality, but she wasn't immature.

She was still clicking through her calls when she heard Jane's voice and then the two women were gone.

Calls concluded a few minutes later, she went back to the office to find Anthony mulling over papers from the printer. "I thought I would wrap up today, but I just spent two hours on other things. If you're going to settle the matter of the future leases I'd like to come back tomorrow so I can make my report as accurate as possible."

It was an excuse, but if Anthony suspected that it didn't show. "Certainly. That makes sense. Would you like to see how the auction goes this evening?"

Toni could think of a thousand things that required her attention but heard herself saying, "That would be fascinating. Six-thirty?"

"Good time," Anthony agreed. "Thank you, Toni. You've been a big help."

He still didn't get it, that she wasn't here to help him. She realized, then, that part of her hoped he never did. She hoped there was a miracle and she didn't have to be the harbinger of doom, not for this business. Not for this family.

She turned away from the public road as she drove away, unwilling to admit that she knew Syrah and Jane had gone this direction. The rental car interior was hot and choked with Caroline's perfume, and she rolled down the windows as she slowly drove along the tree-lined dirt road. Two hours to the south was one of the largest metropolitan areas in the country, but the buzz of insects and racket of birds made it hard to believe she wasn't in a time warp.

She was wasting time, but it seemed more than worth it to coast to a slow stop in a shady wide spot and shut off the engine. The first thing she thought was that the country was noisy, then she was lost in remembering the last summer at the cabin on Lake George. That summer had been painful, but long ago. She simply hadn't understood that her mother was ill and at eleven had had no way to fathom the concept of "gone forever."

Her cell phone rang and she quickly dealt with Valerie's question. She was grateful for the interruption of what would surely have been maudlin thoughts.

One of those country quiets fell. The buzzing ceased and then resumed at half its volume, as if some of the insects had decided on a siesta. In the distance she heard voices, then a scream. Alarmed, she got out of the car and walked through the line of trees. The hill sloped sharply away, too sharply to consider climbing down, but through the spreading branches of oaks she could see two fig-ures—Syrah and Jane, had to be—swimming in a pond. There was another scream as Jane pulled Syrah under, then they both waded out of the water and out of her sight.

It had been enough, that sight of Syrah. No gymnasium waif, she was as curvaceous and sensual as Toni had dreamed she might be.

Her heart was pounding, and it was silly. She got back in the car, resisting comparisons to Botticelli or Raphael nudes. Syrah was more lean but equally as lush.

Last night she had been passive to Caroline's undeniable, forthright passion. Today, having been aware of Syrah Ardani's every move for hours, her palms were sweating. She felt like an idiot for having twitted Missy about her infatuation. Syrah Ardani did not even like her. How could she be sitting here imagining that body spread out on her bed, that voice rising to cry out her name, and the laughter that would embrace them both when their bodies were exhausted?

Rebound. Dementia. Wine poisoning. There had to be some explanation that made sense. She started the car and continued on the road, realizing too late as she dipped down a curve that she was going to go right past the pond where Syrah and Jane were lazing. Lazing naked.

She reversed as soon as she could, but it took a couple of attempts to turn around. Relieved, she hit the gas and would have made her escape had it not been for a forceful, "Stop that!"

Toni looked in her rearview mirror and beheld Syrah Ardani marching toward her car. She wore only her T-shirt, and it was wet in places that made Toni's mouth go dry.

"What the hell are you doing?" Syrah glared down into the car with such fire in her eyes that Toni was grateful she couldn't look away. Other parts of Syrah were tantalizing her peripheral vision and she wanted to take a long, long look. She shoved her hands under her thighs.

"Trying to go back the other way. I thought this would lead to—"

"You're kicking up a mile of dust. Ten years from now we'll be explaining the extra notes of dirt in this year's Cabernets."

"Oh."

"Just go slowly, would you?"

"I will."

"Good." Syrah marched away from the car and Toni watched her go. She would have felt humiliated if it weren't for the beautiful twin curves of Syrah's backside peeking below the T-shirt hem. With a slight smile she watched them swagger out of sight, then finally began the journey back to the winery and on to Netherfield.


"Why is she here?" Syrah tweaked a cookie off the tray Bennett was setting down on the sideboard in the formal dining room that also served as a meeting room.

Bennett swatted her hand. "I'm sure I don't know."

Syrah watched Toni shaking hands with the grower representative from the largest collective in the Napa-Sonoma counties. It had felt good to have a real reason to yell at Toni this afternoon, even if, when she'd gotten back to the pond, Jane had pointed out the impairment a lack of panties dealt to one's dignity.

She munched on the cookie—shortbread, her favorite—as she approached the tasting room, then used a piece of it to lure Hound outside and onto his chain. They were now officially closed and glasses of last year's table zinfandel were being offered and accepted. She slipped into place next to her father and poured a few more glasses, handing them out as she said hello.

When Toni stepped up to the bar, Syrah handed her a glass. "There aren't any notes of dirt in this batch."

"Really?" Toni sipped appreciatively. "No city slicker messing up the grapes that year?"

Syrah was uncomfortably aware that Toni was laughing at her, and she did not want to blush. "Not that year, no."

"All I can say is that if rules were enforced by women in such fetching uniforms, we'd all behave ourselves."

Syrah blushed. "I was protecting the grapes. That's one of the fields we'll be leasing today."

"Toni, dear, there's someone I want you to meet." Syrah watched her father drag Toni over to meet another grower and heard him say, "Toni is the daughter of an old family friend and is helping us out with business matters. I thought she'd be interested in how we handle something like this."

"A pleasure to meet you, Ms. Blanchard. I've read so much about you," the grower enthused.

Toni said something in reply that made everyone laugh and her father beamed.

As if she was an invited guest, Syrah thought, and not running from here to a judge to explain how they'd found a way to keep their heads above rising water. She didn't know why she had to remind herself so forcefully of Toni's role, but she knew it had nothing whatsoever to do with the way that Toni's hands moved as she talked, or the warm, low tone of her laughter.

Syrah plastered a smile on her face and circulated through the room, taking some satisfaction from the turnout. There were at least twenty interests represented here, and that meant they'd get a fair price even at the short notice. Properly advertising and doing a public auction might get them more, but after the costs they would likely net the same amount.

Bennett appeared from the hallway that led to the dining room and gave a significant harrumph. Syrah shooed people in that direction, promising warm shortbread and other tasty things.

Toni remained at the door, and since Syrah didn't want to take a chair from a bidder, she lingered there as well. Some people had to stand anyway, but no one seemed to mind. The bowl of note cards and envelopes was passed from party to party, and in a few minutes pencils had made their notes and envelopes were tucked shut. Syrah took a second bowl around the table to collect the cards, then set it in front of her father.

When she rejoined Toni at the door, Toni whispered, "Is it really this easy?"

"It is for us." She shrugged. "Public auctions are much more tense, with multiple sales and everyone having contingencies. You know, if they don't get their first choice they then need to shore up their bids to fill in what they didn't get. This is one deal and a known quantity. The Bench, Alexander Ridge, Lime Flat—they all know exactly what those plots are."

"Gotcha."

The growers chatted among themselves while her father opened the envelopes and arranged the bids from high to low. By the time he finished most of the wine and all of the cookies were gone.

"This is very gratifying. Thank you all for your serious bids." He quickly named the five top bidders.

"Oh, well," one of the losers said genially on his way out. "It was a long shot. I hoped nobody else would have heard. There's no way I could afford anything off of Ardani Bench."

"Me, too. I stayed for the cookies." A woman Syrah didn't know paused to hand her a business card. "If there's another auction of this kind, do let me know. And I love shortbread."

"I'll remember." Syrah smiled back, vaguely wondering if she was being flirted with.

Toni said, her lips stiff with an obvious effort not to smile, "I think she likes your vines."

"It's just business."

"What would a woman have to do to get you to realize she's flirting with you?"

Syrah wondered why Toni wanted to know such a thing. It wasn't as if . . . Her heart was suddenly pounding. "It doesn't happen all that often."

"That you notice."

Alarmed, and not sure why, Syrah concentrated on the activity in the dining room. The five top bidders were filling out new cards, having been told what the previous high bid was. She already suspected that the lease would go to the collective representative. Her father wouldn't be all that happy; the collective often then sold their residuals to the big conglomerates. It wasn't to be helped. She sighed.

"This isn't easy for your father."

"No." For me either, Syrah could have added. Things weren't supposed to change, not like this. Nature could make change but when people forced change it never felt right to Syrah. "How are you enjoying Napa?"

"I'll admit it's beautiful here. We had a delicious dinner last night at French Laundry."

Syrah was nonplussed. "Really? How did you pull that off?"

"It wasn't me. Caroline can be ingenious when she wants to be."

Good for Caroline, Syrah thought. She glanced again at the bruises on Toni's arm and when she tore her gaze away she realized Toni had caught her looking.

Syrah couldn't begin to decipher the expression on Toni's face. It wasn't a blush, and it wasn't shy admission. It was . . . uncomfortable. She couldn't pry into it, so she asked, "Do you have other business in the area?"

"No, not right now. There is a rumor of a client working out an acquisition in Los Angeles, but I'm well aware that's not really the same state."

Syrah snickered. "You understand Northern California attitudes too well, perhaps."

"That or I'm too cozy with Southern California business interests. Since the Silicon Valley crash there hasn't been the same kind of activity up here to give me balance."

They stopped talking as her father began opening the next round of envelopes. "We have a clear leader this time." He stated the top bid and two of the growers put up their hands in resignation. "One more round?" He glanced at the remaining three.

"I think I'm done, too, much as I hate to be," another man said.

Syrah walked them out, thanking them along the way for their efforts. By the time she returned to the dining room, everyone was shaking hands and her father had a mixed look of pleasure and regret on his face. As Syrah had expected, the collective had won the bid.

"It was fifteen percent more than I thought it would be," Toni said in a low voice. "Excellent."

"That's good news."

"It is. I'm going to see what happens if I project forward five more years of lease—"

"I don't think Dad will agree, I really don't. He's dying inside." Syrah hadn't meant to say so much but at least Toni was nodding with understanding.

"I know. At least we can see how it pencils."

Papers were being signed and then her father walked the two other men to the door. Syrah found herself abruptly alone with Toni and could think about nothing but the fact that Toni had seen her with no panties on this afternoon and what Toni might have been doing to Caroline to get those kinds of bruises on her arm.

"Have dinner with me," Toni said suddenly.

Syrah blinked. "Why?"

Toni's mouth tightened but Syrah didn't know if it was laughter or annoyance. She supposed her blunt question had been a little rude. "Because a girl's gotta eat and I don't know where is good."

"I don't think I can get us into French Laundry."

"Good. It was delicious but far too rich to do every night. Bennett's food is also starting to show on my waistline."

Syrah couldn't help but look. She had no control over her eyes as she studied the flat stomach, lean hips and long, long legs. She brushed her hand over her own stomach. "Oh, you've a ways to go to catch me. I need to stick to a diet."

"No, you don't."

Toni's low tone caught Syrah off-guard. Was Toni flirting with her? No, it was just polite conversation, she thought. She didn't want Toni Blanchard to flirt with her, not at all. "Let me clean up a little, then sure."

In her room, Syrah discarded the T-shirt that had been treacherously too short, and pulled on a red short-sleeved sweater. She brushed her hair, pulling it back into a ponytail. Recalling Caroline Bingley's perfect brows she quickly plucked a few stray hairs, then decided she did not have time for an all-day makeover.

She frowned at herself in the mirror. "This will have to do."

"Have fun," her father called.

It was surreal, sitting in Toni Blanchard's rental car, her father's words ringing in her ears. She had no expectation of having "fun" but her heart was pounding nonetheless. Exactly what was she doing, then?

# Chapter 8

"To tell you the truth, I'd like a drink. From a bar where it's dark, the music is low and the French fries are served with ketchup." Toni gripped the steering wheel with both hands to keep her palms from sliding on it. A drink was probably not the best idea, but she could think of nothing else to say now that Syrah's thigh was a mere six inches from her own.

This feeling inside was ridiculous. She was not fifteen and dying over her first girl.

Syrah was gazing out her window, but Toni thought she heard a hint of a smile in her tone. "I think I know just the place. Go north on the highway to Trancas and head east."

"Gotcha." *What's wrong with me, what's wrong with me*—the refrain wouldn't stop. "I'm glad the auction went well, I really am."

"Obviously, I am, too." Syrah shifted her position so she was now looking at Toni. "I don't mean this as rudely as it sounds, but what's in this for you?"

"In what?"

"What you do. I understand money of course, and I don't think that's a bad thing, mostly."

"A girl's got a right to make a living, doesn't she?" Toni gave Syrah an arch look.

"Yes, of course. But why this living?"

"Good question. I intended to go into business law, but I was just about finished with grad school before I grew up and realized my interest was mostly about following in my father's footsteps. He's a judge."

"I think my father mentioned that. I understand the compulsion to want to follow on well-trod ground. I certainly have."

"You have grape DNA, right?"

"You're quoting my father." Syrah looked down at her hands. "I enjoy spreading manure sometimes. Other times it's the chemistry of it."

Toni had to force her gaze back to the road. Syrah's fingers were as shapely as the rest of her. "I finished the law degree, and it has certainly come in handy. But my first job out of college was with a crook who treated everyone and everything, including me, like a slot machine. Fiddle with it just so, and it pays off for you."

"What did you do?"

"I quit and found another company and the story was much the same. Eventually I freelanced and got to pick and choose. I was lucky in the form of a patron, a friend of my father's. He brought me a chunk of business as a test and when that worked, we went on to bigger and better things. I got flat-out lucky, made a bundle in something I had put my own money into and life, generally, has been good."

"Lots of travel? Adventure?"

Toni grinned. "Lots of hotels and bad food. That's been a delightful change about this trip."

"Netherfield is a lovely old home. I don't know if it's true, but there was a story about its being located on the spot where the first Spanish land grant for the valley was signed."

"I like it. At first I thought Missy was crazy, but it has many charms."

"More than one, yes."

Wondering what that cryptic comment meant, Toni was about to ask when she realized the exit she wanted was coming up. Syrah pointed out the way and they left the main highway behind in favor of a more suburban setting. Stores with matching facades and familiar names gave way to older buildings and a farmer's market. They arrived at an aging strip mall and headed toward a heavy door under a sign with a blinking martini glass.

"This is Nate's. I don't know what it's really called," Syrah added hastily, "but it's run by Nate. Doesn't matter who's behind the bar, the tag says *Nate*."

Toni liked it immediately. The bar was long, worn but well-polished, and the ceiling was strung closely with hundreds of glass prisms. The low light shimmered as if supplied by candles. Banked behind the bar was a wide variety of spirits. A clatter at the far end promised a kitchen of some kind and she quickly identified the aroma of French fries and possibly fried cod. "This is perfect."

"They make a great Reuben or grilled cheese, and the fish and chips are good if you're in the mood. That's the whole menu by the way. There was a foray into cheese sticks a few years back, but it didn't sit well with the regulars."

"Would that include you?" Toni gently pressed her hand to Syrah's back as they followed the bartender's gesture toward a booth.

"No, afraid not. I've just been here on the occasional late night, when everything else is closed." Syrah slid into the booth with a relieved sigh. "This is just what I needed, too. Sometimes living where you work can be a little stifling."

It had taken a great effort not to run her hand up Syrah's spine in time to the slow, silky jazz that oozed from the speakers. "Why did you go to Europe? You were away for, what, four years?"

Syrah's expression shuttered. "How did you know that?"

"Your father told me." She knew Syrah was a good dancer, but the kind of dancing Toni couldn't seem to stop thinking about wasn't upright.

Syrah eased into a slight smile. "I didn't want to be an Ardani. I was certain there was more to life than that, and more to wine-making than the way we did it. So I went to France, primarily, and apprenticed in several places."

"Did you get what you wanted out of it?"

"You ask very probing questions."

"Sorry." The arrival of the bartender startled Toni but she recovered quickly. "Tennessee whiskey, neat."

"Daniels or Dickel?" The bartender—Nate, the nametag said—swiped the table in front of them with a towel that had at one time been white.

"Dickel. And a glass of ginger ale." She nodded at Syrah.

"A mudslide, heavy on the mud."

The bartender grunted and walked off, leaving Toni to remark, "A milkshake in a place like this?"

"It's more than a milkshake," Syrah chided. "It's got alcohol in it."

"It's grownup chocolate milk, frozen."

Syrah sat back against the cushion. "Did I criticize you for choosing a distillate of corn mash? One could argue it's a grownup breakfast cereal."

"Works for me." Toni tried to relax but found herself leaning on the table so she could better see Syrah's expression. "You didn't answer my question."

"About?"

"Europe. Did you get what you wanted out of it?"

"Yes and no. I learned a lot about wine. When I got home I was more of an Ardani than ever."

"Was that so bad?"

"It only seemed so for a while. I wasn't ready to come home but I am very glad that I did."

The drinks arrived and they both ordered fish and chips.

Syrah hoisted her tall, frosted glass. "To business, successfully concluded."

Toni nodded and raised her glass as well. "We've bought some time today."

"I've noticed," Syrah said after a long sip from her glass, "that you say *we*."

"Does that bother you? I don't usually." She generally kept her boundaries much, much cleaner than that.

Syrah shrugged. "Why make an exception for us?"

"I think . . ." She had another sip of whiskey and let it warm her throat before she went on. "I think it's because your father always puts it that way. And I like him. I like him a lot."

Her expression softening, Syrah said quietly, "Dad is special. Sometimes he's in a world so far above ours that it's frustrating, but he is a patient teacher, a kind man. And a good father." She frowned at her drink. "This is going right to my head."

Toni felt much the same about her whiskey. "My father spoke highly of yours. Did you know your dad introduced my parents to each other?"

"No, nobody told me that." She pushed her drink away and reached for the glass of water. "I'll go slow. After Saturday night I don't want any repeats. I was blotto."

Toni didn't agree with her, not aloud at least. In spite of Caroline's criticism, she knew there were times when agreeing with the truth was a bad idea. "I was so hot I thought I'd have heat stroke. Missy didn't give me a chance to change."

"Oh, I thought you were into suffering."

"The beer saved me from heatstroke."

"I should have stuck with beer. I like Missy, by the way. As my dad likes to say, she'd make a good grape."

Toni's heartfelt laugh turned heads. "That is priceless—and perfect. A sparkling white, it suits her."

"Fruity only in the aroma, then warm at the first taste."

102

"Sounds like Missy." Toni wondered how Syrah would describe her as wine. Acidic, likely.

Syrah was having another long sip from her drink, and the way she licked her lips free of the foam made Toni hide a smile. It was a milkshake no matter how much Irish cream was in it, and if Syrah had been in pigtails the picture of a child enjoying her treat would have been complete. "Are you like a Syrah grape?"

"Syrah with a *Y* or Sirah with an *I*?"

"I did wonder what the difference was." She'd been trying to pay attention, and Internet searches had helped, but the more she learned the more it was obvious that years of study would be necessary to become even modestly conversant about grapes and winemaking. That, or personal tutoring, but it really wasn't grapes that were uppermost in Toni's mind.

Syrah gazed into her mudslide as she answered Toni's question. "Petite Sirah and Syrah are both Rhone valley grapes, but they're otherwise not related. In Europe the petites are generally out of favor—they're small and tart, usually, though some argue those are really Durifs. Our petites, though, aren't Durifs and they can act as good agents mixed carefully with less complicated reds. Our Petite Sirahs can be really dark and they have a long-lasting peak."

Toni nodded as if she was following all of it—mostly she thought she understood. "And Syrah with a *Y*?"

Syrah colored slightly. "Well, I think as a youth, I was spicy, but I never thought smoky worked."

Oh, Toni thought, but it did. Smoky—it was exceedingly apt. "And now that you're, what, thirty?"

"Thirty-one."

"Ancient."

"I'm not a child," Syrah said sharply.

"Sorry, I didn't mean that you were." Note to self, Toni thought, avoid that particular sore spot. "Thirty-something can hardly be called your maturity, however."

Syrah gave her a suspicious look. "No, I suppose not. But I

don't think I'm silky violet and rose petals, either. That always sounds funereal to me."

Smoky, silky violet and rose . . . Toni was buying every word. "What's the mature Syrah like, then?"

"Blackberries, pepper and enduring complexities."

Sounds fun, Toni thought. "We could all aspire to that. At least the enduring part."

"My mom died when I was little, but my father says I resemble her."

Thinking of Anthony's broad, regular features, Toni said, "I do like your father, but it's true. You don't resemble him, except the smile."

"I asked him once how he managed to get my mom to marry him and he said it was his smile and willingness to lie through his teeth if necessary."

Toni was again startled by another bartender and she leaned back to let Nate—a woman this time—put two steaming plates of fish and fries down on the table. Two bowls of coleslaw quickly followed and Toni didn't hesitate to grab the ketchup.

"This is a long way from Tavern on the Green," she said without thinking.

"Go there often?" Syrah smoothed the rough surface of the table with one hand.

"I used to. I was dating someone who valued that kind of experience on a regular basis." She hadn't meant to go into her past.

"Did you value that experience on a regular basis?"

"At times. Sometimes a hot dog from a street vendor can be better. I got away from that for a while, that's all." Too much whiskey, too fast, Toni thought. If she told Syrah all her secrets she'd be a goner.

Syrah broke open a piece of the cod and dunked it in the tartar sauce. "We've got fried, fried, mayo, mayo." She nodded at the coleslaw. "Cabbage. There is cabbage."

"You're spoiling my meal, mentioning vegetables."

"Sorry. I've been leaning on Bennett the last month or so. Dad's cholesterol keeps creeping up. It's like talking to a wall."

"I can imagine. Still, olive oil and wine are supposed to be good for us, aren't they?"

"Yes, in moderation. Not with a pound of cheese and cream." Syrah finished blowing on the hot fish and took a tentative bite. "On the other hand, this is perfect comfort food."

"Are you in need of comfort?" A physical jolt surged through Toni at the thought of putting her arms around Syrah, even just to comfort her.

"Isn't everybody?" She swallowed and gazed at Toni for a still moment, then broke the mood by reaching for her drink. "Sometimes comfort can be all we need."

Toni flushed as she realized Syrah was staring again at the bruises Caroline had left on her arm. She hadn't even felt them at the time, but she was well aware of exactly when they had happened. It hadn't been about anything so simple as comfort. "Sometimes."

Syrah looked away and Toni realized she had given the wrong impression and there was nothing she could say to fix it. It was between Caroline and her, and Syrah wasn't . . . didn't figure into that. Except, of course, she did. What Syrah thought of her mattered deeply at that moment, and there was no way to explain what Caroline meant to her without sounding like the cad she was. She ought not to have let Caroline get that close, that involved. She'd known better. She'd like to think she'd been drunk, but that didn't even explain it. How could she explain that she'd felt so detached from Caroline's passion that part of her hadn't really felt anything at all had happened?

They ate in silence for a while and Toni couldn't tell what Syrah was thinking. The black and gold eyes were lowered, focused on her food, while the shimmering light on her hair made Toni want to feel it filling her hands. The sweater Syrah wore molded strong but softly rounded shoulders that Toni suspected could shiver in responsive delight.

"Cabernet Sauvignon, but first growth."

Toni arched an eyebrow and swallowed quickly. "Pardon me?"

"If you were a grape."

"Oh. Is that good, first growth?"

"In France it is."

Toni wanted in the worst way to ask about here as opposed to France, but any answer Syrah might give scared her. "I know that means a dark red wine—but your complexion is darker than mine."

"It's the inside of a grape that matters more."

"Am I that dark? On the inside?"

"Complicated."

That word again. "I really don't think I'm complicated at all. My rules are very simple."

Syrah nearly looked as if she'd ask for a list, but a new Nate arrived to ask if they'd like another drink. Toni shook her head—she wanted another but it would be highly unwise. Syrah also declined but asked for more water. A noisy group entered and they were silent until the bar quieted down a little.

"So, when are you going back to New York?"

"I don't know. I'd like to stay another week at least, mostly because Missy got the pool cleaned and working again and I can't believe what she's doing with the wallpaper." Her eyes were saying more, she could feel it.

Syrah abruptly wouldn't look at her. "Can you be away from work so long?"

"I'm not the least bit away from work. My cell phone is a tyrant."

"I noticed you're on it a lot."

"Irons in the fire—a lot of them. Mostly it's colleagues doing their own contracts and wanting ideas or advice from me. Honestly, I had forgotten I was still listed as a receivership analyst with the Delaware Court. One of the lenders requested me as I'd worked on a deal before."

"Oh." Syrah sipped the last of her mudslide. "How does that all work? I mean—forgive me for being tactless about it, but who pays you?"

"It's not tactless. How do you know if you don't ask? The court, if I take a fee."

"Why wouldn't you?"

She shrugged, not wanting to talk about it in depth. "Sometimes I don't. It depends on the deal. The court is of course paid by the corporation in question and my fee can sometimes make or break the numbers." Shut up, she told herself. *Don't let her know that you can be soft. It's a losing hand.*

Syrah wanted to ask, it was plain in her eyes. Toni wouldn't let herself say that she had no intention of profiting at all from Ardani. She was too involved, and was caring about things having nothing to do with money, which meant she was not serving her clients' best interests.

They gazed at each other for far too long and finally Toni could not hold back a shivering gasp. Never in her life had she felt so examined and so known by another woman. "What?"

"Nothing that we can talk about, I suppose."

"No, not really."

Original Nate stopped at their table. "Dessert for you ladies?"

Toni waited to see what Syrah wanted before she, too, shook her head. "Not tonight." She handed over a credit card and Nate toddled off with their dishes. "This was good, thank you. Just what I needed."

"Comfort food?"

"Yes, and interesting company."

"Interesting? I'll take that as a compliment, I guess."

"It was meant that way."

Syrah's smile with tight. "I was wondering if *interesting* was like the Chinese curse, *may you live in interesting times.*"

"I can promise you I will probably think of people as grapes for the rest of my life." She signed the check, thanked Nate and they got up to leave.

To her surprise the temperature outside had dropped significantly. Syrah shivered.

"I don't even have a coat to offer you," Toni said.

"It's okay. It's good for me—stressing the vine."

Toni opened Syrah's door. "Wouldn't that be bad for you?"

Syrah answered once Toni had the car safely backed out of the parking space. "Stressed vines are stronger and bear smaller, more intense fruit. Weather extremes and too little water are the most common stressors. I think it applies to people. A little discomfort makes us appreciate things that feel good. Like a hot bath."

Toni's thighs clenched at the idea of slipping into a bathtub of hot, soapy water with Syrah. "I will confess, I thought you picked the grapes, stomped them and put the juice in bottles. Later, you open the bottle and drink."

Syrah laughed. "That can turn out something drinkable, but actually, at a minimum, you have to dilute the juice with water. Some vintners can stop there if the grapes are just right."

Hoping she remembered the return trip, Toni angled for the highway on-ramp, but Syrah touched her arm.

"We can avoid the traffic if you keep going."

The country roads were dark, but Toni didn't mind going slow. There were a few other cars out and the lights of the occasional home, set back from the road, flickered in the distance.

"Our land is on the right, now." Syrah's voice, soft and tender, sent a shiver up Toni's spine.

"I read the surveyor's description, but it had no sense of scale to me. Maybe I'm too city-bred to know what five hundred acres here and two hundred acres there really means."

"If you turn here and promise to drive slow, we can go through the back way."

"I promise. Thank you for trusting me after this afternoon."

Her voice was even softer. "I'll get the gate."

Toni didn't know what to do with the ache she felt as she watched Syrah move in the glow of the headlights. She briefly struggled with the lock, then the gate swung open and Toni had the bizarre feeling she was being given entrance to Syrah's world in a way she'd never get walking in through the front door.

She rolled down the windows to let the night in and moments later Syrah slipped into the passenger seat again, bringing with her the damp, heady scent of cologne and earth.

"We won't get lost, will we?"

"I know the way. I thought we had some patchy fog, given how damp it is, but the sky is clear."

"I can't tell you the last time I saw a clear night sky and took the time to notice it."

They drove slowly along the packed dirt road, saying nothing. Toni thought Syrah ought to be able to hear her pounding heart. It's not a good idea, none of this is smart, she tried to tell herself. This was foolish in a way that was different from being foolish with Caroline. *This is going to hurt both of us.*

Syrah made a little noise, then said, "If you stop here, we can stargaze. The moon is just rising, so visibility is good. I know a few constellations."

Dumb, this was dumb, but the voice telling Toni so was helpless to stop her hands from switching off the ignition and turning off the lights.

They got out of the car and for a few minutes, while Syrah pointed heavenward, they were on opposite sides.

"The small one with red tones, see that? Just to the left is a cluster. That's the Pleiades."

"I don't see the red star."

They met in the front of the car and leaned their heads together so Toni could sight along Syrah's finger. "There. It's very small, but tinged in red. Next to the larger blue one."

"I think you see more colors than I do."

"You haven't had much chance to look at stars, that's all."

Toni turned her head to study Syrah's profile etched by the starlight. "And I'm supposedly the complicated one."

Syrah's arm slowly fell to her side. "I'm finding it very hard to understand you."

"I really do think I'm straightforward."

She turned her head sharply, but her lips were curved in a smile. "But not straight."

"Not in the least."

There were stars reflected in Syrah's eyes, flickers of silver mingling with that deep, alluring gold. It's the stars, Toni thought, that make her look as if she wants me. *It's the stars.*

She told herself it was the stars when Syrah leaned into the inches that separated them and their lips met.

They both drew back immediately and Syrah scooted up onto the hood of the car, wrapping her legs with her arms. "I'm sorry, I don't know why I did that."

Toni couldn't help but smile. "Maybe because we both wondered what it would be like."

She nodded.

Toni willed herself to at least look calm as she leaned against the car. "The hood is warm."

"Yes, feels good."

"So I think I see the red star. The Pleiades aren't so much stars as a group glow."

"I know when I was a girl I could count four out of seven. But these days this is the best it gets." She unwrapped a little, sliding to the edge of the hood. "It's hard to see anything clearly with so much interference."

Toni shifted just enough to study Syrah's face again. "Our world is full of noise. But tonight it seems very quiet."

Syrah turned her head and the invitation was there in the tremble of her lips, the unfocused gaze that seemed to reach no further than Toni's mouth and the restless movement of her hands on her thighs.

Toni lost track of the world. The stars might have winked out for all she knew, suspended in that desirous, vulnerable look. She captured one of the restless hands, shivering as she coiled her fingers around Syrah's. She felt the shudder that unfurled in Syrah's arms, then their bodies wound together, close and hard, lips seeking and finding equal pressure.

Toni knew she said something, but she couldn't hear her own voice over the pounding in her ears. Their kisses surged from one to another with increasing intensity until Syrah's legs wrapped around Toni's hips and their rhythm became mutual.

She had not felt this fire for Mira in a long time, and last night Caroline had only blown on low embers. This fire was hot and real, and the little noises Syrah made as they kissed only sent the flames higher.

Toni let herself feel Syrah's bare arms, then the curve of her back just under the hem of her sweater. She wanted Syrah's sweater out of the way, but she still had some control left, though it was rapidly weakening. Every movement of her hands seemed to bring a responsive shudder from Syrah and their hips were locked in a frustrating dance. The sweater wasn't the only thing she wanted Syrah to take off. Her own clothes were too tight and too confining.

She gasped and broke their kiss at the thought of their bare breasts touching and felt a clench high up that stunned her. She moaned, realizing too late how excited she was and Syrah caught her in a fierce grasp, pulling Toni onto the hood, on top of her warm, rolling body.

"Like that?" Syrah's hands were at Toni's zipper. "I didn't think . . . We shouldn't."

"We shouldn't." Toni groaned. "Yes, just like that, please."

Syrah's hands slipped inside Toni's underwear, making space for her hands to move. Fingertips grasped Toni's hips, then nails grazed the sensitive skin of her inner thighs. "That's it," Syrah said softly, then she arched hard under Toni as her hand closed over Toni's swollen, slick center.

"Please." She could find no other word.

"Kiss me," Syrah whispered. "Kiss me while I touch you."

Unraveling, she fell into Syrah's mouth. Their tongues danced in a sensual, intimate give-and-take while Syrah's fingers slowly stroked every nerve between Toni's legs.

I can't protect myself like this, Toni thought wildly. It wasn't the vulnerable position, her legs spread over Syrah's hips. Something else was completely exposed and it was Syrah's gaze that touched it, caressed it. She reared back to try to get away from the way those eyes were trying to possess her and found Syrah's fingers were slipping inside.

"Oh, please," she choked out, her mouth dry.

"Yes," Syrah said through clenched teeth. "Just like that. Let me feel you."

Toni couldn't help but let most of her weight fall on Syrah when the first climax washed over her. Syrah was kissing her, now, fiercely, and she thrust down hard on Syrah's fingers as muscles tried to tighten and relax at the same time. She heard a short, sharp cry, realized it was her and buried her face in Syrah's neck.

She could have melted on top of Syrah, but nerves shivered awake as Syrah whispered, "Please let me have more of you."

Toni shifted slightly, feeling the delicious pressure of Syrah's fingers still inside her. Gathering what strength she had, she pulled her own shirt over her head and loosened her bra.

Syrah moaned, a low, sexy sound that ended as she captured Toni's nipple between her fingers. They kissed, and Toni realized she was dancing for Syrah and she never wanted to stop. She'd never felt this kind of release before, this kind of abandon.

"Oh . . . oh, you feel so good." Syrah's voice was silken. "I don't want to stop touching you. I'm sorry, I didn't think we would do this . . . You feel *so* good."

"Don't stop." Toni silenced Syrah with a kiss and let the searing pleasure of skin on skin claim her. Every time she pushed back against Syrah's fingers she heard one of those wonderful little sounds from Syrah and they were getting increasingly frantic. Syrah's pleasure was so palpable that Toni felt another surge of tightness inside.

It was happening so quickly and Syrah's stunned expression echoed Toni's peak. They both cried out, sharp, sweet, and suddenly they were both laughing, kissing, settling into a comfortable embrace as their hips slowly continued to move.

Syrah's hands smoothed Toni's back. "I really didn't think we would . . . do this."

"Neither did I." Toni kissed Syrah's earlobe, then she nibbled lightly at it to feel Syrah shiver again. "I really wanted to, but I thought I had more control than this."

"I'm glad you don't." Syrah leaned back enough that they could be face to face. "I'm glad I don't either. I'm just feeling . . . well . . ."

Please don't say you feel sorry or foolish or guilty, Toni wanted to plead. She didn't want to hear *inappropriate* or *one of those things*.

"I'm feeling surprised."

"That we're here?"

"No. Okay, well, on the hood of your car, yeah. I'm surprised." Syrah gazed up at the stars for a moment. "What I meant was, though, that I . . . could do that."

"What? Make me feel that good?"

She nodded shyly. "I've never responded like that while touching someone else."

"Oh. You mean you . . ." Leaning close, Toni whispered, "You came with me?" She felt another nod against her cheek. "Wow. I'm sorry I was distracted. I wanted to be quite aware when you came for me the first time."

A shudder traveled the length of Syrah's body. Her voice was a blend of uncertainty and boldness as she said, "Well, I didn't exactly come *for* you. I came *with* you."

"And that's different?"

"It sure as hell felt different. It was quite, quite nice."

"I think we need to be sure," Toni said, trying to tease just enough to help Syrah relax again. "I'd hate for you to be confused on that point."

"What did you have in mind?"

"A little of this." Toni shifted her position so that she could pull Syrah's sweater off. "A little of tha—" Toni bit back a gasp. "Dear heaven, you're so incredibly beautiful."

"Touch me," Syrah breathed as she unhooked her bra. "Touch me."

The womanly swells Toni had glimpsed under the wet T-shirt were under her palms now. Responsive nipples made her mouth water. Syrah was so divinely female. Cupping her breast was like holding a feminine secret. Toni leaned forward to softly kiss one plump tip and shivered when she felt it harden against her lips.

Another of those small sounds, something between a whimper and a plea, brought Toni's head up to kiss the panting mouth as she gathered Syrah's breasts in her hands. Syrah's vulnerability was going right to Toni's head, leaving her dizzy. "You are so very beautiful to touch."

In the starlight Syrah's expression flickered from fear to desire, back and forth, and Toni touched her with all the tenderness she felt inside.

"I won't hurt you."

A cool breeze drifted over them and Toni could feel Syrah withdrawing. "Not tonight, I know you won't tonight."

Not ever, Toni wanted to say. Her hands stilled. It wasn't a promise she could make.

They kissed again but Toni knew Syrah had shut down. The starlight had only lasted so long, Toni thought.

Softly, she asked, "Do you want your clothes back?"

"I think so." Syrah turned her head away.

Toni softly kissed the shoulder nearest her and felt Syrah tremble. "Oh, honey, don't cry."

"It's just reaction. I'm okay." The dark eyes that turned toward Toni were brimming with tears. "This wasn't a good idea for either of us."

"No, no, it wasn't. I don't say that to hurt you, Syrah." She let herself, unseen, touch Syrah's hair as she pulled the sweater back into place. "We both . . . I guess we both need to think what this means."

"If it means anything."

"It does. It does to me."

All the fear Toni had felt earlier, trying to keep some kind of distance from the pleasure of Syrah's company, then the fervor of her kisses, Toni could see all that fear in Syrah's eyes now. It was that same disbelief and worry that by the time she pulled back it would be too late.

She has more than her heart to lose through knowing you, Toni thought as she pulled her own clothes back into some semblance of order. Her jeans were soaked. What had been sexy was rapidly chilling to discomfort. She wished she could take Syrah back to Netherfield, to bed, but Caroline was there and ye gods, what a tangle. Nor did she fancy waking up to Bennett's slashing wit, or Anthony's undoubted hurt to find out Toni had seduced his daughter.

This hadn't been smart, not at all. Her stomach lurched as she recalled the moment she hadn't been able to pull back and had lost herself in Syrah's arms. It hadn't been smart, but nothing in her life had ever before felt so right.

# Chapter 9

Shifting in bed, Syrah knew the alarm was not far off but she still told herself she was trying to sleep. Rolling over with a sigh she scratched her nose and the aroma on her fingertips washed over her.

Toni.

Sleep was impossible. After pulling on work clothes, she made her way through the lower fields toward the oldest and smallest fermentation building. The rough-cut stone created a low temperature for slow yeast reactions, resulting in their most mellow, longest peaking reds.

The interior was damp and cool and Syrah hoped it might mellow her, too, but she doubted anything could. Even though her limbs felt like lead, her heart kept missing beats every time she remembered what it had felt like to hold Toni in her arms.

Methodically working her way through the barrels with the testing meter, she relived the night before, everything from the surprising invitation to dinner and the conversation that had side-stepped important things and left so much unsaid. At times she had felt so unschooled, unsophisticated. She was sure someone like Caroline Bingley was never at a loss for words or actions.

How could she have seduced Toni like that? Even when she'd seen those bruises in the starlight she simply hadn't cared that Toni had been with anyone else. Toni had been responding to her, she was sure of that, not just the romantic spring night and one drink at dinner. Something tingled and ached like never before, but she had been stupid, stupid to grab Toni like that, as if there had been no yesterday and would be no tomorrow.

And then, like some child, she'd gotten scared about what it meant to be making love so intensely and broken the mood. Toni had wanted her and even now Syrah's body felt simply unreal.

She finished her measurements and notes and walked back to the house, hungry but not sure she could eat. Toni had said today was the last day she'd be at the winery, but she wasn't going home for a week, maybe. Would she ask Syrah out again? Should she ask Toni for a date? What did they do now, after that awkward hug and peck good-bye?

Toni's rental car was in the small lot when Syrah regained the house. She braced herself, or tried to, but her stomach still lurched at the sight of Toni casually leaning against the counter, one elegant hand wrapped around a mug of coffee.

At least, Syrah thought with satisfaction, it looks like she got as much sleep as I did.

If anything, Toni's eyes were haunted. "Good morning" was all she said.

"Good morning. How are things penciling today?"

"Better than yesterday, though there's a great deal of uncertainty remaining."

"Not to mention a lot of noise."

Toni nodded, gazing into her coffee. "A great deal of noise." She sighed when her cell phone rang and walked by Syrah without a glance on her way to the patio.

Syrah made herself eat a little toast, and coffee seemed to settle her jumping stomach. Every so often a snatch of Toni's conversation drifted toward them. Syrah wondered who "Crystal sweetie" was and why "Doc" was so happy. It wasn't her business.

She settled at the computer to download the distributor orders for the day and checked her e-mail. With a jolt she recognized the same sender who had sent the mysterious note from "A Friend" yesterday.

Even though she'd showered she felt as if she could still smell Toni on her fingertips. She heard the breath of wonder that Toni had let out when she'd first touched Syrah's breasts. Her finger hovered over the delete button, but again, remembering that more was at stake than anything she might feel for Toni, she made herself open the message.

"Dear Ms. Ardani," she read.

I know what I'm about to tell you isn't going to be easy to hear but if I can save you the torment I have suffered at Toni Blanchard's hands, it will be worth the risk to me. If she ever knows I broke my silence my entire family will be ruined. Below I have included some links to articles about Blanchard's business practices and numerous editorials pleading with her not to close down factories and sell off holdings in small towns all over the country.

Her excuses about her tactics always sound sincere, and to my everlasting regret her charm and attractions got the best of me. Our affair was highly painful for me as I believe she took pleasure in the fact that I was so dependent on her. When I tried to leave her and had to borrow money she promptly bought up my marker and now holds it over my head to ensure my silence.

Don't believe her lies. Don't let her get too close. She is a master of manipulation.

Once again, it was signed, "A Friend."

Numbly, Syrah reviewed the links in the e-mail, then chose the last and clicked. The browser hopped to a page from the *Valdosta Journal* headed by an editorial titled, "Blanchard Pulls the Plug— Factory Closing Tuesday."

Though her eyes blurred with tears, she made herself read every last word about lies and false hope, about promises to help then fading out of sight. The other links led to similar articles, including one that detailed the possibility of a grand jury investigation into the purchase of a bankrupt high-tech company in Silicon Valley. Was that the real reason Toni didn't work in that part of the state now?

She hadn't wanted to trust Toni, hadn't wanted to think she was really here to help them. Yesterday she had let herself think that maybe Toni didn't have a calculator where her heart ought to be, and last night . . . last night . . . she had felt something she'd never known she could.

She closed all the screens, fighting to breathe, and escaped to the vineyard again. Her throat ached too tightly to cry.


"I don't know where Syrah can have gone, but if you like I'll have her call you." Anthony scratched his head, obviously puzzled by his daughter's absence.

"It's okay, I'll call her to say good-bye. I'm glad that we were able at least to solve a few problems, temporarily. I, or one of my colleagues, will be back in two months to review the projections so we can assure the court that everything is going according to plan. At that time . . ." Toni made herself look him in the eye. "At that time we may have to consider some painful alternatives while there are still choices and no one is forcing a course of action on us." Stop saying *us*, she told herself. There was no *us*.

"I am going to think long and hard about what to do, too. We'll be careful with our expenses, that I promise as well."

Toni found a smile. "You've no idea how good that is to hear. A number of companies I've worked with never even want to promise that."

She shook hands, accepted his greetings to be passed on to her father, and then left the Ardanis behind her, or so she sincerely hoped. She regretted last night with Syrah, and she'd been acting out of character from the moment she'd arrived. She needed to apologize to Caroline, too, and then go home. Missy's pool was tempting, and so was the sunshine, but she needed to get home and back into some kind of balance.

She now knew the drive to Netherfield well and was surprised to find, though it was hardly past noon, Missy's convertible in the driveway.

"Toni, you've done wonders!" Missy beamed at her from the common room, surveying the heavy crimson wallpaper.

"All I did was let them in. You need to thank Caroline—she told them what to do around the windows. I hadn't a clue."

Caroline appeared from the direction of the kitchen, glasses of wine in hand. "Hello, stranger," she said to Toni. "You were late in last night."

"I went out to dinner with Syrah and then decided to stargaze. There aren't any stars in New York."

"Really? Was she a good guide?"

"Only for part of the evening." Every word was the truth, but she had a feeling Caroline was hearing more than Toni was willing to admit. "She picked a great pub for dinner, though."

Missy, oblivious to their conversation, continued to chatter about how the room looked. "I've been thinking about the gardens all week, and I'm going to ask Jane for advice. Even if she doesn't have time to mastermind it, I think she has wonderful taste."

"Well, a week of work didn't change that tune," Caroline said in a low voice. "So, darling, I chose a laundry, and she chose a pub. Which of us got it right?"

"It's not like that, Caroline."

"Then why do you look like you didn't sleep? Did she get any sleep?"

"You know I was alone when I got here."

"That doesn't mean I'm pleased to think another woman disturbed your sleep."

"I'm going home tomorrow, Caroline." Syrah had plainly been avoiding her today and Toni got that message loud and clear.

Missy whirled around. "You're not! I just got back, and I'm taking half of next week off—well, working from here. I need you to be here, just a few days."

"You have to stay a little longer," Caroline agreed. "Otherwise we won't be able to chaperone her."

"Guys, really, I need to go—"

"Wednesday. Stay until Wednesday. Then at least I'll have made some plans for this place, too."

"Besides," Caroline added brightly, "tonight's karaoke night for the local girls. It'll be a hoot."

God in heaven, couldn't they just let her leave? She wanted to crawl back to New York and bury herself in nothing but work because there was no telling what would happen if she saw Syrah Ardani again. Her voice flat, she said, "It sounds ever so fun."

"We leave at seven," Missy said. "We're meeting Jane and her friend there."

Toni knew that Caroline didn't miss her sharp intake of breath. "Goodie."

"A party of five," Caroline mused. She sipped her wine, then said, to no one in particular, "I wonder who will end up the fifth wheel?"

"Jane, I'm so tired, can't I skip this month?"

"I need you there. I'm seeing Missy for the first time in ages, and what if she doesn't like me anymore? I can't just be there by myself. Here, you wear this." Jane held up Syrah's only skirt.

"No freakin' way am I wearing a skirt for karaoke. It's jeans or nothing."

"Okay, you can wear jeans. And this top. And have a nap, you look like hell." Jane dropped onto the bed next to Syrah. "What's wrong?"

Knowing Jane would never believe a denial, Syrah said, "I really don't want to spend any more time with the woman. She's done her work. Maybe she's left for home already."

"You and she really rub each other the wrong way, huh? I think she's sharp and witty, but I'm not sure, really, that she likes me much." Jane idly scratched the back of her neck and Syrah thought again that she ought to be in love with Jane.

Now, more than ever, however, she knew that she was not. As perfect as Jane was, she did not make Syrah feel even remotely the way Toni did. "How could anyone not like you? You have the best heart and you're gorgeous."

"You're biased. So you'll come tonight? Please?"

"Okay, if you'll let me sleep now." Syrah closed her eyes as Jane got off the bed.

"I'll be back at six-thirty, and you better be dressed. I'll tell Bennett to wake you."

The next thing Syrah knew there was an aroma of coffee near her nose. "Come on," Bennett said brusquely. "Dinner's going to burn while I'm up here waiting on you."

"Thank you," Syrah mumbled. "Tell Dad I'm feeling better, and thank you for the break from pouring."

"There are still people in the tasting room—busy, busy Friday afternoon."

Damn. Her need for a nap had been ill-timed. She scrambled into the jeans and dark blue top Jane had approved—both a little tighter than she generally preferred—and hurried downstairs to help clear the tasting room. Jane arrived while Syrah was pouring the final red for one of two couples, having sent her father in to dinner. At last she rang up their purchases and turned the door sign to *Closed*.

"Go brush your hair," Jane advised.

"I don't like this shirt," Syrah said as she went up the stairs.

"Okay, pick something else, but no polo shirts, not tonight."

She found a short-sleeved polyester shell that didn't make her feel as if her breasts were popping out to say "Look at us, look at us!" She wasn't twenty anymore. A few minutes later they were in Jane's truck and Syrah examined Jane's pressed khakis and form-fitting muscle T—lucky Jane in cotton from the skin out. "Why can't I be comfortable, too?"

"Well, this will sound dumb, but I think Missy really likes me being butch, and I look more butch if you're not doing that crossover thing you do, that sports jockette act you sometimes pull off."

Syrah gave Jane an incredulous look. "First of all, you look butch *all* the time. As if you could look femme if you tried. And I don't have some kind of 'sports jockette act.'"

"Yes, you do. You do that ponytail thing and you look about nineteen, then the shorts and polo with the boots. It's hot as hell, not like you notice the women following you around trying to lick your ankles. I just wanted . . . to stand out tonight."

Syrah shook her head at the vagaries of being in love. Indicating her shirt, she asked, "So what's this look? Femme tart?"

"No, it's sexy, but classy. I like the boat neck on you. I can't wear that. It makes your shoulders look great. And nobody in this town wears white the way you do."

"I'll probably spill a drink down my front."

"And about six women will offer to mop it up for you."

Syrah laughed. "You are a good friend." She didn't want to think she was going to lose Jane to Missy, but Jane had never worried about how she looked and who thought what of her. She hadn't wanted to say anything, but she was absolutely certain that Jane's lip gloss had color in it and there was a suspicious tint of mascara, too. Gilding the lily, she thought, then recalled that the last thing Jane liked was to be compared to flowers.

"Women pay good money for half what you were born with."

Syrah pushed away the memory of Toni's voice when Syrah had asked to be touched. *Beautiful*, she'd said, uttered as if the realization had been painful.

Her head was still spinning. The fear she'd felt in letting Toni get so close was stronger than ever, yet the words from that e-mail haunted her. She might have been able to ignore it if it hadn't been the newspaper articles that described Toni with words like *avaricious*, *intractable* and *soulless*. Could someone with no soul make love the way Toni had last night?

"Syrah? Don't go zoning out on me tonight, okay?" Jane turned the truck into the parking lot of the Dance House. The lot was already crowded, but Jane spotted the only vehicle that mattered to her. "Oh, there's her car."

They were barely in the door when a cheerful "Yoohoo! Jane, Syrah, over here!" drew them across the floor to one of the better tables with a good view of the dance floor and the stage. Caroline Bingley looked overjoyed to see them.

Syrah couldn't help but notice that Toni sat between Caroline and Missy, and the two empty chairs were on Missy's left. Jane of course took the closest and Syrah, with barely a nod at Toni, slid into the other.

Nobody said much, but it wasn't as if Missy and Jane noticed. They were so rapt with each other, flushed and giggling, that Syrah ordered a margarita with salt on the rim to counteract the free-floating sugar. The lights finally went down and the canned disco music stopped. Milly, who had been hosting karaoke for years, opened the show with her signature Ethel Merman impression.

The night progressed like most of its kind. The less shy were always first up and guaranteed to sing on key. Caroline was effusive in her praise, her eyes sparkling with some kind of glee. Syrah couldn't look at Toni, but she could feel the tension from her. She was like she had been at the dance, aloof and monosyllabic.

Syrah would have enjoyed herself, normally, but she was too aware of Toni to let herself go. She had no problem at all accepting an invitation to dance, however, then laughingly agreed to be one of the Supremes for Becky Argost, her steady two-step partner. Becky's Diana Ross made up for unintentional key changes with a good attitude as they hammed their way through "Love Child."

She excused herself to the ladies' room and waited in line. When she made her way back to their table she realized, with profound horror, that Jane was doing a solo.

Jane, who had said often of herself, "If bricks could sing, they'd sound like me," was singing "Close to You" with her heart out on her sleeve for all to see.

Friends did not let friends do such things.

She grabbed Becky, who looked as nonplussed as Syrah felt, and the other two Supremes with a muttered, "Nine-one-one."

The four of them sandwiched Jane at the microphone, and fortunately she began to laugh, which stopped the singing. Off key they crooned "golden starlight in your eyes of blue" as they swayed back and forth in exaggerated rhythm. The painful silence gave way to laughter, and they bowed their way off stage, playing it to the hilt.

The moment they were in the semi-dark of the nearest alcove, Syrah demanded, "How much have you had to drink?"

"Just the one. Missy loves that song so I said I'd sing it for her."

"Girl, you have got it so bad."

Milly's voice cut across them. "A new face tonight! Everyone, welcome Caroline."

"B-flat, please," Caroline said, not looking the least bit nervous, and after the opening lines of "You Are So Beautiful" it was clear why. Her voice was smoky, like violets and rose petals, deep, rich, intense, and there was no doubt at all to whom she sang. Syrah saw Toni take an almost nervous swallow from her drink, and even from where she stood, Syrah could see the bruises she'd ignored last night. She suddenly felt quite ill and dragged Jane outside with her.

"What's with you today?" Jane stood, hands on hips, glaring at Syrah.

"Something happened last night," she began, but the club door opened and it was Toni who stepped outside. "Oh, hell."

Jane stared back and forth between the two of them. "I think I'm in the way," she said finally, leaving Syrah to look anywhere but at Toni.

"I think we should talk."

"Not now, Toni, I can't. I'm so tired, and so confused."

Toni caught her hand and Syrah felt herself melting inside, but she tried as hard as she could to strengthen her resolve. *Don't believe her lies. Don't let her get too close. She is a master of manipulation.* She shuddered when Toni kissed her fingers.

"I think if we talk, we can find some way to work something out here."

"What do you mean by 'something'? An affair? Until you leave and I stay?"

"No, that's not what I meant. But I can tell you're upset and so am I. Maybe last night shouldn't have happened—"

"It shouldn't have," Syrah said passionately. "It made everything so much harder."

"But it did, Syrah. Meet me for lunch tomorrow, please?"

"It's the growers' trade show tomorrow."

Toni frowned. "I forgot. Your father had mentioned that. Sunday, then. Meet me Sunday for brunch before the tasting room opens. I'll get a picnic."

"Okay," Syrah said, feeling weak. "Sunday. Ten-thirty?" Syrah wanted to ask a thousand questions, starting with what Caroline meant to Toni. Why was Toni doing this to her? She let go of Toni's hand, though it was hard to do so.

"Ten-thirty." Toni stepped back, a muscle in her strong jaw working, then turned quickly to go back into the club.

Released from Toni's dark-gray gaze, Syrah staggered against a car and tried to catch her breath. Her body was so heavy with desire that she couldn't think. She didn't really know who Toni was, so how could she want her? How could she want to drag her into the nearest back seat and see if they could find that incredible high together again?

She managed to pull herself together enough to go back inside. Their table was empty and she spotted Caroline and Toni on the dance floor. Toni was relaxed now, laughing even, as she said something to Missy, who passed by in Jane's arms.

The music changed and before Syrah could sit down Toni had her by the hand. She heard someone say, "Jane, sweetheart, there you are!" and just as she forgot her own name in the tight embrace of Toni's arms she saw one of Jane's old flames pulling her onto the dance floor as well.

Toni, watching Jane, had gone a little stiff, but after a few moments they moved together like they shared one set of bones between them. The thin fabric of her shirt let through all the heat of Toni's body. It felt to Syrah as if she was falling down a well, but the water at the bottom was dark. Shallow or deep, she didn't know, and that fear rose up again, making her shake ever so slightly in Toni's arms.

They tightened around her and Syrah couldn't ignore the swelling of her body and the memory of last night. Toni had been so vulnerable, she couldn't have faked that. She wasn't "manipulating" Syrah with her hands stroking so sinuously along her spine. The look in Toni's eyes was not "a lie."

The song ended and Syrah could not have said what the music had been. She peeled herself out of Toni's arms. Jane gave what's-her-name a polite peck on the lips and extricated herself.

"Off with the old and on with the new?" The woman held onto Jane's arm overlong. "Same old Jane."

Jane was too kind to shake off the restraining hand. She covered it with her own. "Even I can change."

Syrah stayed poised to intervene if what's-her-name turned rude. Jane and the woman had gone out a few times last winter, just after Syrah had arrived home again. All these months later wasn't the time to make a scene.

She was aware suddenly that Toni had gone back to the table. "Let's join the others," she said to Jane, and the woman finally let go. "That was weird. I thought she was the one who broke it off."

"She did," Jane whispered. "But she's had too much to drink."

Jane asked Missy to dance again, and they moved to the floor even though Missy looked subdued. Jane said something and a smile returned. Syrah sat down with relief.

She stole a glance at Toni. Caroline, who hadn't moved throughout, had her hand on Toni's forearm, slowly tracing the bruises there. She looked a query at Toni, who nodded. Syrah heard Caroline say, "I'm so sorry, darling."

She wanted to go home. She hated those bruises and yet they didn't matter at all to what she wanted. If she stayed she'd probably end up on the hood of Toni's car again, willing to do nearly anything. She loved this feeling and yet it revolted her, too. Was she really attracted to Toni or was Toni's attraction to her what was making her so damned hot?

The evening wore on, and Toni did not dance with her again. Aspen, who tended to fall in love over a gesture, asked Syrah to dance and she said yes simply for something to do. Hopefully Aspen wouldn't think it was the beginning of forever. After that more partners approached and Syrah was increasingly aware that she didn't have to sleep alone tonight, but right now the thought of any other hands but Toni's left her cold, even if the heat of another woman against her as they danced was making her pulse pound in her throat.

Missy and Jane were increasingly inseparable, but when it was clearly time to go, Jane made it plain she was taking Syrah home. Missy and she made a date for dinner the following evening, though, and Jane was all smiles when they got in the car.

"I'm going to spend all day tomorrow cleaning up my place. I want her to see it. I told her about it while we danced. I don't think she'll mind it. I just want her to know who I am before we . . . you know."

"I know."

"So what happened between you and Toni? You started to say something happened last night."

"We got carried away. Hands did things they shouldn't have." Syrah knew she wasn't succeeding in making it sound like nothing.

"You're kidding."

"Wish I was."

"And so?"

"Did she seem all that eager to be with me tonight?"

"Yes, for her she did. And you—I've never seen you dance with anyone like that. Like you wanted to breathe through her lungs."

Syrah groaned. "It was that bad?"

"Yeah, what's wrong with that?"

"Jane . . . she's going home. Back to New York. I'm not living in New York. I'm not moving into her world. Can you *seriously* see her moving into mine?"

Jane was quiet as she turned a corner, then she said, "I can't, actually."

"And so . . . nothing. Plus, I don't know if I can trust her. I don't know what she's going to tell the court about us, really." She described the e-mail to Jane, who immediately told her to ignore it.

"Nobody with the truth to say can be believed if they won't give their name."

"The articles had names, places, dates—the number of people who lost their jobs and how much money Toni's investors made. I just don't know who she is."

"Can't you give it time? I think she really cares about you."

"Does that matter? I can't let myself trust her."

Jane pulled around to the back of the house and Syrah slowly got out. "Was the sex good?"

Recalling how Toni's second climax had brought Syrah to one of her own, she said with choked honesty, "Like nothing I've ever felt before."

129

"Then I don't care if the rest of her is made of stone. Grab on with both hands and see where it goes."

Undressing for bed, Syrah tried to hear Jane's advice louder than those compelling phrases in that damned e-mail. Neither could drown out the way she felt, stretched out in bed, replaying the feel of Toni's body against hers.

# Chapter 10

The growers' trade show restored some sense of normalcy to Syrah's battered sensibilities. Chemical suppliers vied for their attention, along with wine distributors and manufacturers of glass bottles. Syrah loved talking about their vines and soil to anyone who would listen. Their bottle manufacturer took them and other clients out to a lavish lunch near Sausalito and by the end of the afternoon, Syrah could even think about Toni without flinching. Toni was a problem-solver. Maybe Toni could figure out how to make everything work.

It was after dark when they arrived at the house. A quick look said the tasting room had been locked up by Chino's wife, who had done the honors for the day. Only when they drove around back did she see Jane's truck, and there was Jane weeping on the porch.

Her father wisely left them alone and Syrah, her stomach in her shoes, sat down next to Jane.

"What happened, sweetie?"

Jane gave a little moan and buried her face in Syrah's shoulder. "She's leaving. Going back to San Francisco. For a long time. Didn't say if she'd ever come back here."

"What? But she loves it here."

"No, no, she doesn't. She said . . ." Jane took a long shuddering breath. "Said her business wasn't going to wrap up like she thought and commuting for at least another year from here wouldn't work. We didn't even make it to dinner. She told me when she got in the truck. Got out again and went inside. And didn't look back."

Syrah felt hot, as hot as Jane's tears soaking through her shirt. "I don't understand."

"I followed her and rang the bell and Caroline told me—told me that I should read between the lines and Missy needed a change of scene already, and they had no plans to return."

"Bitch."

Jane's tears began anew and Syrah held her tight, shushing the expressions of blame.

"This isn't your fault. I don't think it's you. I really thought she cared, but maybe she can't care about anyone but herself. You don't deserve this, Jane."

"I let myself believe her eyes."

I know, Syrah wanted to say. *I know exactly what you mean.*

Eventually, she cuddled Jane in bed, holding her close and talking, dozing, shushing her throughout the night. She wanted them all to go away now, she told herself vehemently. They had upset her world from top to bottom and she wanted them all gone, permanently.

It was a lie, but bravely put forth, and as she drifted off near dawn, Syrah almost believed it.


Jane and she woke to a clatter from the kitchen.

"I feel only slightly better than I did last Sunday," Syrah mumbled. She looked at the clock and was both apprehensive and pleased to know she would see Toni in just another hour.

"I don't want to go home," Jane said. "Can I stay here?"

"Sure. Want some coffee?"

"No. I just want . . . to drift for now."

Syrah showered and picked out her favorite jeans and a thin-strapped tank top fit for a picnic. The day was already turning warm.

She was most of the way down the stairs when Bennett leaned in from the kitchen. "There's someone here to see you."

Her heart leapt for a moment, treacherously, but she knew if it was Toni, Bennett would have said so. And her heart had no business reacting that way, even if it was Toni. She was in no clear frame of mind yet and wasn't about to let her silly heart decide anything for her.

She wasn't expecting to see Caroline Bingley standing on the porch.

Her tone exceedingly curt, Syrah said, "Can I help you?"

"Syrah, dear, I just wanted you to know how sorry I am about Missy and Jane. I know Jane is your best friend, and nobody expected things to turn out this way."

Syrah bit her tongue to keep from offering a choice observation or two about Caroline's fickle sister. "Jane is devastated, if you must know."

"Really? Well, I'm sure she'll find comfort quickly."

"What's that supposed to mean?"

"I hope we don't fight about this, Syrah. Missy and Jane don't have the same . . . values."

"You mean incomes."

"That, too, but that's really not what Toni and I were trying to get into Missy's head all day yesterday."

With a descending feeling of numbness, Syrah echoed, "Toni?"

Caroline's nod was forlorn. "Jane is a free spirit, and a lovely woman, but Missy needs someone who will stabilize her."

"I thought they were doing a fine job figuring out how to balance themselves." Toni had been part of Missy's decision?

"Until Jane's affections changed. Missy is a swan and Jane is more of a hummingbird, isn't she?"

Syrah gaped at Caroline. "Jane is the kindest, gentlest woman I know, and she's also the most trustworthy and thoughtful. There is nothing flighty about her."

Caroline sighed sadly. "As I said, she's a lovely woman, just not right for Missy."

"And you and Toni decided this?"

"It was Missy's decision in the end. I just didn't want it to ruin our friendship, Syrah."

Through stiff lips, Syrah managed to say, "I have work I need to get done."

"Of course," Caroline said immediately. "And you have a date, don't you? Toni was very cute this morning. She always is when she's met someone new."

Syrah stopped just short of telling Caroline to get the hell off her porch. "Thank you for stopping by."

"Toodles, then." Caroline winked and took herself, her matching bag and pumps, designer-casual slacks and sweater set and her beautiful, manicured hands off the porch.

It was all Syrah could do not to throw a flowerpot after her.

She stormed down to the nearest fermentation barn, though she had no reason to be there. Hound wanted to play, but she sent him back to the house—she was in no mood for games. So Toni was "cute" when she met someone new, was she? Did her relationship with Caroline permit the occasional fling? Syrah had a hard time believing that Caroline shared anything she considered hers, and she was no cold fish, not given the bruises on Toni's arm. What could Toni possibly want with her when she had the beautiful, accomplished Caroline Bingley to take care of her every need?

Who the hell was Toni, anyway? Who was she to tell Missy that Jane was no good for her? Oh, Syrah had understood perfectly the hummingbird reference. So Jane had had plenty of fun with a lot of different women. What did that matter?

She growled at the lock on the door and finally flung it open wide. Stomping inside she relieved her anger and tension by pummeling the nearest barrel with her fists. Finally, she slumped against it and muttered, "They're not worth it. None of them."

She rested her forehead against the cool wood for a long while, willing herself to find some kind of calm. She didn't know how she could face Toni, or what she would say.

"Syrah?"

Oh, shit, Syrah thought. She slowly turned around.

"Bennett said you headed this direction. I know I'm early."

"You have a habit of that."

Toni stepped out of the sunlight and blinked uncertainly as she adjusted to the low light. Syrah found herself licking her lips as she noticed the way Toni's jeans clung to her long, long legs. "Are you all right?"

"No. I spent the night comforting Jane."

"I'm so sorry about all of that. I really am."

Syrah only looked at her, unable to formulate a coherent question out of her anger.

"I know she's your best friend."

"Yes, she is. And I love her like a sister."

"I don't suppose we could talk about it and picnic at the same time?"

"I don't feel much like a picnic."

Toni seemed to take that in stride. "I do need to talk to you."

"I'm not sure talking is going to change a thing."

"I'd like to give it a try." Toni's voice was kind, gentle even, and all Syrah could recall was those damnable words from the e-mail: *Don't believe her lies. Don't let her get too close. She is a master of manipulation.*

"You don't have to say anything to me." Go ahead, she wanted to snap. *Go ahead, tell me how my friends and I aren't good enough for you.* At least Missy hadn't fucked Jane before she came to that conclusion. Unlike you, Syrah wanted to snarl.

"I know. I want to say it. I can't help but say it."

Syrah finally looked at Toni and didn't understand Toni's expression at all. "What, then?"

"I love you."

Syrah nearly laughed, the idea was so absurd. "How can that possibly be true?"

"I don't know." Toni stepped closer. "I can't get you out of my thoughts. I've never met anyone like you. I don't know why, and I know I shouldn't, but I love you and even though I tell myself it makes no sense, and I am behaving like a crazy woman, the truth is still there. I love you."

"Is this a 'pity the country girl' moment? What are you trying to tell me?"

Toni frowned. "I didn't think my declaration of love could be construed as anything but just that."

Syrah felt a fury take hold of her as all her fear and worry were sucked into an anger so intense her voice shook. "You stand there and you dare to tell me you love me? That even though it's crazy, and you know you shouldn't, you love me anyway? Against your better judgment? What kind of love is that?"

Toni went pale. "I don't think that's what I said, or I've said it badly."

"That is exactly what you said. You know you shouldn't love me. You're crazy because you do. After what you did to Jane, you stand there and expect me to jump up and down because you haven't got a friend to stop you from making a fool out of yourself over someone like me?"

"Jane and you are completely different women."

"In what way? How do you know I haven't had a string of lovers? How do I know that about you, either! What does it matter how many women she's been to bed with as long as Missy is the last?"

"I don't think Missy would be the last. I don't believe Jane's regard for Missy goes past her checkbook."

Syrah faltered for a moment, remembering Jane's pronouncement at the pond. She had said she was hankering to settle down, even said the new woman at Netherfield sounded rich and ready. But that had all evaporated the moment she'd looked at Missy, even before she knew who Missy was. Jane had *never* been that way with anyone.

"I don't think I'm wrong," Toni said firmly. "And whatever I told Missy or advised her to do I did out of friendship and love for her. I could never do less."

"That's how you define honor? Are you saying you never lie?"

"I try not to."

"So if a bunch of workers in Georgia are told you're going to save their jobs and they end up out of work, who lied?"

Toni's face went still. "You don't know what you're talking about."

"Are you planning to take the Fifth with that Silicon Valley grand jury?"

"That action was punitive and has been dismissed."

"Stupid me, I'm just a country girl with no cash flow."

"Syrah, I don't know where you got—"

"Everything is about money to you. Jane can't love Missy because Missy has money." Syrah felt as if fire was sparking from her fingertips. She had never been so angry in her life. "Maybe the truth is no one would love *you* if you weren't rich."

Toni stepped back as if Syrah had struck her. "Don't."

Syrah couldn't stop, nor did she want to. "You can't tell me that you've never used money as emotional brass knuckles." The details of the e-mail boiled into her brain and she said slowly, clearly, "Is this where you use the family finances to control me? Is this when the poor helpless damsel falls at your feet and pretends she loves you? Is that how the script is supposed to run, because I am telling you right now, I could never love someone as arrogant and as unfeeling as you."

Toni's eyes closed for just a moment, but when they opened again the dark gray was hard as flint. "You've made your feelings quite clear. I won't bother you again."

Then she was gone.

Toni had thought she'd understood numbness after Mira, but she was appreciating the emotional state at new levels. Numb was good. Numb kept her hands on the wheel, the car on the road.

She was so numb she could replay the scene with Syrah and not hurt. Something had gone horribly awry, but it didn't matter what

137

or why. Syrah had made her feelings very plain. So plain that there was no point is asking for further clarification. The merger was rejected and all the players were going home to write off the expenses of the proposal.

Numb was working until Caroline found her shoving clothes into her suitcase. "Maybe I should come with you."

"I really need to be on my own for a while."

"I didn't want to say anything, Toni, but you did just split with Mira and—"

"Rebound, yes, it crossed my mind. Problem is I had to have been in love with Mira to be on the rebound, wouldn't I?"

"Weren't you?"

Toni clamped down hard and tried to get back to numb. Talking to Caroline was peeling away at her. "No. It's abundantly clear that I was not in love with Mira."

"How do you know?"

"Because I didn't hurt like I do right now." To her horror she felt tears start in her eyes. "I've never *ever* put my head down on the block for anybody."

Caroline rose swiftly and put her arms around Toni. "And she chopped it right off, didn't she?"

"Don't, Cari."

"Let me help, Toni. It's all I've ever wanted, to help you and be with you."

"Cari—" Toni was surprised by Caroline's mouth on hers and she responded violently with a bruising kiss that rocked Caroline back on her heels. "Please don't. I'm too angry. I'll hurt you."

"I don't care. I will take anything from you, don't you get that? Take me to bed. Hurt me. *I don't care.*"

The feverish glitter in Caroline's eyes stilled Toni's heart for a moment. "I do. That you don't scares me right now and I can't deal with it."

"But last week you could fuck me."

Toni closed her eyes. "I'm sorry."

"And the other night you fucked her."

"It didn't get that far." It was a half-truth, but the memory of Syrah's body rising under hers stabbed behind her eyes like sharp needles.

"Basically, Toni, you're fucked up. Mira—"

"This is not about Mira! Caroline, please, I need to go. I need to be on my own."

Caroline was breathing hard, her face sharp with either anger or arousal, or both, Toni couldn't tell. Whatever it was, she knew that if Caroline touched her again they'd both get hurt. She looked down at her shaking hands and couldn't believe she was even considering how she might take out how she felt on Caroline's body. It was violent, it wasn't her and she was not going across that line.

"The answer is no, Cari. No."

Caroline flounced out of the room with "Just don't fall for the stewardess, too."

Fifteen minutes later Toni tossed her bags into the rental car. Missy followed her forlornly.

"How did it all go so bad so fast, T.B.?"

"Women are unpredictable."

Missy sighed. "If a man said that we'd deck him."

"It's still true."

"I thought we'd both . . . gotten lucky."

"Maybe you did. Maybe I was all wrong about Jane. Look at me—not exactly the expert on relationships here." She felt her Blackberry buzz and glanced at the screen. The weekend on-call Admin Queen, Valerie, had sent three flight numbers out of San Francisco, one out of Oakland and the number of a helicopter charter service at the Napa airport.

"At least you tried," Missy said. "At least you gave it a shot. That's more than I did before I broke it off."

"I told her I loved her and she was insulted."

"I just don't believe it." She ran her hands through her hair, destroying what was left of her curls. "Call me when you get in. Please. Promise me you'll call."

"I will. I have to go, Missy. I can't seem to stay still." They crushed each other in a mammoth hug, both shaking a little. "We're going to be okay."

"A week," Jane murmured. "How does life go from okay to completely screwed up in a week?"

Syrah stretched out on the old blanket, hugging the ground. It was the only thing that felt real. "She loved you and just like that, she didn't."

"She never said she loved me."

"But she did." Syrah clenched the blanket with her hands. "I saw it. She did."

"How can you know for sure?"

*Because Toni looked at me that way before I killed it.* "It was in her eyes, plain as day."

"Then why is she going away?" Jane wiped her eyes and Syrah could not say that it was because Jane had a past too recent for Missy's comfort zone.

"Maybe because she's scared."

Jane turned her head to gaze woefully at Syrah. "Did she really say that she loved you even though she knew better?"

Toni's face was everywhere Syrah looked. "That's nearly a direct quote. She said she was crazy. How was I supposed to take that? And she'd just convinced her best friend that my best friend wasn't good enough for her. So how could I be good enough either?"

"You're worth two of her."

"So are you." They shared a mutual sigh, Syrah certain neither of them believed it.

"What do we do now?"

Wiping away a tear, Syrah had only one answer. "We hurt. And then we get over it."

She dragged herself back to the house after their swim and Jane departed listlessly for home. The tasting room was crowded, including a buyer for a supermarket chain in the southern part of the state. Syrah took over the room and let her father retire to talk business. Her shoulders felt as if her head was a boulder and she knew she moved with all the oomph of a banana slug.

She joined her father and Bennett for dinner, hungry at last but taking no real enjoyment from her meal. She didn't want to explain her mood, and she knew they both noticed. Bennett, however, knew who had called this morning and in what order, and knew, too, that Syrah's black mood and blotchy eyes had appeared only after the second visitor.

"I can't say they've been any credit at all to the neighborhood," Bennett pronounced. "All that money and a lovely house, but what have they done? Poor Jane Lucas is heartbroken and you, I must say, look as if you'd like to murder someone."

"Leave Syrah alone, Bennett," her father advised. He looked up from the steaming fricassee to regard her seriously. "It's been a stressful little while, but things are better. Tomorrow we'll work out the chemical order."

"And when will Ms. Blanchard be back," Bennett demanded. "How long will things be better?"

"She said two months. I'll look forward to meeting with her again."

Syrah observed, with a strong hope it might be true, "Perhaps she'll send one of her colleagues next time. We're small potatoes to her regular deals, I would think."

"It would be just like her best friend, that Missy Bingley, who has broken Jane's poor heart. They cut and run, these types." Bennett stacked dishes, leaving Syrah to muse on the staunch fluidity of Bennett's loyalties.

"She'll be back," he father said. "Her pride won't let her leave things half-completed."

That's what I'm afraid of, Syrah thought. Feeling better for the hot meal, she sat down at the computer hoping for anything entertaining. She didn't expect another missive from "A Friend" and wasn't disappointed. What she did find sent her heart into her throat. Hesitantly, having no real expectation of what the message might say, she clicked open.

Dear Syrah, I hope you will at least read this letter, especially if I assure you that I won't repeat what I said this morning. It was clear you found my words offensive and that matter will not arise between us again. I'm writing you from someplace over Denver wishing to clear the air on the other matters you brought up. We will, most certainly, have to face each other again in the course of business, and my hope is to ease those later meetings with information now.

Syrah scrolled down, consumed equally with curiosity and anger.

You accused me of several things of differing magnitude, and I will deal with the smallest matter first. Though I do not want to offend you or Jane, you cannot blame me for wanting to protect my friend from a woman I thought would ultimately hurt her. I was not and still am not convinced that Jane feels any deep or lasting feelings for Missy.

You do know her better than I do, but I know Missy better than you. I saw nothing in Missy's manner that I hadn't seen before. Though she repeatedly told me she believed she was in love with Jane, she quickly agreed that leaving the area for a while was the smart thing to do, especially after I told her I didn't think Jane's feelings ran very deep. I related the ease with which Jane flirts with other women and even you did not disagree that Jane has liked to the play the field.

That's right, Syrah thought. Not everybody ran cold, unlike some financial types she could mention. The thought was unfair, she knew that immediately, remembering the heat of Toni's body. Nevertheless, the lofty, lecturing tone brought out her most childish responses, and she read on, less and less willing to believe a word of it.

> I won't apologize for doing what I thought best for a friend, and I'm sorry that you think badly of me for my part in it. But I would do it again, and since Missy ultimately agreed with my assessment, it seems to have been the right thing to do. I acted out of concern for Missy, and I can't seriously believe that this matter alone would have caused you to be so repulsed by my feelings.
>
> That brings me to the other charges you laid at my feet, interrelated. You mentioned workers in Georgia, which means you received or sought out information about me. I certainly don't blame you for typing my name into a search engine—it was a sensible step to undertake. But if you read any of the articles about the Georgia affair you would, I think, not have said what you did. I deeply regret that the deal fell apart. I did all that I could to make it work. You have only my word for that. There was nothing more I could do, and the other parties refused to make any concessions. They wanted their business to remain unchanged and so it did, until the day it closed its doors, just a few days after I withdrew the contracts offered by the consortium I represented.

"Only your word for it, that's right," Syrah said to the screen. "Everybody would say how unfortunate when our vines were sold, but they'd praise you for getting money for the lenders." She scrolled down again, still angry, and read the closing paragraphs.

The grand jury affair was a long time ago, not the first of its kind and probably not the last. People with hurt feelings try to find recourse any way they can. Every action against me, my firm and my colleagues has been easily dismissed.

As for the idea that I would use my position somehow to blackmail you into a relationship with me, I must say that I am grateful to you for suggesting it. Only when you said that did I truly comprehend how little you respected or understood me. I pride myself on my honor and it's clear you do not believe I have any. I can offer no evidence to change your mind, but rest assured, I have never, and will never, force any woman into bed with me. I do not know how it is we have misunderstood each other so badly, but I think we may have to each take a small amount of blame for letting our baser desires get so out of hand. It will not happen again.

Syrah stared at the signature, "T.B.," for several minutes, then read the letter a second time. The assertions about Jane's feelings were patently false because any fool could have seen Jane was crazy about Missy. If Missy had been so easily persuaded to part company with Jane, then Missy was the one with no substance.

It was harder to read the part about the business deal. With chagrin, she realized she had not performed even the most cursory search for information about Toni. Instead, she had relied on a stranger's word, one she had no reason to believe beyond a moving and well-written letter.

She opened a browser window and typed "Toni Blanchard" into the search box. Within seconds she had links to hundreds of articles, and the counter was still rising.

Some of them were the same articles that "A Friend" had sent, but she chose instead links that went to magazines and journals. She was prepared for it all to boil down to a matter of "she said/they said" but it quickly became apparent that it was not so simple. The most vitriolic words against Toni were, in fact, the very ones that "A Friend" had sent. But for each of those there were a dozen that told the story Toni's way. One journalist even concluded, "Given Blanchard's history of saving the day for medium and large enterprises, this surprising failure will no doubt rankle all concerned for some time."

She sat there for a long while, trying to sort through what she ought to take from Toni's letter. If she found some of it to be true, shouldn't she believe it all? Since "A Friend" had sent only the most slanted information about Toni to be found, could Syrah really believe the assertion that Toni had in some way blackmailed someone into a relationship with her?

With a growing sense of shame, Syrah read Toni's letter one more time. Toni said the matter of Jane and Missy was the least important and that was where, Syrah thought furiously, she was wrong. Jane's feelings and well-being were important to Syrah, and having wounded those, Toni could not expect Syrah to look upon anything else she did with favor.

Toni had seen her hung over, angry, indiscreetly naked, and if Toni wanted to think she was some kind of trash, that was one thing. It hurt, but she could see how Toni might feel that way and truly regret having any kind of feelings at all for someone she didn't respect. But to tar Jane with the same brush, Jane who had never hurt a fly and never would, that was too much to bear.

"Maybe I was unfair, and maybe I should never have read those e-mails," Syrah said to her reflection as she brushed her hair before bed. "Maybe I shouldn't have touched her and shouldn't have wanted to find out why she felt so good. But she should not have hurt Jane."

She brushed her teeth and shut off all the lights. Hound's steady breathing and the warm bed were welcome and yet she didn't sleep, not right away. She had behaved badly and Toni was now on the other side of the country.

Perhaps she would come back. If she did, Syrah would apologize for what she could. Maybe since Toni had put such emphasis

145

on her love for her friend she would understand how Syrah had had to do the same.

She wished her father hadn't been unwise with money that people had had no business lending them. Part of her wished she was back in France, watching grapes die on the vine for another spring. Even that would be less painful than what she felt right now.

# Chapter 11

The sterility of her apartment was the most welcome thing Toni had ever experienced. No smell of loamy earth, no buzzing of insects, and the small fountain in the living room, when she switched it on, did not truly resemble the real sound of running water. The June skies were dark and heavy with heat, so sunshine wasn't even a reminder of the gold she'd been so aware of in those fine, dark eyes.

She hadn't meant to insult Syrah, hadn't even thought she would say what she'd said until the words were spoken. She hadn't been herself from the moment she'd stepped into the winery that first day. But she was herself again, back at home. Balanced. Steady.

Not in love with anyone. *I could never love someone as arrogant and unfeeling as you.* No, she was not haunted by Syrah's last words.

It had been a week of insanity. Some virus in the spring air, some potion in the wine.

Monday morning was normal in every respect. A quick report

from Kyle on the way into the office. A pit stop at the deli, then a brief glance at the *Wall Street Journal* headlines on the way up in the elevator.

Crystal smiled broadly when she saw Toni and saluted with her latte cup. Pleased to see such an improvement in Crystal's manner, Toni was glad of every minute they'd spent chatting in the last week. She sincerely hoped that Mira's vicious game wouldn't keep Crystal from dating soon.

As if, Toni thought, dating has turned out so well for you.

Even as she considered the first of Tracy's hot-list items, part of her was wondering if one dinner had constituted dating Syrah. Had that been her mistake? Not enough courtship, enough roses and chocolate and sweet nothings?

"What?" Tracy was waiting, pen poised over her notebook. "What's so funny?"

"I just remembered something, that's all." She hoped the rental car company had checked the trunk and if so, someone had enjoyed the picnic lunch on dry ice. Wine, cheese, salads, crackers and fresh chocolate chip cookies had been her foray into courting Syrah.

"Gonna tell me?"

"No." She had known Syrah would be upset about Jane but had never dreamed they wouldn't be able to at least talk about it.

"And you're not going to tell me why now you look as if someone just stomped on your favorite doll, are you?" Tracy's eyebrows had disappeared behind her bangs.

"No, not that either. What's next?"

"Henry wanted a moment."

"Let him in, then I'll see Barth's list."

She answered two e-mails while she waited for Henry, who lingered nervously at the door.

She waved him in. "What's new?"

"I was hoping to really quickly—quickly, Toni, promise—run through my deck for Orly? I think I've got it right."

"Sure, give me twenty to settle up with admin and we'll do it."

Toni regarded him thoughtfully. "If I hadn't come back today, what would you have done?"

"E-mailed you the deck and if you didn't have time, just gone with it."

"Good. That's exactly what you should do."

Barth shooed Henry out of the office, took Toni's receipts and the Ardani files while running through the most urgent matters on his list. "I'll get you those reservations to North Carolina—same hotel?"

"Yes, and make sure Doc gets an invitation to dinner the first night I'm there."

"Will do." Barth gave her a long look. "I'd have thought a week in the wine country would have shown more, boss."

Obviously, the Admin Queens were noticing far too much about her today. "Oh, gee, thanks. I look like crap?"

"You look tired."

The infuriating part of her day, her week, the next several weeks, was waking up every morning knowing she looked tired. Her own foolishness to make some wild declaration of love wouldn't let her sleep. She'd known the woman for only a week, and so yes, the adrenaline every time she'd breathed in Syrah's cologne had been intense, but how could she have been so reckless with her own heart and Syrah's life? Caroline's professions of attachment bothered Toni, so how must Syrah have felt listening to professions from someone she so disliked?

*Maybe the truth is no one would love you if you weren't rich.* Had she told Missy that Jane only wanted her money because it had been true of Mira?

The vision of the last minutes with Syrah followed her through a successful, lucrative deal for Doc—who told her she looked tired—and back to New York again where she welcomed even more work. The court in Delaware, of course, approved her application for a creditor's stay, and she put Ardani Vineyard, Inc., out of her head for the nonce. She would get over Syrah Ardani even if it meant never drinking wine again.

In a matter of a week, the fields that formed Syrah's horizons went from green to gold. Grape leaves darkened and the fruit began to swell. Finally, clusters she sampled began to tell of the late spring rains and the promise of a rich, ripe harvest.

Walking the vines with her father was a daily adventure, as were their sojourns into the fermentation buildings. They tasted, took readings, broke soil in their fingers so they could practice the most difficult part of viticulture: trusting their instincts enough to do nothing.

Syrah looked up from one of Bennett's hearty sandwiches to see Jane's truck pulling into the crowded lot. Thankfully Chino's wife was enjoying control of the tasting room and Syrah could focus on the vines and the business end of things more than ever. Slowly, her father was letting her weigh in on bills to pay and decisions to make. As the summer progressed, every day's list of things to do would grow longer until harvest would play out over a month where sleep was scarce.

Maybe harvest results would be more than anyone dreamed. Maybe it would be enough to keep Toni Blanchard and her business interests on the other side of the country.

Hound bounced excitedly around Jane, but Jane had no enthusiasm for a game of fetch. She had lost a few pounds, weight she could not afford to shed. Syrah, on the other hand, knew she had put on a few. Once her initial turmoil had subsided, her hunger had returned and she seemed to have no end of craving for things like macaroni and cheese, oatmeal with cream and Bennett's mashed potatoes and gravy. Comfort food, plain and simple.

"Job's done," Jane confided as she helped herself to the other half of Syrah's sandwich. "I am officially seasonally unemployed."

"There'll be some more jobs."

Chewing thoughtfully, Jane said, "Of course. This year I might take them. I don't feel like painting, that's for sure."

Syrah patted Jane's hand. "I understand."

"You'll never guess what I just heard." Bennett joined them on the porch outside the kitchen. "Wine for Dimes is still having an event at Netherfield, in three weeks."

Jane winced. "I know someone who is working on the landscaping. I thought it was being prepped for sale. The owner hasn't been near it."

"I was told that she is back, and I must say, Jane, you don't need to go near the place." She hauled Hound's snout out of a bag of potting soil. "Missy Bingley might be able to buy the affection of some people with a little charity event, but we know the truth about her."

Jane put down the sandwich and Syrah knew she wouldn't have another bite. She reclaimed it for herself and said, around a mouthful, "She could still be getting ready to sell."

"Maybe," Jane said.

"That poisonous sister of hers will be there."

"Probably."

"We're not going anywhere near the place, are we?"

"That's where you're wrong," Bennett said with equal conviction to her opposite declarations of only moments earlier. "You should march right in the front door, dressed to kill, and show all of those outsiders that local women do not need them to be happy. You should wear that morning suit of your mother's, Syrah. It's all the rage, vintage clothing. And you, Jane, should perhaps try a dress."

"Never," Jane said with a flicker of a smile. "But I will brush my hair—that is, if I go."

A timer dinged and Bennett hurried away. They shortly heard her say, " . . . and Jane Lucas refuses to wear a dress when she could score the last word if she did."

"She's remarkable," Jane said.

"Believing two conflicting things at the same time is hard work, and Bennett makes it look so easy. But it's nice to have someone in your life who thinks you're right about everything for a few minutes every day."

Jane touched Syrah's hand. "Yeah, it is. Don't be going off to foreign lands again, okay?"

"Who me? Never."

The afternoon mail brought an invitation to the Netherfield Wine for Dimes auction and reception. Syrah nearly threw it away. She finally stuck it on the business events calendar, wondering if Missy would select them for the wine, and she made herself think of the party strictly in those terms. When a caterer called to order their Riesling Syrah felt very much in control. She also included, as promised, two bottles of their 'ninety-three Cab reserve for auction. Since it wasn't available for general purchase, she sent out a few e-mails to collectors in the area, urging them to attend the event.

Life had reached a semblance of neat and tidy. She and Jane looked happy and whole again, and even a trip to Nate's didn't fill Syrah with pain and regrets. They were both all better. Syrah assured herself of that fact often, but was careful not to look over-long into her own eyes.

Not having to manage the tasting room was a great relief. Syrah could come and go as she pleased. The early June afternoons, however, were increasingly warm, and it had always been her habit to come in from the fields and have a half-glass of a light white and cool off.

Two days before the party at Netherfield, she followed her usual routine. The afternoon was airless and warm, warning of a thunderstorm during the night, and she was looking forward to the Gewürztraminer she knew was chilled. As always when the weather allowed, she lifted her glass to the sunlight and looked at the color it cast onto the stone floor.

"You look pleased."

Syrah smiled, then nodded at the elegant woman who had spoken to her. "I am. The color is uniform and lustrous. The grapes were small and intense that year."

"Stressed vines." Clear, delicate skin was shaded by a wide-brimmed white hat.

"Yes, exactly. Are you a grower?"

The woman's British accent was as charming as her smile. "No, just a wine scrounge." She held out her hand. A very real-looking amethyst bracelet circled her wrist but she wore no rings. "Mira Wickham. You must be Syrah Ardani."

"Yes, I am." She gave Mira an inquiring look.

"We have a mutual friend of a friend, Caroline Bingley. Caroline waxed rhapsodic about the valley and the wine, so I decided it was high time I visited my uncle. He has a—what's your American word for it? Spread? We'd call it an estate."

"Spread works." She was taken aback to meet someone who called Caroline even a friend of a friend. The world was small indeed.

"So here I am and I have had the most wonderful tour so far."

A customer distracted Syrah and it was several minutes before she again found herself within chatting distance of Mira Wickham. As soon as it seemed polite, she asked, "How do you know Caroline?"

"Oh, I don't. Caroline and I have never . . . run in the same circle." Mira's look held some significance but Syrah wasn't sure how to read it.

Syrah offered to pour the next white for two cozy men at the bar before turning to Mira again. "I'd have been surprised if Caroline were to mention us to anyone."

"Actually, it's not Caroline I know, but Toni."

Syrah felt herself stiffen. "Toni Blanchard?"

Mira was studying Syrah intently. "Yes, unfortunately, but I shouldn't say that."

"Oh, don't be polite on my account." The words were out before Syrah could stop them, but she didn't really regret them.

"I knew Toni was out here on business and I made inquiries of mutual acquaintances. I suppose I ought to let it go, but it all turned out so badly . . ."

Against her will, Syrah wanted to know more. Maybe it was the idea of knowing someone else who had the Toni Blanchard blues.

"I guess I'm not surprised. She was very good for our vineyard, but . . ." She shrugged. "Other things didn't go well."

"Are you sure she was good for your business? How do you know?"

"We're not getting letters from banks anymore." Syrah drew back then, realizing she was being indiscreet with a stranger.

Mira only nodded and seemed to know not to pry further. "That certainly seems like a step forward. I hope all does go well for you, then."

Syrah would have chatted with her some more, but customers divided her attention. She noticed Mira speaking to her father for some time, then she left.

The encounter depressed Syrah as she tried to sort out if she'd really wanted to know Mira's history with Toni or if she'd merely been grateful for any news of Toni, good or bad. Like Mira, she ought to let it go. After the Netherfield party, the last reason she had to mingle in any way with the Bingleys, she would make forgetting Toni Blanchard her number one priority.

"It's just a short plane ride," Missy pleaded. "Fly up here, stay for the party and fly home again. I need you here, please, Toni."

"You don't know what you're asking, Missy." Toni paced the Los Angeles hotel room, liking its anonymity. "There are people I don't want to see so soon."

"You have to face her sometime. You were going to be back next month anyway, right?"

"I was hoping to send someone else for the two-month follow-up."

"Please, Toni." Missy sounded near tears. "I'm so weak and I know if we talk I can stick to my resolve."

"You invited her?"

"Of course I did. I've invited every lesbian on the planet, it seems like. If I left her out it would be obvious why."

Toni dug her toes into the thick carpet. "I think she'd have understood. And I doubt she'll come."

"Syrah R.S.V.P.'d and where Syrah goes . . ."

"I can't, Missy."

"If you can't face Syrah, how am I supposed to face Jane?" Missy's sniff was audible. "You weren't even in love."

Yes, I was, Toni wanted to say. "We don't need to face either of them. You don't have to show up to your own party. You're selling and moving, aren't you?"

"Yes, though I love what's been done. You should see it—"

"Missy . . ."

"Just get on a plane, would you? I'm only asking for a one-hour plane flight and Saturday night. Call me when you're boarding at LAX and I'll meet your flight. Just do it or I'll tell Caroline where to find you."

"Please tell me Caroline won't be there."

"Of course not. She's not speaking to me since I somehow forced you on her. She'll forgive me at some point."

"I really am sorry about that." Toni idly reviewed the room service menu. No Laundry salmon, no pub fish and chips.

"Caroline is consoling herself with some singer in Texas. But she could get to L.A. in twelve hours or less, I'm guessing."

She knew Missy wasn't serious, but maybe she was right. She had to face Syrah sometime, so why not get it over with? It was her second weekend in Los Angeles, and it was going to be as dull as the first.

It was a short, painless commuter flight and sure enough, Missy was waiting in her convertible at the curb. Unlike the last trip, there was no race to get to a dance and Missy took the long way around, treating them both to a nighttime drive across the Golden Gate Bridge.

"I can't quite afford both houses," Missy said. "I don't want to give up either."

"But you're ready to get out of advertising, aren't you?"

"I have been for three years. I liked owning my own shop but now that I'm in my forties—"

"The horror."

"You know what I mean. It seems silly to work so hard when I can enjoy life. There are so many good books I haven't read and places I haven't been. Caroline had that part right, I think. Why work?"

Toni relaxed in the night air, liking the way it whipped through her hair. "I think working gave you a lot of character that Caroline doesn't have."

"Why do you work, Toni? You could have retired after that Silicon Valley deal fifteen years ago."

"The deal was why I didn't. It was pure luck, absolutely pure luck, that we bought the bankrupt holdings, and that I used my own money to get it over with. I just wanted away from the place."

"And then the empire from Redmond wanted the patent."

"Another piece of pure luck. And pure luck that it was just after Black Monday and they had to give us ten times the stock in trade. It wasn't me, it was luck. And what luck gives, luck can take away. I couldn't stop working until I felt like I had enough."

Once they were clear of the last large town, Missy moved into the fast lane and set the cruise control. "And now that you have enough and you've proven that luck has nothing to do with your success? You're still working."

"Yeah. I'm not done yet."

"Done with what? Bailing people out?"

"If you put it that way. Maybe I'm just kidding myself, Missy, but especially after all the accounting scandals it seems like somebody ought to be doing honest business."

"You're a sentimental fool, T.B., and I love you for it."

Toni studied her friend in the passing highway lights. She was thinner but still delightfully femme with her curls wrapped back by a pink scarf. Wild horses wouldn't make her point out that Missy also looked older. She felt a pang—was it because of Jane? Had Missy cared more than Toni had understood?

The bed at Netherfield was familiar and she slept better there than she had at the hotel. She stirred reluctantly in the morning, awakened by hammering. When she opened her eyes she realized the change that had been wrought in this guest room. Faded wallpaper had been replaced with lustrous fabric. The furniture was the same but the ceiling was refitted with new lighting and the mirror reframed in heavy gold gilt. Simple changes, but Toni felt as if she woke up in another century.

She pulled on a T-shirt and running shorts and wandered the house. Missy had pulled off an amazing transformation. Netherfield now seemed like the lovely old estate home it had once been. The common room was broken into several seating areas, all looking inviting and comfortable. It suited Missy, every stick of it.

She was sipping coffee in the remodeled kitchen, staying out of the way of a testy caterer, when Missy appeared.

"It's fresh," she said, indicating her cup.

"Have you seen the garden? Come on!" Missy pulled Toni after her, and even though there were still heavy lines around her eyes, she seemed happier than she had the night before.

They strolled through some newly paved cobble walkways as well as freshly cleared paths between tall box hedges. "You should be so pleased with yourself. The house is beautiful."

"It just took hold of me." Missy sighed. "I don't think I can stay here and watch Jane be with other women. But I love this place."

Toni could still hear Syrah demanding why it mattered how many women Jane had been with if Missy was the last. Tonight, she thought, she'd watch them together and, who knew, maybe change her mind. Missy was not happy, and she'd never failed to quickly get over her previous broken hearts, infrequent though they had been. As surely as she had thought Missy was nothing but a checkbook to Jane, she'd also thought Jane was nothing but a hot time to Missy.

She'd been a fool about her own heart, and all of her perceptions had been wrong. She could admit that to herself now. She had no need to admit it to anyone else. That thought was no sooner formed than she called herself a liar.

Jane's wolf whistle was heartening. The vintage suit Bennett had unwrapped from a chest in the basement was unlike anything Syrah had worn before, but she did have to admit it looked . . . good.

"Girlfriend, you'll break hearts tonight. Who knew your mother was such a babe?"

"Oh, she was." Syrah realized her father had come out of the office and was gazing at her somewhat mistily. "You look as lovely as she did in that suit. I'd strut around with her on my arm, the proudest rooster in the farmyard."

"It's not too long?" Syrah didn't like skirts, as a rule, but when she did wear one she liked the hem above her knee. The pencil line of the thick sapphire silk ended halfway down her calf.

"Hound, stop that!" Bennett snapped her fingers and Hound reluctantly left his adoration of Jane's slacks.

Jane sighed as she picked a few hairs off her pants leg. "You look like a movie star, but watch the dog hair."

"So do you," Syrah said. They'd shopped the secondhand stores in Petaluma for something Bennett would agree was "dressed to kill" for Jane. The charcoal pinstripes with the button-up bib front white shirt was stunning. "That suit is perfect. You look very butch and very female. Yowza."

"You make a charming couple," her father said. "Have a good time."

"And come back with your hearts in one piece," Bennett said from the kitchen doorway. "I'm sure those high and mighty types at the party won't appreciate either of you." She darted over to Syrah and settled the collar on the tight-fitting jacket. "Your mother wore it just like that."

Syrah took one last glance in the hall mirror. The jacket allowed for no blouse underneath and draped off her shoulders to display an expanse of chest that nearly made Syrah blush. Then she thought of the possibility of competing with the likes of Caroline

Bingley. In the chest department, at least, there was no contest, and sometimes a girl just had to lead with her best assets.

"Shall we?" She turned to Jane with a brave smile. They didn't have a care in the world, did they?

The first familiar face Syrah saw at the party was Mira Wickham. Not that she knew Mira, really, but the friendly smile made her feel much less foreign.

"What a wonderful suit," Mira said sincerely. "You look ravishing. Ravishable, even, though I'm not sure that's a word."

"There might be a person or two I wouldn't mind leaving wanting." Syrah snagged a glass of wine as a uniformed waiter went by. "What do you think of it?"

Mira lifted her own glass and the light caught earrings that matched the amethyst bracelet she once again wore. "It's lovely. Light and party perfect. Missy chose well."

"I'm glad we've met again. I wanted to ask you—"

"Oh, heavens, what's *she* doing here?" Mira's consternation was so complete that Syrah knew to whom she was referring before she turned around. "I had no idea."

"It was a possibility," Syrah said calmly. At least she thought she sounded calm.

Mira gave her an odd look. "Shall we move to the garden for a while?"

"Certainly," Syrah agreed.

Toni saw Jane almost right away. She was smiling congenially at a pretty redhead who was all but draping herself on Jane's arm. She studied both of them for several moments, then saw the little motion that said Jane was trying to extricate herself.

"Jane," she said jovially. "It's a pleasure to see you again." She detached her from the redhead and steered her away.

"Thank you, but you didn't have to do that."

159

"Did she matter to you?"

"Of course not. I just hate to be rude to anybody." Jane stopped walking and Toni had to admire the way she didn't flinch from meeting Toni's steady regard. "I'm in love with Missy and I don't know why I should have to convince you of that."

"Convince Missy and I'll be convinced."

Jane stared into Toni's eyes without flinching. "Give me a chance to, then. That's all I want."

"Don't hurt her. She's too sweet."

"Don't you think I know that? I want to spend the rest of my life making the perfect pillow so I can put her on it and protect her from everything mean and rotten in the world." Jane spread her hands in front of her, openly pleading. "I know she won't let me do that. She's strong and smart and independent. But I think she'd like to let me try."

Toni took a deep breath and then did what she had rarely done before in her life. "I apologize. I was wrong to interfere. I think, however, all is not lost."

Jane likewise took a deep breath, then she said steadily, "Apology accepted. Where is she?"

"Probably in the kitchen. There was some last-minute catastrophe with the . . ."

Jane was no longer looking at her, and likely no longer heard Toni, if she was even aware Toni was in the room. She made a tiny little gasping sound and walked past Toni without a word.

Turning, she watched Jane cross the room, making a beeline toward Missy, who stood frozen in the doorway.

People in the way didn't matter to Jane, and when Missy hurried forward, the layers of her cocktail dress shimmering, they didn't seem to matter to Missy either. She fell into Jane's arms and Jane's whoop of joy brought all conversation to a halt. Even the string quartet stopped playing.

Missy's tears sparkled on Jane's face and Toni found herself dabbing surreptitiously at her own eyes. She'd been wrong and looking at the two of them, holding each other tight, was somehow

160

breaking her heart. How could one look make it all so simple between them? As the musicians resumed playing she glanced around to see if anyone had noticed her emotional display, and that was when she saw Syrah.

Syrah was alternating between dabbing at her eyes and looking as if she wanted to clap for joy.

She looked amazing, Toni thought, when she could breathe again. Her hair was up, revealing the long line of her neck, and *smoky, sexy* didn't even begin to capture the beauty of her nearly bare shoulders and curves of her tummy and hips. Toni was suddenly awash with the memory of touching that body, of having been the focus of Syrah's black and gold eyes, even if only for the few minutes in the starlight.

Missy and Jane finally drew apart and Toni's gaze met Syrah's at last.

Syrah smiled defiantly, her eyes flicking to Missy and Jane, then back to regard Toni again. Toni nodded and made a small clapping motion with her hands, thinking it more discreet than a thumbs-up.

Syrah stiffened nevertheless, then turned to say something to the woman next to her. They moved toward the window, and Toni shifted position to see who Syrah was with.

She looked again.

Mira Wickham put her hand on Syrah's arm and said something that made Syrah laugh.

# Chapter 12

"That's just amazing," Mira said, her gaze resting on Missy and Jane. "You Americans are so demonstrative."

"I'm so happy." Syrah wanted to go somewhere and cry. They made it look so easy, as if being in love was all that was necessary for happiness. Maybe, for them, it was. "Jane and I have been friends for a very long time, and trying to get over Missy was killing her."

"They weren't together until now?" Mira easily juggled her fresh glass of wine and dainty plate of hors d'oeuvres as she sat down on the cement bench that ringed the dark oak tree.

"Well, they were—I mean they'd dated a little. But people convinced Missy that Jane wasn't serious, and I think Missy had to go away and think about it."

"I hope she's not easily convinced again."

"Me, too. I don't think Jane would survive it. She's an artist but not a dark one, you know? Her canvases are all about light and texture." She smiled at Mira. "Like wine but with paint."

Mira's laugh was throaty and full. "Everyone goes on about the Queen's English but I love the way Americans talk. I think, perhaps, Missy needs new friends."

Syrah seized on the opportunity to bring up Toni. That little clapping thing Toni had done stung, as if Jane had pulled off some grand performance. "Maybe she does. Toni Blanchard had a hand in turning her against Jane."

"I'm not surprised. She's an opinionated woman and not afraid to share her views, even when they're not wanted." Mira sighed. "I have a confession to make. I hate being deceptive and it seems that fate threw us together tonight. You sent my uncle a note about the wine being auctioned and he was adamant that I should be here to secure it."

Puzzled, Syrah sat down next to her. "I don't understand."

"It was no accident I stopped in at the winery the other day. I feel the most curious affinity for you, that's all. You see, I'm the one who sent you those e-mails about Toni."

"What?" She'd envisioned a woman from a small town, like herself, but Mira was hardly the small-town type. She'd heard someone call her "Lady Wickham" and the amethyst jewelry she wore did not speak of financial need.

"I know what you're thinking," Mira said quickly. "Believe me, I am quite dependent on the generosity of family, and I have only these few pieces of my mother's to carry on the charade of wealth. Toni knew that when we met and she made it very easy for me to think I loved her and she loved me. That is, until I didn't do what she wanted and she threatened to take away her support."

Syrah made herself focus on Mira's words. She had nearly decided that the author of the e-mails had been telling lies, but here was a flesh-and-blood woman, no longer anonymous, telling her story. Through lips that didn't want to move, she asked, "How long were you together?"

"Two years and then some. I finally had to leave. I borrowed money from a business associate and Toni—as she so often does—Toni paid off my debt and now holds it over me, trying to control

163

me forever." Mira was focused on the amethyst bracelet, turning and turning it on her wrist.

"So why are you telling me this?" *Why are you making me hate her again when tonight I wanted to run across the room, just like that, to be in her arms?*

"Because I try to figure out where she'll be so I won't be there, and I knew she had an assignment to oversee the sale of your winery. Your picture is on the Web site, and she . . . is predictable in her . . . predilections. I thought I would be able to warn you, and Toni could never trace it back to me." Mira's beautiful face was streaked with tears. "Please—you can't tell her. She'll ruin me. She's threatened to put her barristers on me."

Syrah leaned back against the tree, trying to breathe. She put her hand on her stomach, trying to find a way to speak.

"Oh, no." Mira was gazing at Syrah in sympathy. "She . . . got to you. You're so beautiful. Exactly what she likes."

Too bludgeoned to move, Syrah didn't even nod.

"I know how persuasive she can be. Strong, powerful."

Syrah shook her head. She felt Mira studying her intently and wanted to hide.

"And then she's vulnerable and soft. She makes you think you've knocked her for a loop and no one has ever made her feel the way that you do."

I've been such a fool, Syrah thought. Toni was here to sell the winery, and anything she arranged must have just been a prelude. The owner's daughter was part of the deal. *Messing me up, making me want her even though I hated everything she was doing, was just part of the fun.*

"I've upset you, and I'm so sorry." Mira finally looked away. "Believe me, you're better off hating her. The wounds heal that much more quickly."

Fighting back tears that felt so hot her eyes burned, Syrah could only turn her head away.

"I'm so sorry. Shall I leave you alone for a bit?" Syrah felt Mira press a handkerchief into her hand. "I'm *so* sorry."

164

Conflicting impulses were at war inside her. Part of her wanted to find Toni and wipe that superior, haughty look off her face permanently. Part wanted to slink away someplace dark and die. Another part, to her disgust, clung to an absurd hope that none of it was true.

She still had no idea who Toni Blanchard was, and trying to find out left her in this horrible state, caught between revulsion and desire.

"Syrah."

I can't, Syrah thought. *I can't face her. She always does this, makes me talk before I'm ready.* She got unsteadily to her feet and walked toward the house.

"Syrah, please. I can only imagine what Mira told you—"

"So you do know her." Syrah paused but would not look at Toni.

"Yes, I don't deny that."

"You were lovers?"

"Yes, I don't deny that either."

"Busy girl, aren't you? Mira, Caroline, me."

"I'm not particularly proud of some of the things I've done, no."

How could her voice sound so calm, almost tender? "No doubt you think I shouldn't listen to Mira."

"No, I don't think you should. I don't think you could begin to comprehend someone like her."

"Am I that naïve? That unsophisticated?"

"You're that innocent, Syrah. I never meant to bring Mira down on you or anybody."

Where she found the strength, Syrah didn't know. She turned, aware that her eyes were full of tears, but at the moment her voice was steady. "Answer me this, just this. Does she owe you money and are you using that fact to make her do what you want?"

Toni stared at her for a long minute, jaw working and her eyes slowly going to concrete. Finally, with a little gesture that might have been defeat, she said, "Yes."

Syrah walked away. Surely, part of her wailed, there were extenuating circumstances. And so what if there were? Blackmail was blackmail and she could not, would not want someone who could do that.

She paused at the door to the kitchen, looking for Jane. The caterer was fussing over trays of food as if such a thing could possibly be important. She found Jane, finally, dancing with Missy to a rhythm the string quartet wasn't playing. It hurt to look at them, to see eyes that shone with emotion and bodies merged as if they had been made that way by a most benevolent deity.

The enormity of Jane's happiness washed over her. Syrah loved her too much to ruin the moment with her own tears. She needed Jane but they were, now, forever divided. Jane's heart was whole and she had all she wanted in life right there.

Please, she thought, don't let me be bitter because Jane is happy. It was a shock to think she could be so petty. Was this what knowing Toni Blanchard had done to her?

She quit the house for the cool, shadowed front porch and tried not to feel anything at all. Even if Jane was free to talk Syrah did not know what she would say. She hadn't been in love with Toni, that wasn't possible. This was just crushed expectations, dashed dreams.

She could not tell her father that Toni Blanchard had never been his friend and had never planned to help them. He would find that out soon enough—let Toni herself break his heart. She was oh so good at it.

Her skin told her that Toni was behind her, suddenly, and she didn't want to react that way. In a low voice, she said, "Blackmail is blackmail, though I'm sure you can explain everything. I'm sure you think you've behaved in the only way possible. But you can't save our vines, can you? We're going to have to gut our holdings, aren't we?"

Toni's voice was hoarse. "I can't see a way around it, no."

Syrah wouldn't turn around. She didn't want to see those eyes or fall, helpless, into those arms again. There was nothing but pain for her there. "Do you really want to know what I did in Europe?"

"Only if you want to tell me," Toni said quietly.

She searched the night sky for something more than cold starlight. "I watched the vines die. It wasn't what I went there for at all. I can't even talk to Dad about it. Record drought, record heat."

Somehow, finding happiness as simple as a dancing embrace had eluded her.

"The fruit went brown and shriveled in the matter of a week. Then the leaves dried but they didn't drop like they do in fall. They crumbled, still attached, then hot winds beat them to ash."

Toni made a sound, but Syrah was lost in what had been, until now, the most painful days of her adult life.

"The vines . . . died. At first, some of the growers brought in rototillers, turning them under as if they'd be able to start again next season with the survivors. But when it became clear that entire fields were going to die, kilometers of first-growth vines, nobody had the heart to till it all. So they twisted tight. And then they died."

"Syrah . . ."

"The thing is, that while I was watching those vines die, while I made myself take in the enormity of that kind of loss and I cried with people whose wine lineage goes back centuries, the vines were dying at home. My father just didn't know it. But you knew. You knew when you got here they would soon be dead to us. And I don't know how you could just watch it happen without a single tear."

"What you must think of me." Toni sounded as if tears threatened, but Syrah steeled herself not to look. "I hardly know what to think of myself."

The string quartet's energetic launch into a new piece startled Syrah. She realized she was shaking. But she would not look at Toni and did not look when she heard, finally, Toni's footsteps fading away.

"What is it, pumpkin? You've been morose for days and I don't think my old heart can take it anymore. Jane seems so happy and you are so sad."

"Jane is over the moon." Syrah kept her gaze on the hills where the sun was still dusting them with light. "It's a good thing Missy grows on a person, otherwise I'd be very upset."

"As would we all. So why are you watching the fields like you expect marauders?" Her father joined her at the porch railing as Syrah watched the shadows lengthen on the nearest fields.

"I think I do, Dad." For nearly a week she had tried to keep her knowledge of their inevitable losses to herself, but her desire to have it be Toni who told him the news now seemed petty. "I talked to Toni Blanchard last week. She flew up from some business in Los Angeles for Missy's party."

His smile was still affable, though a small crinkle of concern flickered across his brow. "Oh? How was she?"

"I don't know. I didn't ask. But I know for a fact that she's understood all along that we're going to have to sell off whole pieces of our land. If we don't the lenders will foreclose and we'll get not even a fraction of their worth."

"No, I think you've misunderstood, pumpkin. Besides, Toni is going to be back in a couple of weeks, and we'll see what more magic she can work."

"The only magic she's going to work is getting the lenders paid. She's not on our side, Dad." Syrah gazed at him, marveling that he could be so wonderfully obtuse and loyal. "She's always been on their side. We're going to have to sell. She told me, when she was here, that based on the latest appraisals, we'd have to sell half, eventually."

"I should call her."

"Don't! Dad, you have to understand, she's not our friend. She doesn't want to help. We're in a totally screwed-up position here, and we can't trust her, any more than you should have trusted investors offering free money."

Her father abruptly sat down in the porch rocker and Syrah wanted to bite her tongue out. "I thought I was doing the right thing."

"I know. I didn't mean it." Syrah felt her tight clamp on her despair loosen and she quickly dashed away the tears that had threatened all week. "You've done nearly everything perfectly, all these years."

"I shouldn't have bought the Tarpay fields."

"We'll sell them."

"Who would buy them, pumpkin? The fruit isn't even ours for two years and the people I bid against have gone on to other purchases."

Syrah perched on the rocker's arm and took his hand. "We can always ask around, can't we?"

"Find another investor who'll promptly want their money back, too?"

Syrah really did not know what they were going to do. "I'd at least like to feel as if we have some choices here."

"I wonder . . ." He said nothing more, but stiffly got up from the rocker looking a decade older than when he'd joined her on the porch. Syrah watched him take the long way to the kitchen, then turned her gaze out to the vines again. What were they but another small company in trouble and no way out?

Every sunset, just like this one, seemed like the last.

Toni knocked a second time, briefcase in one hand. She knew Mira was there. She was expected, even. It was like Mira to keep her waiting, though.

Finally, the door of the Central Park apartment Mira was "borrowing" from a friend opened and Toni was invited in with an arch smile. Mira was clad in white silk pajamas, and Toni's amethyst bracelet and earrings were the only color on her besides her lipstick.

She was so bloodless, Toni thought irrelevantly. "Thank you for seeing me."

"How could I refuse?"

"With a simple no."

Mira laughed mirthlessly and gestured at the living room sofa. "Do sit down."

"This won't take long."

Mira lowered her gaze to the coffee table as she gracefully sat down at the far end of the sofa from Toni. "I can't imagine why you needed to see me so urgently."

"It wasn't urgent, but it needs resolution."

"Really?" Mira raised her gaze to Toni's. "Not urgent? Have you come to scold me for my California trip? I had no idea you'd be there and my uncle insisted I go to that pastoral soiree. Getting to tell the little winery girl all about you was a bonus, though."

"My visit is not about that." Toni could feel the muscle in her jaw jumping, but they would get to Syrah after business was done. She opened her briefcase and got out a single piece of paper. "This is what I should have given you when you were leaving town."

Mira refused to take it. "Another demand for me to be a good little girl?"

"No. A bill to your trust, due when you get control of your funds for the money you owe me. That's it."

Mira's eyes narrowed. "What's the catch?"

"There is no catch. You owe me thirty thousand dollars and I will wait until you can pay me from your trust."

"What about Crystal?"

"Please stay away from her. But the money and Crystal have nothing to do with each other." Toni closed her briefcase. "I was wrong to try to make you do anything just because you owed me money."

Mira's expression clouded. "I know there's a catch here. This isn't you. You're not in love with that Italian tart, are you? How droll."

"Just because I won't blackmail you doesn't mean I've forgotten what you did to Crystal. I can guess what lies you told Syrah, too."

"I told her no lies. I just told her a fraction of the truth and she was absolutely horrified."

More than horrified, Toni wanted to say. Syrah had accused Toni of killing the Ardani grapes, and there was no more serious charge Syrah could level. "Listen to me very carefully, Mira. The bracelet and earrings you can keep. The matter of the money is no longer between us."

"Why, thank you. This is all very pleasing."

Toni went on as if Mira hadn't spoken. "I will not be silent about your character any longer. I was afraid if I told people what you were really like they would think badly of me for loving and supporting someone like you. But I can't afford pride, as you so ably demonstrated. You have lied, cheated, used people and shown no remorse. Anyone who asks will hear that from me from now on. Say what you like about me in return, but I will be honest."

"Am I supposed to believe you?" Mira coiled into the couch. Abruptly she laughed. "I rather liked crossing swords with you. I can't believe you have gone so soft. Talk all you want. Nobody cares."

Toni allowed herself a little smile. There were people who would care and those who didn't could make their own fortunes with Mira's tender mercies. Syrah had been right—blackmail was blackmail. She hadn't realized she had fallen to Mira's level, and there was no way she could expect Syrah to respect or believe her until she rose above it again.

"I've sent a copy of the billing to your trustees for their record-keeping. I know you could protest it wasn't owed, but the money trail from Crystal to you to me to Crystal is clear."

"I won't protest it, Toni darling. You're finally behaving reasonably, after all."

"Not for your benefit, Mira." She had taken money out of the equation, and Mira no longer had any reason to interfere in Toni's life.

"Oh, that hardly matters." She rose as Toni did. "I don't care why you do anything. All that matters is how it affects me."

"At last," Toni said quietly, "I understand you perfectly."

"You think you do, at last. Syrah Ardani is a beautiful woman. You didn't do right by her, though." Mira's eyes glittered. "I think she really wanted you to be masterful, but you weren't, were you?"

Toni wasn't about to let Mira discuss anything about Syrah.

"Stay away from her, Mira. There's nothing in it for you to make her hate me more."

"Oh, all right. I'll stay away from the adorable creature. She is a bit young for you, isn't she? What—thirteen, fourteen years?"

Toni shrugged. The decade or more gap in their ages was the least of the problems between her and Syrah. "It's really none of your business."

Mira moved to within Toni's grasp. "Was she sweet? You were with her so soon after me. Was it just that she was so different from me? But now I fear she'll have nothing to do with you."

Toni was afraid of that, too, but she wasn't going to show it to Mira. "I intend to tell her all about you, Mira, and all about me with you. And then we'll see what happens."

"You do that. You go right ahead. I'm not going anywhere near the girl, Toni. You've given me what I wanted."

With a nod, Toni let herself out. She heard Mira laugh, as if pleased, and then she let it go. Mira was the past. The present needed some fixing. Then she would see about the future.

Another sunset, another day closer to harvest and another day closer to the inevitable arrival of Toni Blanchard or someone just like her. Syrah leaned on the porch railing, musing about how the hills of their holdings were curved like a woman could be.

Her father's step, surprisingly quick, brought her out of her reverie. "Still guarding the grapes, pumpkin?"

"Yes." She gave up the view in favor of looking at her father. He seemed happier than he had been in over a week. "You do have a bit of a cat-that-ate-the-canary look on your face. What's up?"

"I've just sold the Tarpay fields. For nearly what I paid. There's enough at least to pay off that loan. Or nearly."

"You're kidding!" Syrah stared at her father in shock. "To whom?"

"Do you remember a charming woman who visited us a week or two ago? Petite, pale skin, British accent?"

"Yes," Syrah said warily.

"She said that day she was hoping to invest in a vineyard, and she liked ours. She asked me if there was any chance of being a part-owner in our winery and I told her no, but she still left her business card. Then, after our talk last week I sent her an e-mail and she wrote back."

Syrah wished she could close her mouth. Mira Wickham had bought the fields they had for sale? "If she bought the Tarpay fields she owns them, right? And she knows the fruit is pledged, right? And when the time comes, she has to harvest or face rotting grapes by Thanksgiving?"

"What we've discussed is her being an advisory partner. We keep control of the Tarpay vines, which is the best part of the deal."

"I don't get what's in it for her."

"I asked and she said she wanted to be part of 'art in a glass.' Said you would get that."

Oddly flattered that some portion of their conversation had remained in Mira's memory, Syrah asked him for the sale papers. She tried to read them carefully but the small print from Mira's attorneys was difficult to decipher.

Missy and Jane were dropping by to pick Syrah up for dinner. She hurried upstairs feeling cautiously hopeful that Mira's investment was a turning point in this horrible year. At the last minute she grabbed the sale papers and put them in her pocket. Missy might be able to help make sense of them.

"Barth, I need a flight to California." Toni leaned on Barth's desk, trading receipts and old files for new ones.

He tapped his keyboard to call up Toni's calendar. "Your next free day is not for a week, unless you want me to juggle something."

"No, a week is fine. And I'll be there three days at least."

"Got it."

Valerie joined them, holding out a sheath of papers. "I think you should see this."

Toni took the stack. A fax cover sheet was on top. All it said was "TONI! HELP! Call me! Missy."

"Thanks." She nodded at Barth. "I'll let you know if this is something to log."

As she walked to her office she read the first page of the legal document Missy had faxed. She sat down in a daze, then checked the last page. Damn it, the sales agreement was signed.

"Anthony, Anthony," she whispered, "how could you do this to us?"

But it wasn't trusting, simple Anthony who was at fault, Toni knew that. How could she have thought that Mira was done? Mira had promised to leave Syrah alone, but not her father, and Toni knew better than anyone else how subtle Mira could be about truth and promises.

She called Missy once she had the import of the entire agreement in her head.

"I'm not wrong, am I?" Missy sounded frantic. "It's a horrible deal!"

"You're right, unfortunately." Toni cleared her throat. "Mira has bought the fields, contracted with Ardani to service the fields for which she pays them *nothing*, and she gets all the revenue."

Missy said quickly, "And she doesn't pay them for the land for another four years. So they've kept the expense, given away the income and won't have anything to show at the end of the year."

"That's it exactly."

"I don't know how Mr. Ardani thought he could trust Mira after the way she's behaved. She screwed Crystal over, royally. Mr. Ardani never said a word about this to Syrah until it was done. Syrah looked like she wanted to kill someone."

"Me, she wanted to kill me. He didn't know about Mira. I never got around to telling him or Syrah about Mira's finer qualities."

"Why not, T.B.?" Missy sounded shocked. "I was so wrapped up in Jane I never realized Mira was even at my party. Now I want

174

to make it my life's work to precede her wherever she might go and be the town crier shouting, 'Lock up your silver, the reech beech is in town.'"

Toni stared at the sales agreement and called herself a fool for still being able to be surprised by the depths of Mira's malice. She must have been chortling inside last night, when Toni had thought she had the upper hand. Mira had already trumped her, and she had known it all along. She'd even kept it legal by delaying the promise to pay money she did not currently have.

With a groan, Toni recalled the language of the loan on the Tarpay fields. It was hardly unusual. Now that the fields had been sold, the loan principal was payable in full. Ardani Vineyards did not have the cash to pay for another four years. The lenders would sue and all the other creditors, including the shareholders, would descend in a feeding frenzy that would terrify a piranha. Meanwhile, Mira had the land and it wouldn't cost her a dime for four years.

"Missy, I think she covered all the angles," Toni admitted. "Damn her but she's smart. All I can think of is that failure to use a proper title transfer company for completion of the sale might actually invalidate it. You can't sell something a bank has a lien on without telling the bank."

"So how did he get away with it?"

"The sale was handled privately. They do that all the time with grape auctions. I don't think he thought anything of it."

"I can see that," Missy said tiredly. "That damn sales agreement hurt my head it was so convoluted. We must have studied it for hours last night. So you think the sale might be invalid?"

"Maybe, but the damage is still done. Mira really thought it through. If we petition to invalidate the sale, the lenders will find out that Anthony Ardani, certified babe-in-the-wood, tried to pull a fast one. It's enough to call the loan due anyway. And they have no buyer, so the fields go on a public auction block."

"And they get screwed, again. I could kill that bitch!"

"Imagine if she put that intellect to use on world hunger."

"I'll imagine nothing of the sort," Missy replied sharply.

"This was my fault," Toni said. She had had the power to prevent this. If she'd been honest with Anthony about their circumstances and not found a way to string along his hopes, they would not be in this position. If she'd been honest with Syrah about her past and at least *tried* to explain what kind of woman Mira was, they might not be at this crossroads.

"Toni? Toni? What are we going to do?"

There was only one thing to do, and Toni told her.

# Chapter 13

"I do believe this may kill your father." Bennett pressed her hand to her heart. "I've never seen him this way before, in all my days. You can't trust these people, these outsiders." Bennett poured another cup of coffee for Missy. "Not one of them has an ounce of worth."

Bennett stomped over to the stove, leaving Jane, Missy and Syrah alone at the kitchen table.

"She doesn't include you as an outsider, Missy, just so you know." Syrah chewed a bit of apple pie without really tasting it.

"I'm glad to hear that. I wish Bennett had a sister because I could really use someone like her at Netherfield. I am getting so tired of Pop-Tarts for dinner."

"I made you chili just last night," Jane protested. "It may be the only thing I know how to make, but it was good, wasn't it?"

"Oh, sweetie pie." Missy stroked Jane's arm. "You're always good."

Syrah restrained an inner *blech*. Missy and Jane could put anyone into insulin shock.

An overnight delivery truck creaked up the road to the house, bringing Hound out to bark in a ferocious show of protective instincts that lasted until the usual driver stepped down, laughing as Hound licked her knees. Syrah met the woman at the door and for the first time the sight of shorts, tanned legs and a clipboard didn't set off a little fantasy about changing places with Hound.

She went back to the kitchen with the large, heavy envelope. "I may not survive this either," she announced. "I just had no lascivious thoughts whatsoever about the delivery woman." She pushed the package to one side, having no heart to cope with it.

"Are you ill? Do you have a fever?" Jane played mother hen to the hilt, making a show of feeling Syrah's forehead.

"Aren't you going to open the delivery?" Missy closed the landscaping book she and Jane had been discussing at length. "It looks like documents of some kind."

"I don't want to," Syrah said childishly. She glanced at the label. "Hell, it's from some bank."

"Can I open it?" Missy reached for the container. "I can't stand unopened mail."

Syrah shrugged. "Okay by me."

Jane promptly supplied her Swiss Army knife so Missy didn't risk a fingernail.

"Let's see," Missy said. "We have a lien. We have an assignment document. Here, look." She pushed the papers toward Syrah.

Even with Jane and Missy to help her, it took some time to make sense of it. "This lien is canceled, isn't it?" Syrah showed the paper to Missy again.

"That's right," Missy confirmed with a shining smile. "It's marked *Paid in Full*, just like these others."

"How can that be? And this—why was there a transfer of shares?"

Missy seemed hesitant but then said quickly, "All the shareholders have sold their interests to something called Crystal Clear

Holding Company. It and your father own all the shares there are."

Syrah looked at Missy expectantly. Surely something would make sense to her if spelled out another way.

"So," Missy said earnestly, "someone paid off the loans Ardani had. That same someone is also the sole shareholder of Ardani Vineyards—that is, except for your father. Instead of all those nagging voices there's just one for him to make happy now."

Jane got up to add some cool water to her tea. "How does this affect Mira's purchase of the Tarpay fields?"

Shaking her head, Missy said, "As far as I can see, it doesn't. Mira's sitting pretty. She'll even make money. But she has no one to make trouble with now, except your father and whomever owns Crystal Clear. Of course, if a court eventually agrees the sale was invalid, she gets a big, fat nothing. Either way, she's got nothing to do or say of any influence on Ardani."

"That's too good to be true," Syrah said. Her barely banked anger at Mira threatened to consume her for a moment. She took a deep, steadying breath. "Why would someone do this? Why would someone want to spend all that money to get so much control if we don't *pencil* any longer?"

"With no debts, I bet the winery pencils just fine." Jane scooted into the chair next to Missy again.

"Maybe," Missy said softly, "someone was doing the right thing for once."

More than a little overwhelmed, Syrah escaped to the porch for a few minutes, lips pursed in thought. Another sunset and she didn't know what to think. She had braced herself for losing the vines, the barrels, the heritage of her family. She wanted to hope they had been saved but couldn't let herself believe it, not quite yet.

Missy and Jane were smooching at the table when Syrah went back inside. "How do we find out if this is all real?"

Missy patted Jane on the collarbone. "You hold that thought." Looking up at Syrah, she asked, "Call the banks tomorrow?"

"Yes," Syrah agreed. "That's what I'll do." She looked at Missy speculatively but Missy suddenly wouldn't meet her gaze.

Over the next few days, Syrah received confirmation after confirmation. Yes, the loan was paid off. Yes, it had been paid off by Crystal Clear Holding Company, LLC.

She could find out nothing about Crystal Clear. With summer ripening toward harvest it wasn't as if she had a lot of time to spend on the mystery, either.

The change in her father was palpable. He walked taller, moved faster. Syrah tried to caution him that even though the bankruptcy receivership had been ended and no disgruntled creditors sent consultants to study their every move, one day somebody from Crystal Clear was going to show up and want something for their money.

"It's all going to be okay now, pumpkin," was all he would say and as the days ticked by Syrah actually began to believe it, too. They'd been delivered from the fire by an anonymous hand. Syrah suspected who it was, and the idea pleased her.

Jane and Missy were increasingly inseparable. Summer eased into moderate temperatures, but Syrah joked that if Missy and Jane walked in the fields, the grapes quickened on the vines.

Of Toni Blanchard she heard nothing. A single sheet of paper from a Delaware court arrived stating a petition to end receivership had been approved. She knew now that Mira Wickham was no reliable witness regarding Toni's character, and she discounted everything the woman had said as a half-truth at best, and more likely outright lies.

Toni's own admission—that she had been using Mira's debts to compel her behavior—was the harder issue to think about. She could understand why Toni might have done that, given how duplicitous Mira was, but it was difficult to reconcile the hard consultant who could make such a decision with the soft, vulnerable woman on the hood of the car.

Gay Pride came and went, then Independence Day brought the

county fair and fireworks. Grapes darkened, sweetened. The time had long passed when she might have asked questions and discussed it like a rational human being.

Harvest descended in the first week of September for the shortest-season fruit. Those grapes were no sooner picked and processed into crushers than the next to ripen were ready. Chardonnay, Riesling and Gewürztraminer were harvested in a flurry of round-the-clock activity.

Syrah ached in her bones after two weeks, and they were only through the whites. The reds, slower to ripen, were showing all good signs that they were also due for picking and processing. Petite Sirah, zinfandel and Merlot finished together though their locations on the grounds were far apart. Carlo was frantic trying to get enough temporary labor to pick, and Syrah pitched in as best she could, despite the amount of time she spent in the office, recording the harvest statistics.

"Can we spare anyone to cull the Chardonnay vines?"

Chino dropped into the desk chair. "I don't think so."

Syrah looked up tiredly from her intake estimates of pounds of grapes by vine group and what that would result in for finished liquids. It hit her that not having the fear of foreclosure hanging over her head was making her more proactive. As soon as she finished with the estimates she was ready to place the bottle orders for each of the varietals ready to come out of barrels and spend the winter going cool. "Even one crew?"

"The Pinots are ripe. Your father pulled half the people from the Cabernets this morning."

"Dang." Culling the vines of all remaining grapes was good for them, and the wine that resulted from grapes left to overripen on the vine turned out their highly prized noble and late-harvest dessert wines.

"Maybe we can borrow someone else's crew for a night shift. Drag out the generators and set up lights."

It was a lot of work, but perhaps the only way to manage it. It would cost money but the harvest volumes were so high that she couldn't believe that such measures wouldn't be offset by the rewards.

Her boots had never felt so heavy, but she could not recall a time when she'd felt more like an Ardani.

When the massive labor effort finally began to wane, there was time to enjoy the early October air. One relaxed evening Syrah coaxed Missy and Jane out to the last of the unculled vines, her own Syrahs.

"If it's fruit, pick it," she told Missy. "If we get enough we'll make our own little batch and this time next year we'll be sipping it and feeling pleased with ourselves."

Missy, who had stopped to watch Jane carry a loaded basket to the bed of the truck, said, "I've never made wine before. Are we going to stomp it?"

"Only if you want to. I have to warn you, though, I'm not drinking anything you and Jane fall down in."

Missy laughed. "I wasn't really thinking about that—"

"Sure, you weren't."

Missy was still chuckling when Syrah could stand it no longer. With Jane out of earshot she touched Missy's arm and said, "I know you didn't want me to know, but I figured it out. And I will never know how to repay you."

Puzzlement was plain on Missy's face, even in the fading sunlight. "What are you talking about?"

"The loans. Crystal Clear Holding Company. I just . . . thank you is so inadequate."

Missy gaped at Syrah. "It wasn't me."

"Well, if not you, then who?" Syrah's hands continued their roaming journey among the grape leaves, searching for more soft grapes.

Her eyes expressively wide, Missy just stared at her. "Why did you think it was me?"

"You seemed so shy when the papers arrived. Like you were

trying not to say too much, but you made sure I read them right away."

"Oh. Well, I knew about it before it all happened, but it wasn't me. She didn't want you to know, but I think that's silly at this point. It was Toni, of course."

"Toni?" Syrah looked at Missy incredulously. Even as she protested the plausibility it was patently clear that Toni had been in a position to fix it all. "Why would she?"

"She felt responsible for Mira. It was the only way she could think of to once and for all protect you both from her. Mira was quite capable of convincing the other shareholders to sell some shares to her. She was going to use you to needle Toni for the rest of her life."

"Why? What did Toni do to her?"

"As far as I know, all Toni did was stop loving Mira before Mira was done walking on her. Mira dumped her but it would be so very Mira to expect Toni to beg for her to change her mind. Toni didn't beg."

Syrah blinked. "I don't imagine that she did."

Syrah went on culling grapes and mulling over this new, surprising information. She ought to have seen it on her own, and it wasn't a happy conclusion that she hadn't figured it out because she was bent on not admitting that Toni might have a heart. Knowing Toni could do something so generous hurt, too, but the reason for her distress seemed beyond her unraveling.

But where she had been comfortable, pleased even, to think that Missy had been the one who had masterminded everything, she found herself resentful of Toni's interference. "Nobody asked her to do that, you know."

"Toni has a mind of her own. And she obviously thought it was the only way to atone for not having warned you about Mira's tactics."

"I wouldn't let her. I know she's your friend," Syrah said with a flash of anger, "but she can't buy me."

"I don't think she means to." Missy looked shocked at the thought.

Syrah knew she was being irrational, but she couldn't fight the feeling. "Besides, my father is a grown man, and he takes responsibility for his own mistakes. I'm a big girl, too. If I want to listen to someone's lies and make a fool of myself, that's my decision!"

Missy's laugh made Jane hurry back and Syrah, in all her frustrated confusion, had to watch yet another display of affection.

When Jane wheedled Missy up to the truck, then behind it, out of Syrah's line of sight, Syrah shouted, "That's it! You two get a room. I'm out of here!"

There seemed to be no way to calm down. She didn't want to be obliged to Toni Blanchard for anything, and it appeared that every single person affiliated with Ardani Vineyards now owed Toni Blanchard eternal gratitude.

Well, she wasn't grateful. She refused to be bought.

"A commitment ceremony? Already?"

"Toni," Missy said patiently, "Jane and I have been seeing each other for nearly six months, and living together for three. I've sold my business, and we are officially a couple. I want the world to know."

"Hence a lavish ceremony? Isn't knowing you're a couple enough these days?"

Missy hissed with exasperation. "Do you want to stand up for me or not? Caroline can do it all by herself, you know."

Toni's only reluctance was over the one thing she wasn't going to bring up. It was her problem, however, not Missy's. Given that Missy and Jane were in fact turning into an old married couple, meeting Syrah again was inevitable. "Of course I'll do it. Give me the date again."

"The week after Thanksgiving. The weather is still really wonderful here, Jane promises me. We'll do everything at Netherfield."

"How many people are you inviting?"

"Like I said, the whole world. Mostly." Missy's contented sigh poured through the phone. "I want the world to see how much I love her. You should see the mural she painted in our bedroom. And you need to get to know her."

"I'm not against that, Missy. You know why I'm hesitant."

"I know exactly why. You're both pigheaded."

Toni resisted the urge to whine back, "Am not." Instead she turned the topic to the scary subject of what they would wear. "No peach, no pink. I love you but I'm not doing that for you."

"No navy blue, no gray, no black," Missy fired back. "You can pick something out but I get final approval. We're not doing a whole wedding fancy dress thing. Though does Jane look hot in a tuxedo or what?"

"I wouldn't know."

"She looks even better out of it."

"Missy . . ."

"Spoilsport. Anyway, send me pictures of what you're going to wear. And you have to arrive the day before at least."

Fine, Toni had said as she e-mailed a request to the Admin Queens for air tickets. She had no idea what she'd wear and she knew she'd spend the whole time dreading and wanting to run into Syrah.

Maybe a miracle would happen. Maybe she'd see Syrah and not want her. Maybe she'd be able to move on.

"Maybe," the hopeful voice inside she could not quash murmured, "maybe Syrah will look at you and it won't be with contempt."

"I thought this whole thing was supposed to be spontaneous." Syrah tugged a shepherd's sweater over her head and gave Jane a harried look. "What the heck is a rehearsal dinner all about if we're being spontaneous?"

"Wouldn't you rather meet up with Toni again after all this time with as few people watching as possible?" Jane was looking exceedingly dapper in her slacks, shirt and vest.

"I'd much rather it was a big crowd," Syrah said. "Then I can just avoid her."

"You're being foolish. Look, you don't have to be in love, but you don't hate each other either. Why not get over whatever it was that you each thought the other did?"

Syrah felt a familiar mulish expression steal over her face. "Maybe I don't want to get over anything."

Jane rolled her eyes and Syrah realized that the power in their relationship had completely shifted. Now Jane was the mature one lecturing Syrah on how to behave, Jane doing serious, grown-up things even as Syrah refused to give up being a child.

And it was, to Syrah's way of thinking, Toni Blanchard's fault.

She did not decide on a different sweater or brush her hair a third time before hurrying out the door with Jane. She most assuredly did not immediately sense that Toni was at the far end of the hotel's banquet room, on the left.

She made her way up the right side and chose a seat midway down the long table.

"There you are," Missy called. "Members of the main wedding party are on this end, Syrah."

Muttering, Syrah gave up her wonderfully anonymous chair and slipped into the one Missy was waving at. Oh, joy and happiness, she was seated right next to Caroline and Toni sat directly across, next to Jane.

"It's so wonderful to see you again, Syrah." Caroline was the picture of elegance and taste in a sage green sundress, but her gaze went back and forth between Toni and Syrah more than once.

Syrah made suitable noises and concentrated on her meal. She was just there for the food.

"I'd like to know," Toni said, "how we can have a rehearsal dinner without a rehearsal."

Missy, with no attempt at pretension, gave up the truth. "It's another excuse for a party. Now will you enjoy yourself, please?"

For some reason Syrah found her gaze meeting Toni's. Toni shrugged a "they're nuts" and Syrah blinked back an "absolutely."

She concentrated on her food again.

186

Caroline chattered throughout with Jane, talking about various places she had been during the fall. "What's the name of that little place in San Antonio, Toni? I can't remember it."

"The San Antonio Grill?" Toni was also concentrating on her meal. Syrah realized they would both be done long before anyone else.

"Syrah," Caroline said abruptly, "how is the wine business these days?"

"Very good. Our harvest was exceptional this year."

"What a relief." She dropped her voice so only Syrah could hear her. "And to be out from under all those worries, that must be a blessing."

So Caroline knew. Was it pillow talk or what? She saw nothing overtly amorous between Toni and Caroline, but then again she hadn't back in the spring either. All she'd seen were those bruises on Toni's forearm.

A quick glance confirmed that Toni was wearing long sleeves. Dang.

"Yes, it's a blessing," Syrah said. "Someone went to a lot of trouble."

"Oh, we don't have to be coy, do we?"

"Caroline, would you like some more wine?" Toni hoisted the bottle toward her glass, but Caroline demurred.

"I've had plenty and now I want to chat with Syrah."

Missy tapped her knife against her wineglass. "The hotel disco is open later, everybody, and Jane and I hope everyone will join us. But no terribly late night or we'll all be sorry in the morning. And we're getting married in the morning!"

There was a cheer of approval and Syrah felt the prickle of déjà vu. She'd known all along she'd be making a toast at this particular wedding and now the day was nearly upon her.

A large party did go toward the disco, but Syrah begged off. Work, late night, headache, no dancing, see you tomorrow . . . she headed for the door. Missy and Jane were going home together and she was free to leave any time she liked.

She was more than halfway across the hotel lobby when Toni rose up from a chair.

Syrah didn't stop. It was annoying that Toni easily kept pace with her.

"We need to talk, don't you think?"

"No, not really."

"Jane and Missy think we're pigheaded."

They were right, Syrah thought. "What is there to talk about?"

"Past. Present. Future?"

"I'm too tired for all that." Syrah cleared the hotel doors and welcomed the cool night air.

"Me too. How about this, then?" Toni caught Syrah's hand and Syrah stopped.

They stood there, just holding hands, and a million things ran through Syrah's mind—all the confusion and anguish, all the misunderstandings and relentless prejudices.

She tightened her fingers around Toni's and didn't know what to do when Toni drew their bodies closer together.

"We don't have to talk right now," Toni said. "But we do have to talk eventually."

Shakily, Syrah managed to say, "This is enough for now." She squeezed Toni's hand.

"Yes," Toni whispered, "it is."

The kiss was sweet, nearly unbearably so. Syrah wanted to cry because there was so much to let go of and it was getting in the way. She finally stepped back, blinking back tears. "Enough for now," she repeated, and Toni let her go.


She thought of that kiss all the while she dressed for the ceremony the next morning, and thought of it again as she stood next to Jane in the large common room at Netherfield. Her summery, cotton and linen lavender dress was a foil to Jane's boxy pinstripe suit. Missy was beautiful, luscious even, in a patterned white gown that clung to her curves, but Syrah could not stop glancing at Toni in a silk suit the shade of ripe eggplant, her hair twisted back in that knot that at one time Syrah had found haughty. She hardly noticed Caroline, except for the one gloved hand that possessively grasped Toni's sleeve.

Today Toni was real, with dark luminous eyes that threatened to mist over as the minister said true and profound things about love. At least Syrah was certain she'd have found them true and profound, if she'd been listening.

But she was thinking about that kiss and Toni's tenderness and the look in her eyes. The kiss had simmered with all the heat Syrah had felt in the spring, but there was something more there. Whatever it was, it didn't scare her now.

Missy's sumptuous bouquet divided in two, and she and Jane lobbed their halves at the same time. Syrah stuck both hands behind her to avoid catching either. She noticed that Toni had caught hers with a surprised look, but then Missy had thrown it directly at her head. Jane at least had thrown it a little on the low side.

Thoughts of that kiss pursued Syrah all day. The reception was unhurried, with a mellow band performing sweet love songs while guests danced or stood in clusters enjoying food and wine from long, overflowing tables.

Toni asked her to dance. She agreed. They moved together, but not tightly, and Syrah thought about that kiss.

"Thank you," Toni said when the song ended.

Syrah had no idea what had been playing. "I was rude and completely misjudged you. I'm sorry."

Toni swallowed hard. "I didn't protect you and your father—and your vines—when I should have. Forgive me."

"Oh, Toni." Syrah leaned into the tall, lean body and breathed in Toni's seductive, wonderful cologne.

Toni said, her voice more formal, "Oh, that's my cue. Be back in a bit."

Toni took up a position at the singer's microphone. "Okay, Missy, you can stop giving me that look. You might be sorry for making me do this. Yes, everybody, we've reached the portion of the evening for Missy's best friend to make a speech. Fill your glasses, because it's time for a toast."

Syrah noticed waiters were circulating with trays of Champagne and she accepted a glass with a smile.

Toni cleared her throat and gave Missy an affectionate look. "I've known Missy longer than either of us can believe, all the way back to a time when we could stay up all night at a dorm party and turn up for an eight a.m. class. I won't pretend I haven't seen her in and out of love in all those years, and ended up with the occasional wet shoulder when things didn't work out. But this year I saw something I'd never seen before and frankly, it made me envious. The way Missy looks at Jane was, for me, understanding what love is all about for the first time."

There was a shared *oh* of sentimental response from the crowd. Toni smiled and Syrah wondered if anyone else saw the small, nervous gesture as Toni unnecessarily smoothed her hair. She was so poised, Syrah mused, but underneath all that was a real woman.

"I've learned a lot about wine since the spring, and I think that Missy and Jane are bottling something very special today. I plan to be around to pull the cork with them in twenty years, thirty years and more, because what they have ripening is that good and will be that special. Jane and Missy sparkle. They blend. They dance."

Moved by the tiny quiver in Toni's voice, Syrah found herself blinking back tears.

Toni lifted her glass. "To love, to fortune, and to Jane and Missy for showing us all how to be happy."

Syrah echoed, "To Jane and Missy" and sipped her Champagne—sharp, clear with a mellow burn, distinctively French. Her own turn at the microphone had come and she still wasn't quite sure of everything she was going to say.

"Jane and I have been skinny dipping together since middle school," Syrah began, pleased when everyone snickered and Jane blushed. "All that time it was so unfair that no matter what happened, Jane was cool about it. Bug in the water? She just swooshed it out. She thought someone was attractive? Jane could walk up and say hi. She did so many things I wished I could do, and she did it easily. She has always been the essence of cool."

She gazed at Jane for a long moment. "Then, one spring day, Jane wasn't calm. She wasn't nonchalant. She was at a loss for words, didn't know what to do. And all because she'd met Missy and in a single instant fallen head over heels in love. Honestly, I remember it well, and Jane stood there for at least two minutes with her mouth hanging open. And I knew right away that I'd be here, making this speech."

There was a ripple of laughter.

"Love, I guess, can be like grapes. It can die on the vine or turn to vinegar in the wrong hands." Her voice faltered. "I didn't know . . . I didn't understand that love isn't just when the grapes are growing. There's the terrifying decision to pick the grapes and risk making them into something else. Because you can pick them too soon and nothing turns out the way you planned."

Her gaze met Toni's and she wondered if she would ever be able to say everything she felt.

"But you can come back to the vines again, later, for another try. But then the decisions have to be made about how to blend the different flavors together so it tastes right to both of you. The waiting and hoping and mistakes and praying that at least one bottle turns out, that there will be one good bottle to share, the kind of bottle that is never empty." She tore her gaze from Toni's to wipe away a tear. "I'm so glad that Jane and Missy found it right away, the perfect blend that still has all the individual notes of who they each are and leaves the rest of us to partake in their abundant happiness." She lifted her glass. "To Missy and Jane, and all the years ahead of them."

She noticed as she slowly lowered the glass to her mouth that Toni mirrored her movements and they sipped in unison.

The music began and she was claimed by Jane—who said it was tradition—and watched Toni leading Missy.

"Thank you," Jane said. "What you said was sweet. And true."

Syrah found a broad smile, though part of her was lost in thoughts of that sweet kiss she and Toni had shared. "I could have been really mean, you know, but I was good."

"I appreciate it. Missy knows all my flaws by now, but she didn't need to hear about some things."

"Like the fact that I was responsible for introducing you to grooming? You were such a tough butch—you didn't need conditioner and moisturizers."

"You civilized me, and I thank you." Jane smiled that wide, easy smile of hers, and Syrah felt a pang of pure envy. "Missy likes me civilized."

"It's a good thing we didn't ruin our friendship by sleeping together," Syrah said seriously.

"We were never drunk enough at the same time."

Syrah thought about it. "You know, you're probably right."

Jane squeezed her tightly as the music ended. "We're still best friends. You can't get rid of me."

Syrah's ache of loss eased. "I feel just the same way."

"Good. Because I think I'll be using this suit again soon."

Syrah wanted to pretend she didn't understand what Jane meant, but finally said truthfully, "You could be right. If I don't screw it up again."

"And when I toast you and that certain someone," Jane said, her eyes twinkling, "I am going to remind you that you were dead set against the 'mania to get married.'"

She thought about Toni's kiss and the look in her eyes again, and she let herself wonder, for the first time, if there was no reason to envy Jane's happiness. Could she really trust that the same kind of happiness was within her grasp? "If there is a time and place for you to make that comment," she said slowly, "I'll be too happy to care."

Jane squeezed her. "I think you're beginning to get the hang of this love thing."


"So, when are you going to actually date the woman?" Missy leaned back in Toni's arms.

Toni, watching Syrah dancing with Jane out of the corner of her eye, shrugged. "I don't think we're going to date."

"Toni, don't be pig—"

"I intend to court her, maybe for the rest of my life. Just wish me luck. I think I can use it, given how things have gone."

"You don't need luck," Missy said firmly. "You need to talk. Communicate. Be afraid of no topic."

Toni laughed and pulled Missy against her for an affectionate squeeze. "I have to say I do not see you and Jane talking all that much."

"We do." Missy's smile was impish. "We talk after. The best part is that it's hard to tell when the talking stops and the lovemaking begins again. Talking makes for great afterplay and it leads to more foreplay."

"I really am happy for you, Missy."

"I just wish the courts would move faster ruling the sale to Mira invalid. She'd be completely out of your life if they did. It would be a relief."

"Yes, it would be," Toni agreed. "But I'm starting to realize that business deals can end neat and tidy, but relationships do not."

As she twirled Missy one last time Toni let herself wonder if she and Syrah would ever find love so easy. Maybe. Certainly, sitting in the restaurant wanting to dump salad dressing on Mira seemed like a lifetime ago. *If Syrah ever says those words to me I won't walk out.* She would listen, talk, try anything to keep Syrah in her life. She didn't want to play at a relationship with Syrah, she wanted more.

It was crazy to picture a time in the future when she'd introduce Syrah to her father and tell him she was in love with the little girl he'd met long ago. It was positively insane that their fathers would likely be delighted.

She couldn't help but envision it and she realized that what she felt was amazement. Her feelings about Syrah had no metrics or annual projections. No merger proposal, but instead a desire for inseparable union. There was nothing crazy about it after all. She had never felt more sane in her life.


"That was a wonderful speech, pumpkin. Dance with your poor, old father."

Syrah happily moved into a precise box step with him, the first and only dance move he'd ever taught her. "I might be figuring out why you and mom were so happy."

"Not something you can learn from a book." He regarded her kindly. "I didn't realize raising a daughter would be so much like tending grapes. It's been hard to leave you alone to grow."

"Oh." Syrah blinked back tears—weddings seemed to bring them out. "How am I doing so far?"

He favored her with one of his slow, charming smiles. "I think the vines were stressed this past while, but there's no reason to think harvest won't be just fine."

For you, Dad, Syrah wanted to say, life was meant to be that simple. "I am hoping for less stormy days."

"I hope so, too, pumpkin. I really do."

# Chapter 14

"I've got birdseed in my bra!" Missy shook the front of her blouse as she scrambled for the limo.

"I'll help with that in the car," Jane said, prompting hoots from the well-wishers who continued to pelt them with seed.

With a cheery wave they were gone. Toni watched the limo slowly make its way down Netherfield's drive and blinked back yet more tears. Their happiness was so palpable that it could turn a person's stomach—unless that person was just as much in love herself, she thought ruefully.

She turned to find Syrah, who had single-handedly plastered Jane with a couple of pounds of birdseed, right behind her.

"Hi." It was all she could think to say.

"Hi." Syrah's smile and arched brows said she found Toni's incoherence just a little bit amusing.

"I have to see to the clearing up and pay off the caterer and such. Will you stay?"

Syrah said simply, "Yes."

Emboldened, but feeling fifteen, Toni was mortified when her voice cracked. "All the houseguests are leaving today."

"Are they?" Syrah was making no effort to hide her amusement now. "Toni Blanchard, is that an invitation to stay the night?"

"Yes, it is." And longer, she wanted to add, but she'd made enough of a fool of herself. "I know you have obligations and stuff tomorrow . . . and things like that."

Syrah laughed. "Who would have thought you could be nervous?"

"You make me very nervous."

"Good. I like that." Those beautiful, wonderful, absolutely *fine* eyes sparkled. "Don't worry, I understand the invitation is for tonight only. Oh, my father is ready to go. I'll just tell him not to expect me."

The invitation was for more than tonight, but Toni wasn't sure she could find the words. She watched Syrah make her way through the thinning crowd, remembering, vividly, the way Syrah had felt under her. The rest of her imagination was occupied with visions of their bodies in a great many other positions.

"Roll up your tongue, Toni." Caroline stepped into Toni's line of sight. "I don't think it'll work. Do you think she's going to leave her father and the Ardani fields?"

"She doesn't have to," Toni said slowly.

Caroline's smile was like cut diamonds. "As if you'd leave Manhattan. As if you're home more than a week out of every month. She's going to want more than that. She's so . . . young and idealistic."

"I'm trying to be worth some idealistic values. Besides," she added quickly, "compromise is the hallmark of every successful relationship."

"I'm never giving up, Toni. I think we were meant to be together."

"What about love?"

"What about it?" Caroline's laugh was unamused. "I thought we were grownups."

"I think I'm just now growing up in that department."

Something flickered in Caroline's eyes. "Temporary insanity. I forgive you."

"No forgiveness is needed." Very seriously, so that Caroline could not claim to have misunderstood, she added, "I don't know who you love, Caroline, but it's not the real me."

"Oh, Toni," she said with a pretty laugh, "that only makes me want you more."

Toni didn't have to look around to know that Syrah was now in earshot. It was very Caroline, to say something ambiguous but salacious—if one was inclined to take it that way. Caroline loved mischief as much as Mira. In a low voice, she said, "I'm very sorry if I ever misled you."

"See you back in Manhattan, where you belong," Caroline said before waving at someone and abruptly leaving Toni's side.

Toni turned to look for Syrah, but if indeed she had been there, she no longer was.


People were making obvious signs of departure. Syrah agreed with one and all it had been a lovely ceremony. All the while part of her thought about the scene she'd just overheard between Toni and Caroline. She hadn't meant to eavesdrop, but Caroline had suddenly raised her voice, obviously so that Syrah could hear what she said.

Tired of small talk, she tried to help the caterer repack the wine bottles in crates but was shooed away. She found herself outside, looking at the pattern of sparkling light on the house as it reflected off the pool. She'd point it out to Jane—it was the kind of thing Jane liked to capture in her paintings.

"Syrah, dear, there you are. We were just getting ready to go, and I didn't want to miss saying good-bye to you." Caroline had changed into more casual clothes and carried an overnight bag in one hand. "Can I tell you a secret?"

Syrah wanted to say no, couldn't say yes, but her silence was enough for Caroline.

"I think that today really put Toni in mind of finally doing something public for the two of us. I've cared about her for years, even when she and Mira were a walking disaster zone." She shrugged, looking coy.

Syrah could tell Caroline wanted her to comment, but she didn't see the point. She very much wanted to believe that Toni only spent time with Caroline because she was Missy's sister. As for Mira, well, it was to Toni's credit that she hadn't been able to believe that Mira was so evil. In that one way, Toni was like her father, and the idea that the two of them were anything alike made Syrah smile to herself.

Caroline gave Syrah a curious look before continuing. "We've been so off-again on-again throughout the years, and last night . . ." Another coy look. "Last night she made it so clear that we need to think about a permanent future."

Syrah blinked. Slowly, she replayed in her head what Caroline had just said. Then she thought about the kiss and the look in Toni's eyes when she'd asked her to stay the night. She weighed that look against all of Caroline's half-truths and innuendoes. She, like Toni, didn't want to believe someone could lie to her face and look like an angel, but part of her understood wanting Toni enough to be that desperate.

She studied Caroline's face, thought once more about the kiss, and it was suddenly the easiest thing in the world to say, clearly and firmly, "Caroline, I don't believe you."

She glanced past Caroline's shoulder and saw that Toni had paused in the nearest doorway, looking at them quizzically. Syrah shrugged a "she'll never change" and Toni spread her hands in a clear "*mea culpa* but it's never going to happen again."

"What?" Caroline looked at Syrah in stunned surprise.

"I don't believe you. Toni wouldn't lie to me, so you must be. I'm sorry. Excuse me."

She saw that Toni was in motion as well and they met in only a few seconds. She tipped her head back and met Toni's steady, dark gray gaze.

"Do you remember," she began clearly, forgetting that Caroline existed. "Do you remember the day you told me you loved me?"

"Vividly." Toni's eyes were shining with laughter.

"Can we do that over?"

"As many times as you like."

"How about until we get it right?"

"Even if it takes a thousand tries—you got it."

Syrah arched her back so she could gaze up into Toni's face. "That pencils just fine for me."


From the large picture window in the great room they watched the last rental truck, laden with chairs, disappear into the falling night at the end of the drive.

"No stars tonight." Syrah swallowed as Toni's fingertips trailed lightly over the nape of her neck.

"I think I'm glad. I can't blame anything on the stars."

"Did you, before?"

"I tried." Toni's hands were gentle on Syrah's shoulders as they shifted to face each other. "I never meant to insult you. I never meant to imply that loving you was bad for me or against anything I believed in. I realize, though," she added before Syrah could speak, "that you could have taken what I said that way."

"I listened to lies and part of me wanted to believe them." Syrah realized she'd have to go slightly up on her toes to kiss Toni.

"I don't know how this will work out, Syrah. My business is demanding."

"So is mine. And will be over time as my father gets a little less involved." Syrah shivered as Toni's hands feathered over her throat and shoulders.

"Truthfully, I don't have to work." Toni was breathing hard, and her words slurred as if forming them was difficult. "You wouldn't have to either."

Syrah smiled broadly then bit her lower lip as Toni's hands drifted over her ribs. "Like either of us would stop at this point in our lives."

"I'm thinking there are times we could. And that I don't have to live in New York twenty-four-seven, obviously. But I do want you to see my world. Meet my father."

Syrah nodded. "Yes, Toni. Yes, I'd like that."

"I love the way you say *yes*," Toni breathed. "Can we agree to a transitional stage of negotiation?"

Syrah could feel her lips trembling. The house had settled into quiet and it felt as if their heartbeats were the only sounds for miles. Alone—they were very alone. "I agree, with one caveat."

Toni brushed her cheek against Syrah's forehead as she pulled Syrah firmly into her arms. "And that would be?"

"Our goal isn't transitional—I don't want some kind of together until we're bored thing. I want . . ." Syrah ached to say "forever" but her voice broke and she feared she would cry. She didn't want Toni to think she was frightened or sad.

"You want hundred-year vines by the time we're done?"

"Oh." A tear spilled over in spite of her efforts. "How did I ever think you had no heart?"

Toni's eyes sparkled. "There was a time I tried not to have one. I thought a lot of money meant I had to be unsentimental. But your eyes, the moment I saw your eyes I felt like I'd found myself again—"

Syrah could stand it no longer. On her tiptoes she pressed her lips to Toni's with a decidedly unladylike sound.

Toni crushed Syrah in her arms with a ferocity that sent ripples through Syrah's stomach. "Tonight I want to leave the lights on. I want to see your face. I want to watch your eyes. I want you naked and mine."

Syrah couldn't breathe. She felt a stab of that familiar fear that if she let Toni get all the way inside her heart she'd end up so hurt she wouldn't survive.

She wanted to hold part of herself aloof, to keep one last escape, just in case. But a frozen moment of panic melted with the revelation that the only way to save her heart was to give it all. She would be breaking it herself, this very moment, if she gave Toni anything less than the whole.

Toni whispered into her ear, "Syrah, please."

She groaned "Yes" against Toni's mouth. With that single word she could finally feel Toni's uncertainties and fear, too. Flooding with tenderness, she said it again. "Yes. Yes, Toni."

Toni's hand trembled in Syrah's when they finally eased apart. "How about a nice mattress instead of the hood of a car?"

Syrah smiled and loved the way Toni's mouth crinkled into a matching grin. "I'd have already dragged you to bed if I had the slightest idea where your room was."

"Really?" Toni pulled Syrah against her again. "Does that mean you want me, too?"

"I want the lights on. I want skin." She kissed Toni's collarbone with a little moan. "I want to get out of these shoes."

Laughing, Toni pulled Syrah toward the staircase. "I have an idea—what about a bubble bath?"

"Oh. That sounds divine," Syrah conceded. She slipped out of her heels at the foot of the stairs and carried them with one hand while Toni held the other. She could picture doing exactly this on any future night, eager for bed, but relaxed, knowing there really was no hurry.

Toni slipped out of her jacket and hung it on the knob of the closet door. "I'll start the water running."

"This is a lovely room," Syrah said truthfully, loud enough to be heard as Toni disappeared into the bathroom. Drawn to the window, which overlooked the gardens, she enjoyed the sparkle of party lights strung through the hedges. She stretched to undo the hook at the top of her gown's zipper and shuddered as other fingers joined her own.

"Let me help with that," Toni murmured.

The slow sound of the zipper, followed by Toni's warm breath on her spine made Syrah wonderfully dizzy.

"Oh, and with this, too," Toni added.

Her bra was suddenly loose and Syrah gasped. She grasped the windowsill as Toni's hands slipped inside her dress, pushing it and her bra off her shoulders. Kisses began at the nape of her neck and moved slowly down her spine. "Toni . . . oh my."

"Yes, the lights are lovely, aren't they?"

Syrah gave a half-laugh. "Lights? What lights?" The windowpane was cool against her forehead.

"The tub takes a long time to fill."

Toni's body pressed against the length of Syrah's back, washing her with warmth and Toni hugged her tightly from behind. "Oh," Syrah said faintly. "I guess we'll have to find a way to amuse ourselves."

Firmly, Toni turned Syrah to face her. Brushing her lips against Syrah's she said, "I have a thought or two."

"You can still think?"

Toni's grin turned wicked. "Yes, I can. For now, let me do all the thinking. I want you to enjoy . . . everything."

Syrah's arms quivered as Toni pulled the sleeves of her dress down all the way. The sound of the fabric crumpling in a heap at her feet was eclipsed by Toni's moan as she slid her hands over Syrah's hips.

"I assure you," Toni said softly, "there will be a time when I will need you to do the thinking, but not right now."

Syrah nodded and closed her eyes as Toni's hands cupped the sides of her breasts.

"Please," Toni whispered. "Please open your eyes."

It was hard, but once her gaze locked with Toni's Syrah couldn't look away. Her lips trembled and a little sound of need escaped her as Toni's fingers found her nipples.

"Your eyes are so expressive."

Syrah managed to say, "I didn't think it was my eyes you were admiring right now."

Toni didn't glance down, but her fingers squeezed each nipple gently. "Your body makes me sweat. I'm afraid of being too . . ."

"Too what?"

"Primal. I want you. I want to feel you move the way you made me move for you." Toni's hands slipped under the waistband of Syrah's panties.

"The water."

"Hmm?"

"Water. Bathtub." Syrah swallowed hard as Toni's fingertips brushed lower. "Overflow."

"Oh. Be right back."

When Toni let her go Syrah thought she might faint. There was no air in this room, and she was so swollen with desire there was no blood in her brain. She pressed one shaking hand to her eyes and then felt the welcome strength of Toni's arms around her.

"Who needs a bath?" Toni pressed Syrah gently down onto the bed.

Only when their bodies were entwined did Syrah realize Toni had taken off her clothes. She groaned as her hands explored the muscles in Toni's back. Toni's thigh slipped between her legs and Syrah lifted her hips, craving more intense contact.

"Please, Syrah."

She opened her eyes to find Toni smiling at her. "You make it hard to keep them open."

"It's not a fetish. Well, at least if it is, you're the first time I've felt it. But when I touch you, I can see it in your eyes. Like that." Toni's fingertips slipped alongside her thigh, sinking into Syrah's puffed, soaked center. "Just like that."

Their lips brushed as they shared air and Syrah kept her gaze locked with Toni's, even as Toni's fingers opened her, swirled around all of her wet skin, and then went inside. She didn't recognize the sound she made and the waves of response inside her were also foreign.

Toni whispered, soft and low, "Beautiful."

Fighting to breathe, Syrah asked, "Do you feel that? Feel me?"

"God, yes."

Syrah shuddered and fought to keep her eyes open, clinging to the adoration and passion in Toni's eyes as the sensations inside her seemed to surge beyond her muscles and nerves and skin, enveloping parts of her she had not realized could be touched.

"Yes," Toni groaned. She kissed Syrah hard and quick and her hand moved faster. "I can feel everything."

"Yes, kiss me." Syrah panted against Toni's mouth, aware of the rising pressure as she arched into Toni's embrace. Her skin felt burning hot, as if all the sensation was too much to hold in and she shook, cried out. Their bodies froze and she marveled at the tears in Toni's eyes before she could stand it no longer.

"Toni, please! More . . ." Syrah shoved her pelvis against Toni's hand. "More."

Toni's earthy groan drew a matching one from Syrah. Her hips pushed Syrah's legs apart and she went inside her again as Syrah's climax peaked. "Always more, anything you want."

Syrah's head pounded as she shuddered one last time, then everything seemed to melt into the bed and she finally could not keep her eyes open.

Ragged breathing in her ear was a welcome sound as Toni settled half on top of her. Another shock wave rippled through Syrah and she laughed.

"I'm assuming that means you feel good."

"Oh, it does." Syrah sighed. "Bath time?"

Toni sounded all too smug. "Not quite yet."

Syrah turned her head and caught Toni slowly licking her fingers. "There's more where that came from," Syrah said shyly.

"Is there?" Toni trailed her wet fingers over Syrah's breast as she waggled her eyebrows. "Can I check?"

Syrah started to laugh but other emotions overwhelmed her. "I'm sorry I sent you away. I'm sorry I hurt you. I'm sorry—"

Toni quickly kissed her. "You were right to do so. Neither of us was ready for this."

"I lose my temper and I'm not tidy." Syrah suddenly felt it was important for Toni to know all her flaws. "I make mistakes all the time."

"Darling, I'm not perfect, either, but I am trying to be worthy of your respect."

"I do respect you, Toni. I didn't understand at all who you were, but now I think I'm beginning to."

Toni made that little noise that Syrah was quickly growing to love but said nothing.

"Do you remember when I said I could never love you?" Syrah drew Toni's still wet hand to her breast.

"I try not to."

"I was wrong." She grinned. "I may never say that to you again, so savor it."

"Oh, believe me, I am savoring everything about you, and I fully intend to go on doing so for a very, very long time."

"I'm in love with you, Toni." Syrah said the words softly and hoped her eyes were saying them, too. "I hope you still love me."

Toni exhaled as if she'd been holding her breath for months. "I think I loved you from the moment I saw you, but it was the middle of loving you before I even knew I'd begun."

Touched, and once again wondering how she had ever thought Toni cold, Syrah wrapped both arms around Toni's waist. "I think, given time, that you could cry over grapes."

*The End*

# About the Author

Karin's first crush on a woman was the local librarian. Just remembering the pencil through the loose, attractive bun makes her warm. Maybe it was the librarian's influence, but for whatever reason, at the age of 16 Karin fell into the arms of her first and only sweetheart.

There's a certain symmetry to the fact that ten years later, after seeing the film *Desert Hearts*, her sweetheart descended on the Berkeley Public Library to find some of "those" books. The books found there were the encouragement Karin needed to forget the so-called "mainstream" and spin her first romance for lesbians. That manuscript became her first novel, *In Every Port*.

The happily-ever-after couple now lives in the San Francisco Bay area, and became Mom and Moogie to Kelson in 1995 and Eleanor in 1997. They celebrate their twenty-ninth anniversary in 2006.

All of Karin's work can now be found at Bella Books. Details and background about her novels, and her other pen name, Laura Adams, can be found at www.kallmaker.com.

# Publications from
# BELLA BOOKS, INC.
*The best in contemporary lesbian fiction*

P.O. Box 10543, Tallahassee, FL 32302
Phone: 800-729-4992
www.bellabooks.com

JUST LIKE THAT by Karin Kallmaker. 240 pp. Disliking each other—and everything they stand for—even before they meet, Toni and Syrah find feelings can change, just like that.
1-59493-025-2      $12.95

WHEN FIRST WE PRACTICE by Therese Szymanski. 200 pp. Brett and Allie are once again caught in the middle of murder and intrigue.      1-59493-045-7      $12.95

REUNION by Jane Frances. 240 pp. Cathy Braithwaite seems to have it all: good looks, money and a thriving accounting practice . . .      1-59493-046-5      $12.95

BELL, BOOK & DYKE: NEW EXPLOITS OF MAGICAL LESBIANS by Kallmaker, Watts, Johnson and Szymanski. 360 pp. Reluctant witches, tempting spells, and skyclad beauties—delve into the mysteries of love, lust and power in this quartet of novellas.
1-59493-023-6      $14.95

ARTIST'S DREAM by Gerri Hill. 320 pp.When Cassie meets Luke Winston, she can no longer deny her attraction to women . . .      1-59493-042-2      $12.95

NO EVIDENCE by Nancy Sanra. 240 pp. Private Investigator Tally McGinnis once again returns to the horror filled world of a serial killer.      1-59493-043-04      $12.95

WHEN LOVE FINDS A HOME by Megan Carter. 280 pp. What will it take for Anna and Rona to find their way back to each other again?      1-59493-041-4      $12.95

MEMORIES TO DIE FOR by Adrian Gold. 240 pp. Rachel attempts to avoid her attraction to the charms of Anna Sigurdson . . .      1-59493-038-4      $12.95

SILENT HEART by Claire McNab. 280 pp. Exotic lesbian romance.
1-59493-044-9      $12.95

MIDNIGHT RAIN by Peggy J. Herring. 240 pp. Bridget McBee is determined to find the woman who saved her life.      1-59493-021-X      $12.95

THE MISSING PAGE A Brenda Strange Mystery by Patty G. Henderson. 240 pp. Brenda investigates her client's murder . . .      1-59493-004-X      $12.95

WHISPERS ON THE WIND by Frankie J. Jones. 240 pp. Dixon thinks she and her best friend, Elizabeth Colter, would make the perfect couple . . .   1-59493-037-6      $12.95

CALL OF THE DARK: EROTIC LESBIAN TALES OF THE SUPERNATURAL edited by Therese Szymanski—from Bella After Dark. 320 pp.      1-59493-040-6      $14.95

A TIME TO CAST AWAY A Helen Black Mystery by Pat Welch. 240 pp. Helen stops by Alice's apartment—only to find the woman dead . . .      1-59493-036-8      $12.95

DESERT OF THE HEART by Jane Rule. 224 pp. The book that launched the most popular lesbian movie of all time is back. 1-1-59493-035-X $12.95

THE NEXT WORLD by Ursula Steck. 240 pp. Anna's friend Mido is threatened and eventually disappears . . . 1-59493-024-4 $12.95

CALL SHOTGUN by Jaime Clevenger. 240 pp. Kelly gets pulled back into the world of private investigation . . . 1-59493-016-3 $12.95

52 PICKUP by Bonnie J. Morris and E.B. Casey. 240 pp. 52 hot, romantic tales—one for every Saturday night of the year. 1-59493-026-0 $12.95

GOLD FEVER by Lyn Denison. 240 pp. Kate's first love, Ashley, returns to their home town, where Kate now lives . . . 1-1-59493-039-2 $12.95

RISKY INVESTMENT by Beth Moore. 240 pp. Lynn's best friend and roommate needs her to pretend Chris is his fiancé. But nothing is ever easy. 1-59493-019-8 $12.95

HUNTER'S WAY by Gerri Hill. 240 pp. Homicide detective Tori Hunter is forced to team up with the hot-tempered Samantha Kennedy. 1-59493-018-X $12.95

CAR POOL by Karin Kallmaker. 240 pp. Soft shoulders, merging traffic and slippery when wet . . . Anthea and Shay find love in the car pool. 1-59493-013-9 $12.95

NO SISTER OF MINE by Jeanne G'Fellers. 240 pp. Telepathic women fight to coexist with a patriarchal society that wishes their eradication. ISBN 1-59493-017-1 $12.95

ON THE WINGS OF LOVE by Megan Carter. 240 pp. Stacie's reporting career is on the rocks. She has to interview bestselling author Cheryl, or else! ISBN 1-59493-027-9 $12.95

WICKED GOOD TIME by Diana Tremain Braund. 224 pp. Does Christina need Miki as a protector . . . or want her as a lover? ISBN 1-59493-031-7 $12.95

THOSE WHO WAIT by Peggy J. Herring. 240 pp. Two brilliant sisters—in love with the same woman! ISBN 1-59493-032-5 $12.95

ABBY'S PASSION by Jackie Calhoun. 240 pp. Abby's bipolar sister helps turn her world upside down, so she must decide what's most important. ISBN 1-59493-014-7 $12.95

PICTURE PERFECT by Jane Vollbrecht. 240 pp. Kate is reintroduced to Casey, the daughter of an old friend. Can they withstand Kate's career? ISBN 1-59493-015-5 $12.95

PAPERBACK ROMANCE by Karin Kallmaker. 240 pp. Carolyn falls for tall, dark and . . . female . . . in this classic lesbian romance. ISBN 1-59493-033-3 $12.95

DAWN OF CHANGE by Gerri Hill. 240 pp. Susan ran away to find peace in remote Kings Canyon—then she met Shawn . . . ISBN 1-59493-011-2 $12.95

DOWN THE RABBIT HOLE by Lynne Jamneck. 240 pp. Is a killer holding a grudge against FBI Agent Samantha Skellar? ISBN 1-59493-012-0 $12.95

SEASONS OF THE HEART by Jackie Calhoun. 240 pp. Overwhelmed, Sara saw only one way out—leaving . . . ISBN 1-59493-030-9 $12.95

TURNING THE TABLES by Jessica Thomas. 240 pp. The 2nd Alex Peres Mystery. *From ghosties and ghoulies and long leggity beasties* . . . ISBN 1-59493-009-0 $12.95

FOR EVERY SEASON by Frankie Jones. 240 pp. Andi, who is investigating a 65-year-old murder, meets Janice, a charming district attorney . . . ISBN 1-59493-010-4 $12.95

LOVE ON THE LINE by Laura DeHart Young. 240 pp. Kay leaves a younger woman behind to go on a mission to Alaska . . . will she regret it? ISBN 1-59493-008-2 $12.95

UNDER THE SOUTHERN CROSS by Claire McNab. 200 pp. Lee, an American travel agent, goes down under and meets Australian Alex, and the sparks fly under the Southern Cross. ISBN 1-59493-029-5 $12.95

SUGAR by Karin Kallmaker. 240 pp. Three women want sugar from Sugar, who can't make up her mind. ISBN 1-59493-001-5 $12.95

FALL GUY by Claire McNab. 200 pp. 16th Detective Inspector Carol Ashton Mystery. ISBN 1-59493-000-7 $12.95

ONE SUMMER NIGHT by Gerri Hill. 232 pp. Johanna swore to never fall in love again— but then she met the charming Kelly . . . ISBN 1-59493-007-4 $12.95

TALK OF THE TOWN TOO by Saxon Bennett. 181 pp. Second in the series about wild and fun loving friends. ISBN 1-931513-77-5 $12.95

LOVE SPEAKS HER NAME by Laura DeHart Young. 170 pp. Love and friendship, desire and intrigue, spark this exciting sequel to *Forever and the Night*. ISBN 1-59493-002-3 $12.95

TO HAVE AND TO HOLD by Peggy J. Herring. 184 pp. By finally letting down her defenses, will Dorian be opening herself to a devastating betrayal? ISBN 1-59493-005-8 $12.95

WILD THINGS by Karin Kallmaker. 228 pp. Dutiful daughter Faith has met the perfect man. There's just one problem: she's in love with his sister. ISBN 1-931513-64-3 $12.95

SHARED WINDS by Kenna White. 216 pp. Can Emma rebuild more than just Lanny's marina? ISBN 1-59493-006-6 $12.95

THE UNKNOWN MILE by Jaime Clevenger. 253 pp. Kelly's world is getting more and more complicated every moment. ISBN 1-931513-57-0 $12.95

TREASURED PAST by Linda Hill. 189 pp. A shared passion for antiques leads to love. ISBN 1-59493-003-1 $12.95

SIERRA CITY by Gerri Hill. 284 pp. Chris and Jesse cannot deny their growing attraction . . . ISBN 1-931513-98-8 $12.95

ALL THE WRONG PLACES by Karin Kallmaker. 174 pp. Sex and the single girl—Brandy is looking for love and usually she finds it. Karin Kallmaker's first *After Dark* erotic novel. ISBN 1-931513-76-7 $12.95

WHEN THE CORPSE LIES A Motor City Thriller by Therese Szymanski. 328 pp. Butch bad-girl Brett Higgins is used to waking up next to beautiful women she hardly knows. Problem is, this one's dead. ISBN 1-931513-74-0 $12.95

GUARDED HEARTS by Hannah Rickard. 240 pp. Someone's reminding Alyssa about her secret past, and then she becomes the suspect in a series of burglaries. ISBN 1-931513-99-6 $12.95

ONCE MORE WITH FEELING by Peggy J. Herring. 184 pp. Lighthearted, loving, romantic adventure. ISBN 1-931513-60-0 $12.95

TANGLED AND DARK A Brenda Strange Mystery by Patty G. Henderson. 240 pp. When investigating a local death, Brenda finds two possible killers—one diagnosed with Multiple Personality Disorder. ISBN 1-931513-75-9 $12.95

WHITE LACE AND PROMISES by Peggy J. Herring. 240 pp. Maxine and Betina realize sex may not be the most important thing in their lives. ISBN 1-931513-73-2 $12.95

UNFORGETTABLE by Karin Kallmaker. 288 pp. Can Rett find love with the cheerleader who broke her heart so many years ago? ISBN 1-931513-63-5 $12.95

HIGHER GROUND by Saxon Bennett. 280 pp. A delightfully complex reflection of the successful, high society lives of a small group of women. ISBN 1-931513-69-4 $12.95

LAST CALL A Detective Franco Mystery by Baxter Clare. 240 pp. Frank overlooks all else to try to solve a cold case of two murdered children . . . ISBN 1-931513-70-8 $12.95

ONCE UPON A DYKE: NEW EXPLOITS OF FAIRY-TALE LESBIANS by Karin Kallmaker, Julia Watts, Barbara Johnson & Therese Szymanski. 320 pp. You've never read fairy tales like these before! From Bella After Dark. ISBN 1-931513-71-6 $14.95

FINEST KIND OF LOVE by Diana Tremain Braund. 224 pp. Can Molly and Carolyn stop clashing long enough to see beyond their differences? ISBN 1-931513-68-6 $12.95

DREAM LOVER by Lyn Denison. 188 pp. A soft, sensuous, romantic fantasy.
ISBN 1-931513-96-1 $12.95

NEVER SAY NEVER by Linda Hill. 224 pp. A classic love story . . . where rules aren't the only things broken. ISBN 1-931513-67-8 $12.95

PAINTED MOON by Karin Kallmaker. 214 pp. Stranded together in a snowbound cabin, Jackie and Leah's lives will never be the same. ISBN 1-931513-53-8 $12.95

WIZARD OF ISIS by Jean Stewart. 240 pp. Fifth in the exciting Isis series.
ISBN 1-931513-71-4 $12.95

WOMAN IN THE MIRROR by Jackie Calhoun. 216 pp. Josey learns to love again, while her niece is learning to love women for the first time. ISBN 1-931513-78-3 $12.95

SUBSTITUTE FOR LOVE by Karin Kallmaker. 200 pp. When Holly and Reyna meet the combination adds up to pure passion. But what about tomorrow? ISBN 1-931513-62-7 $12.95

GULF BREEZE by Gerri Hill. 288 pp. Could Carly really be the woman Pat has always been searching for? ISBN 1-931513-97-X $12.95

THE TOMSTOWN INCIDENT by Penny Hayes. 184 pp. Caught between two worlds, Eloise must make a decision that will change her life forever. ISBN 1-931513-56-2 $12.95

MAKING UP FOR LOST TIME by Karin Kallmaker. 240 pp. Discover delicious recipes for romance by the undisputed mistress. ISBN 1-931513-61-9 $12.95

THE WAY LIFE SHOULD BE by Diana Tremain Braund. 173 pp. With which woman will Jennifer find the true meaning of love? ISBN 1-931513-66-X $12.95

BACK TO BASICS: A BUTCH/FEMME ANTHOLOGY edited by Therese Szymanski— from Bella After Dark. 324 pp. ISBN 1-931513-35-X $14.95

SURVIVAL OF LOVE by Frankie J. Jones. 236 pp. What will Jody do when she falls in love with her best friend's daughter? ISBN 1-931513-55-4 $12.95

LESSONS IN MURDER by Claire McNab. 184 pp. 1st Detective Inspector Carol Ashton Mystery. ISBN 1-931513-65-1 $12.95

DEATH BY DEATH by Claire McNab. 167 pp. 5th Denise Cleever Thriller.
ISBN 1-931513-34-1 $12.95

CAUGHT IN THE NET by Jessica Thomas. 188 pp. A wickedly observant story of mystery, danger, and love in Provincetown. ISBN 1-931513-54-6 $12.95

DREAMS FOUND by Lyn Denison. Australian Riley embarks on a journey to meet her birth mother . . . and gains not just a family, but the love of her life. ISBN 1-931513-58-9 $12.95